HEART OF SHADOWS

Hearts of the Highlands
Book Two

Paula Quinn

Books from Dragonblade Publishing

Dangerous Lords Series by Maggi Andersen
The Baron's Betrothal
Seducing the Earl
The Viscount's Widowed Lady
Governess to the Duke's Heir

Also from Maggi Andersen
The Marquess Meets His Match

The St. Clairs Series by Alexa Aston
Devoted to the Duke
Midnight with the Marquess
Embracing the Earl

Knights of Honor Series by Alexa Aston
Word of Honor
Marked by Honor
Code of Honor
Journey to Honor
Heart of Honor
Bold in Honor
Love and Honor
Gift of Honor
Path to Honor
Return to Honor

The King's Cousins Series by Alexa Aston
The Pawn
The Heir
The Bastard

Queen of Thieves Series by Andy Peloquin
Child of the Night Guild
Thief of the Night Guild
Queen of the Night Guild

The Book of Love Series by Meara Platt
The Look of Love
The Touch of Love

Dark Gardens Series by Meara Platt
Garden of Shadows
Garden of Light
Garden of Dragons
Garden of Destiny

Rulers of the Sky Series by Paula Quinn
Scorched
Ember
White Hot

Hearts of the Highlands Series by Paula Quinn
Heart of Ashes
Heart of Shadows
Heart of Stone

Highlands Forever Series by Violetta Rand
Unbreakable
Undeniable
Unyielding

Viking's Fury Series by Violetta Rand
Love's Fury
Desire's Fury
Passion's Fury

Also from Violetta Rand
Viking Hearts

"It is in truth not for glory, nor riches, nor honours that we are fighting, but for freedom – for that alone, which no honest man gives up but with life itself."

Extract from the Declaration of Arbroath 1320

CHAPTER ONE

Cumberland, England
Summer
The Year of Our Lord 1320

IN A QUIET corner in Storey Tavern, Commander Torin Gray of the Scot's army surveyed the men around him from beneath his black hood. He'd been coming here for the last pair of nights looking for the same thing: border guards from Carlisle Castle enjoying the night off.

Having practically grown up in taverns, Torin knew that if one wanted to find someone or something, the best place to look was in the local drinking spot.

He'd wait, no matter how long it took. They would come for a drink, or to forget the dreaded monotony of patrolling relatively peaceful borders every day or night, waiting for something to happen, growing fat and lazy when nothing ever did. Some wine or whisky, mayhap a willing lass to soothe their weary souls.

He knew where to find them. He'd prepared to wait. He needed them to help him gain entrance into England's last mighty stronghold.

He looked into his cup, at the ale he hadn't touched. He wasn't here to forget anything. He remembered the English soldier who had lifted his weeping mother and carried her away after another had jammed his blade into Torin's father and killed him. He could no longer remember faces, but he never wanted to forget what the English had done to his family.

He flicked his gaze to a table across the room, where five men sat drinking together. He'd been watching them all evening. They were thieves, possibly reivers—a more organized alliance of lawless raiders who lived along the borders. Torin could spot a thief anywhere, since he had once been one—and sometimes still was.

These five were rude and unruly. Perfect for what he had planned.

After another quarter of an hour, the tavern door swung open and, at last, his prey swept inside with the cool night breeze. There were three of them. They wore the red and blue pattern of the English king on their tabards, and swords tucked into scabbards at their sides. Their lids drooped over tired eyes as they pushed their way around other patrons and sat at a small table near the hearth.

Torin lifted his finger to the serving girl when he caught her eye. She smiled and sauntered over.

"A drink for my friend there." He pointed her in the direction of one of the thieves and slipped an extra coin into her palm.

Her smile remained as she stared into his shadowy eyes, but then he looked away and she went about her task. Torin waited while she brought the drink over to the man he'd pointed out.

The patron turned to acknowledge him. Before he had the chance to turn back to his friends, Torin waved him over and hoped the thief would come. He couldn't take the chance of the guards seeing him at the table with *all* the thieves. They would not remember one.

"What is your name and what do you want?" the hulking thief asked a moment later, standing over Torin's table.

"Torin Gray," he told him. "I'm lookin' fer work." He didn't usual-ly sound like a Scot when he spoke to the English, but he didn't want to be trusted by this particular man.

The thief stared down at him with deep-set, suspicious brown eyes. "Remove your hood. Let me see your face in the light."

Torin did as he was bid, pushing back his hood and releasing a mop of chestnut curls shot through with streaks of gold. He wasn't afraid anyone would recognize him. Very few knew he was one of the Bruce's most lethal weapons.

"What kind of work?" the thief asked when he was satisfied Torin wasn't someone he knew.

Torin let his grin shine as he slipped his gaze to the soldiers. "I saw their purses. They are fat. Their sharp swords and swift horses would be highly desired among the reivers."

The thief narrowed his eyes on the soldiers and then turned back to Torin. "So? What has that to do with me?"

"Ye are a thief," Torin said boldly. "Are ye not?" He held up his hands when the man reached for a knife in his belt. "Easy, Brother. I'm a thief as well. But I canna take three of them down on my own."

The man laughed at his proposal, just as Torin had suspected he would. "There are five of us, Scot. What do we need you for?"

Torin blinked in surprise, as if he hadn't thought of that. "But 'twas I who told ye aboot their heavy purses."

"You are a fool, but then most Scots are, and not a very good thief." The man laughed until his gaze fell to a brooch clasped on Torin's léine, beneath his cloak. "What is this?" he asked, growing serious and leaning forward to push the edge of the cloak aside. "A bug?"

Torin's blood went cold. He dipped his chin and looked up from beneath his dark brows. "Take yer hand away before I remove it fer ye," he warned on a deadly whisper.

The thief smiled at him. "If you do anything to stop me, I will cry out to the guards that a filthy Scot sought to rob them and I tried to stop you. My cousins will vouch for me."

Torin was going to kill him, him and all his cousins. He hadn't planned on killing thieves, but he was going to.

First, he had to see this through first. He would not be distracted. It was too late to turn back.

So he remained still while the thief took his brooch. It was a moth, expertly crafted in bronze. He had snatched it from his home while it burned, before he ran away. It was his mother's, though he didn't know for certain.

He didn't fight for it now or chase the thief when the man slipped it into a pouch hanging from his belt and then walked away. Torin wouldn't throw away a perfect opportunity to get himself not only into the castle, but *invited* into it. He had a promise to keep to himself.

His smile was cloaked in shadows as he pulled his hood back over his head and rose from the table to leave.

He went the stable and waited with his horse. It was going to be a long night. He was a wee bit less patient since losing his brooch, but he would wait.

He turned his gaze to Carlisle Castle in the distance, where resided Alexander Bennett, Warden of the Western March, defender of Carlisle.

King Robert the Bruce and his forces had attacked Carlisle five years ago but had failed to take it.

This time, they would not fail.

This time, they had him.

He'd come to Robert shortly after the king's defeat in Carlisle, after he'd written to the Bruce, promising to hand him Till Castle, home of the Governor of Etal. And then he'd done it. His prowess at infiltrating any military stronghold and delivering his enemies to the Scottish king, weakened and vulnerable, had earned him the name *Shadow* among the Bruce's forces.

His skills included things he'd learned as a child while trying to survive alone—things such as lifting valuables from any pocket, and all sorts of thievery.

But his greatest skill was gaining trust and friendship from his enemies while planning their demise. He was in and out of their lives within weeks. He felt no shame or regret for the things he'd done, the people he'd killed. He wanted no reward. Just revenge.

Aye, Shadow was the right name for him, but Torin thought it was better fitting for his heart. For it was not completely black. There were glimpses of light shining along narrow paths but, most often, he refused to take them. The light tempted him away from his purpose, and though he enjoyed what he could find in the light, he chose to stay in the shadows cast by it.

His purpose right now was taking down Carlisle Castle. No Scot had been able to penetrate its stone curtain walls. Little was known about Bennett's forces. How many men guarded the borders, the battlements? How well did they fight? What could he do from within to ensure the Scot's victory?

He would soon find out.

He set his gaze toward the eastern sky aglow in pale moonlight and endless stars, making the red sandstone keep harder to define. For a moment, the beauty of it took his breath away. He might be one of the Bruce's most proficient killers, but he always stopped to appreciate what the light revealed.

He'd been thirteen when he'd broken into Till Castle, home of Governor Henry Alan, and was caught stuffing valuables from the governor's private chambers into his breeches. He'd been beaten and thrown into the castle's pit for four days. Two of those days were spent living in the horrors of his past, swearing vengeance, promising the wee lad inside him that he would avenge his family and make amends for leaving them, that he would kill every English soldier he met for the lives of his friends in the woods. Finally, he'd collapsed on the cold stone floor and pondered a field of endless flowers and a sky as vast as his imagination.

Mayhap he'd gone mad in those eternal days of darkness and hunger and nothing to do, but he'd learned how to escape his life and enter another, filled with sunlight and beauty—and a family, a place to belong.

He'd had to escape in order to live and take down as many fortresses he could.

He'd used the next five years in the governor's garrison, learning to fight, disguised as a friend—

He heard men leaving the tavern and blinked back to the present. He bent to look around the stable wall and saw the three soldiers step outside and begin the walk toward the stable. He waited for the thieves to leave the tavern next. It didn't take long.

He watched as they came up around the soldiers, their faces covered, and surrounded them, knives held outstretched in their hands. He didn't usually kill thieves, but there was no room in his heart for forgiveness. He had a task to achieve and nothing would stop him. Nothing ever had.

"Hand over them purses and we will not kill you," one of the thieves demanded.

The soldiers reached for their swords and fighting quickly ensued. One of the soldiers managed to take down a thief, but Bennett's men had had too much to drink and they were weary. As a result, the four bigger thieves soon overtook them.

Torin watched two of the soldiers fall to their knees and the third lose his sword. He waited another moment until it seemed hopeless for the soldiers to come out of the encounter alive.

He stepped forward out of the shadows and snapped his dark mantle over his shoulders. Reaching behind his back, he unsheathed his long blade and brought it down hard on one gaping thief, killing him where he stood. He turned for the next and twirled his wrist, making the blade dance at his command in the few shards of sunlight. It was the man who had stolen his brooch. The thief opened his mouth and pointed at him. Torin swiped his sword across his throat with one hand and reached for a dagger at his belt with the other. Before the man's body hit the ground, Torin slipped his fingers to the small pouch hanging from the man's belt, cut it free, and dropped it into his boot. He flung the dagger at the fourth robber and didn't wait to see where it landed when he blocked a blow to his skull from the last.

By this time, the soldiers had gained their feet and watched him smash the pommel of his sword into the brawny thief's face and then swipe his blade across the man's belly, bringing his knees to the dirt, and then, his face.

With the last of them dead, Torin plunged his blade into the ground and leaned his hands on his thighs to breathe.

"Stranger," one of the soldiers said with awe in voice. "Who are you?"

Torin looked up from his hands and smiled. "Sir Torin Gray. I seek an audience with the Warden of the Western March."

The soldiers stared at him and then shared a brief look with one another. "Why? What do you want?"

"I want to fight in his garrison. Fight alongside his men."

Their eyes opened in surprise and…gladness. "You fight well, Sir Torin," one said, stepping forward. He was the one who had killed the first thief. He was the oldest of the three, mayhap ten years older than Torin. His chin was strong, his shoulders wide, and his nose looked to have been broken numerous times. He bore six different scars on his face that were visible to Torin's eye. Some of the scars were deeper than others. "I'm Rob Adams, this is Sir John Linnington, and Geoffrey Mitchell."

"You saved our lives," Sir John said. "I will make certain Lord Bennett hears of your courage and skill." He looked around at the dead bodies and ran his palm across his forehead. "You took down four men in less time than it took us to figure out what the hell had happened. You did not hesitate once."

"Hesitation gets folks killed," Torin told him, believing it.

The knight nodded and studied him for another moment before he spoke again. "We can use a man like you against the border reivers. Presently, the Carruthers' and Irvines are thorns in our sides. They try to get across the border to rob us at least twice a month. No one's cattle would be safe from them if not for us and some of the other border families."

Torin had heard much about the reivers. The wars between Scotland and England had left the border towns and villages devastated. In order to survive, kinsmen on both sides along the north, west, and east Marches had formed small armies of raiders. They raided with no regard to any laws, save their own—they could not raid their own kin in different regions.

Torin had nothing against them, save that they gave their allegiance to whoever paid the most—which wasn't always the Scots. They were fierce fighters with a cause. To eat. Torin understood it, but it wouldn't stop him from killing them if he had to. He wondered if the thieves he'd killed tonight were reivers.

It didn't matter. He was here to begin the takedown of England's last mighty stronghold.

"You will see our porter, Charles Corbet, first," Sir John told him. "He is the one who decides who may join the garrison. But he will require more than just my word."

"Of course," Torin agreed and reached into a pouch at his belt to produce a folded parchment bearing a wax stamp. "I have this letter from the Earl of Rothbury, Lord William Stone." He had no idea, nor did he care, who the earl was. He only knew the earl lived at Lismoor Castle in Rothbury. He hadn't broken the seal and read the letter. He'd never fought for the earl a day in his life. The Bruce had provided the letter after he likely forced Rothbury to write it. As long as it aided Torin in his cause, he didn't care where it came from.

"Come." Sir John urged him toward the stable. "Do you have a ride?"

Torin went to a large chestnut and white mare with feathered hoofs and a long silky white mane and tail. She was called Avalon, a name he remembered from a story in his childhood. A story his mother used to tell him.

Avalon had been patient through the night while he saw to his task. Now, as he set her free from where she was loosely tied to a post, she nudged him and he stroked her neck, giving her the attention she sought.

"That is a fine beast," Mitchell complimented, walking around her.

"Avalon is no beast," Torin corrected, planting a kiss on her nose when she presented it to him. "She is a lady, born with power and grace, and she is loyal only to me."

As if to test his declaration, Mitchell reached his hand out to touch her—and almost lost two fingers.

Sir John and his companion laughed, and then Mitchell joined them and gained his own saddle.

Torin whispered into Avalon's ear when he passed it, then leaped to his saddle.

He didn't have to flick his reins; a slight touch of his stirrup set her running. She raced along the River Eden and past the three soldiers with her mane flowing behind her, her powerful hooves tearing up the earth.

"Dinna show off, Avalon," Torin said, leaning in and letting his tongue roll naturally for her ears alone.

They arrived at the castle and passed through the massive gates that entered into the outer ward. Torin examined the battlements, counting how many men patrolled. There were not many. Less than twenty. He studied which men had keys and which were aware and awake though the hour was late.

They took their horses to the large stable and Torin left instructions that no one was to touch his horse. After that, he was taken to the gatehouse. He would meet the porter in the morning. Tonight, he would sleep with the rest of the men.

Torin thanked the three who had taken him in and smiled as he lay his head down to sleep. He was in.

He was taken to the keep early the next morning and hired by the porter after a careful examination of his letter of highest recommendation from Rothbury, and news of what he'd done and how he'd fought the night before.

When word came that Corbet was wanted in the great hall, Torin was dismissed and took the opportunity to investigate the rear tower and the weapons house—though he would need the key to get inside from none other than Geoffrey Mitchell, whom he couldn't find at the moment.

In the meantime, he had other things to discover. How many men were housed here? How much food did they store in case of a siege?

But soon Sir John found him in one of the long corridors and pulled him aside. "The Hetheringtons are here. The warden has called you to the great hall to give an account of last night."

Perfect. Torin had been waiting to meet the great defender of Carlisle Castle. He'd found that he enjoyed getting to know his victims before he took them down.

"Rowley Hetherington, the leader is here with two of…" Sir John paused with resignation in his gaze and in his voice when he continued. "…his best warriors. They say the men at the tavern last night were their kinsmen and they know we killed them. Adams has told them nothing. He says he awaits you."

"Good," Torin said as they entered the keep. "I will tell them I did it. Do not trouble yourself over it."

"Sir Torin," the knight said, stopping him before they reached the great hall. "I think 'twas foolish for Lord Bennett to agree to speak with them. No matter what you say, they will find a reason to fight. Have you met reivers? No? They are wild, like rabid dogs—"

"You fear them." Torin didn't know whether to smile or give the knight the look of disgust he deserved.

"They are hungry. Five of them attacked soldiers of Carlisle last night. They do not care who they rob, or who they kill to get what they want. I know you fight well, but a word of warning—when you set eyes on the leader's daughter, Braya, do not be fooled by what you see."

"What do you mean?" Torin asked, fighting the urge to grin at the fool. Was this guardian of Carlisle admitting to being frightened of a common thief? A *woman* thief?

"She is one of the Hetherington's fiercest warriors."

Torin couldn't help the chuckle that escaped his lips as they picked up their steps. "And what might I be fooled by? Is she beautiful?"

Sir John said nothing but pushed open the doors to the great hall.

Torin stepped inside. His gaze found Alexander Bennett first. The warden was taller than Torin had expected, and older. His eyes darted first to Torin and then to another hulking brute standing behind a line of Bennett's men.

The reiver was broad-shouldered and muscular in his *jack,* a short jacket made up of small iron plates sewn between layers of canvas. He wore trews and riding boots, and a sword at his side, as did the two hooded figures behind him. His head was bald and under one arm he carried a steel bonnet. His eyes were the color of an early morning storm. His weathered skin did nothing to lessen the threat of his stance. Of the two behind him, one was much smaller than the other. They both wore jacks beneath their mantles.

"My lord." Sir John moved toward Bennett. "This is Sir Torin Gray. Corbet has accepted his service in your name. He comes with a letter from the Earl of Rothbury."

Bennett waved Torin forward. "Sir John says he and some others were attacked and you came to their aid?"

"That is correct," Torin told him, stepping closer.

"Then explain to Rowley Hetherington and his son what happened last eve."

Torin turned his gaze toward the reivers, to the smaller one—the woman. He thought he saw fire flash in her hooded gaze. He felt the sting of not being acknowledged.

But he wasn't here to call Bennett a fool. Not yet.

He slipped his gaze to the leader. "I saw five thieves attack the warden's soldiers. The soldiers managed to fell one man but they were in poor condition to fight four more. So I killed the rest."

The woman pulled back her hood, exposing long, flaxen waves loosely woven into an unkempt braid dangling down her left side. She had enormous, almond-shaped eyes that pierced through him like blue, flame-tipped arrows.

"That is a bold and arrogant statement, Sir Torin," she said with a voice that fell across his ears like the sting of a whip.

"And a deadly one," the other reiver said, pulling back his hood as well. He resembled the lass in face only, for the hair falling loose to his wide shoulders was as black as the glare he aimed at Torin.

Torin didn't know which one to scowl at, so he scowled at them both. "If you find the truth bold, arrogant, or threatening, then I truly fear for the state of our borders."

He was certain he heard every man in the great hall sigh when the lass smiled and exposed a mischievous dimple in her right cheek. She gave Torin her full attention again and, for an instant, he forgot what they were all doing standing there in the great hall. He could see nothing but her, a beguiling light in the midst of deathly shadows. He thought of Sir John's words, but no warning was sufficient. This slight wisp of a lass, more beautiful than a sunrise after a battle, was one of Hetherington's fiercest warriors?

She opened her mouth to speak but the leader held up his hand to quiet her.

Damn it, Torin would like to have heard what she was going to say. He offered her the slightest of smiles.

"Do you expect me to believe that you killed four of our men with no help from the warden's guardsmen?" the leader demanded in a gravelly voice, dragging Torin's attention away from her.

He looked at the leader and tried to remember what his question was.

"He had help from me," Rob Adams saved him. "Your relatives thought to rob us after all we have done for your family against your enemies. If I had not been so drunk, I would have helped him kill more."

Arguing and threats erupted. Torin turned his attention away from them—from her when she caught his eye again. She was English. He had no interest in her, or her family. He returned his attention to the warden. "Should I have allowed their kinsmen to kill your men?"

Bennett looked from him to the reivers and finally at the ground. "No, of course not. Men, please escort these people out.

CHAPTER TWO

BRAYA UNTIED HER cloak and her scabbard and hung them by the door of her mother's kitchen then removed her heavy jack and hung it up next. She had to get Carlisle's new knight out of her mind. He was arrogant and he'd killed four of her cousins. But he'd looked at her with those large, luminous, frosty green eyes as if he understood things about her—things no one else understood, or wanted to.

"Tie up that hair, gel," her mother called out softly while she set two bowls on the wooden trestle table in the center of the kitchen.

The fragrance of mutton roasted with turnips and carrots wafted from the bowls to Braya's nose. She closed her eyes and breathed in, then slid into her seat on the bench. She looked up upon hearing her father and brother enter the cottage a few moments after seeing to the horses. She knew her father was angry over how they had been treated by the warden; tossed out on their arses as if her kinsmen hadn't fought with Bennett during the attempted Scottish invasion, and countless times after that. She was angry, too.

"The warden has forgotten all he owes to the Hetheringtons," said her brother, Galien, as her father took a seat opposite her. Galien had his own small cottage close by. Braya wished he'd gone to it. He was rash and would try to lead their father into something that could get them all killed.

"We will help him remember," Rowley Hetherington promised. He smiled at his wife when she set the last bowl on the table.

Braya tossed her brother a solemn side-glance. Galien was now the oldest. He was going to inherit all this mayhem and misery. She didn't envy him. Though, she knew he enjoyed robbing and raiding as much as her father did. What happened last night and this morning was more than that. It would not, and should not, be forgotten. But her kinsmen would want more.

"Well," May Hetherington huffed at them and wiped her hands on her apron. "Which one of you is going to tell me what happened? Who is to pay for killing our kinsmen?"

"The reports were correct. 'Twas the warden's men, including Rob Adams, who turns out not to be a friend at all," Galien growled and tore a hunk of bread from the loaf in the center of the table, ignoring the hand his father held up. Mr. Adams had been their friend for many years. "And Sir Torin Gray, a stranger," he continued, bringing the arrogant bastard's face to Braya's mind. "He admitted to killing four of our cousins!"

"Mr. Adams claimed our cousins were trying to rob them," Braya reminded him.

"Which we know is untrue," Galien argued, giving her a hard stare. "Henry and the lads would not have robbed Carlisle's soldiers knowing the pact between us is a fragile one. They were not fools."

They were if they let one man kill all of them.

Braya didn't speak what was on her mind. Where was the sense in it? The men did what they wanted. They didn't listen to her or ask her what she thought. No matter how skilled she was she hadn't earned the respect of any of the men, including her father and brother.

But she had her opinions! Of course, her cousins would have robbed soldiers. They would have robbed anyone who didn't bear the

Hetherington name. Besides, they didn't live in her village but farther up north in Hethersgill. They didn't know the guards the way her immediate family did. They hadn't been raided by the Armstrongs and Elliots. What did they care of the pact made five years ago to fight with the warden against the Scots in exchange for being protected from more powerful families?

"The warden sat there," her father said with leashed fury in his gravelly voice. "He sat there knowing that his men killed ours. He offered no apology. He had us thrown out!"

Galien slammed his fist down on the table then apologized to their mother. "We must make them pay, Father. They killed Henry. He was like a brother to me. I wish to avenge him."

Braya's father nodded and leaned in to pat his son's broad shoulder. "I know. Do not fear. This offense will not go unpunished."

Braya wanted to rise up from her seat and shout at them not to do what they were thinking of doing. Alexander Bennett was too great an ally to lose—not for five rash, rowdy fools!

But she said nothing. She sipped her milk and ate her mutton and listened to a plan that was sure to get them killed. When breakfast was over and the men left the table, Braya helped her mother clean up. There had to be something she could do to stop this.

"Mother?" she asked while they cleaned. "Do you think it wise for us to gather our kinsmen and attack the castle? The warden?"

"What else is there to do?" her mother asked, narrowing her keen blue eyes on her daughter. "Someone must pay."

"But at what cost to our kin? And do you truly believe that Mr. Adams would lie to us? He has sat right here in this kitchen and supped with us. What if he is telling the truth and our men attacked them? A man is not guilty for protecting himself, is he?"

Her mother shook her head. "Not in our laws. But what can we do? You heard your father and Galien. They want blood."

"Their pride is not enough reason to cast away the support of the defender," Braya pointed out. "Who will stop the Armstrongs or the other reivers from robbing and warring with us if we lose the warden? If we must seek revenge, we need only seek it against Sir Torin. Lord Bennett did not even know who he was. He is new to the garrison. The warden will not care if he loses him. As for Mr. Adams, I'm sure Father will forgive him after a while. Perhaps he will even come to believe him."

"Why did you not bring up these concerns to your father?"

"I will," Braya assured her. "But not with Galien around. He will try to talk Father out of whatever I suggest. You know he is jealous that I beat him at so many things."

"He loves you, Braya," her mother admonished tenderly, sweeping her daughter's hair over her shoulder. Her smile was warm, her round, full cheeks were rosy. "Never forget that. Family is everything. Galien would die for you He is prideful, that is all."

Braya loved her. She loved them all. She couldn't let them start a war with the border guards. There must be something she could do. "I must stop this before word is sent out to our kinsmen."

She kissed her mother's cheek, grabbed her cloak, and stepped out into the warm summer air. She looked to the right, toward the rolling hills, where her brother herded the cattle, and to the River Eden beyond the trees. She knew where to find her father. She turned to the left and hurried toward the cemetery behind the house.

She found him standing before a gravestone with the name of her eldest brother, Ragenald, engraved on it, though Ragenald himself was not in the grave. The Bruce's soldiers had killed her brother at Bannockburn. His body was not recovered.

As if to remind the living that the earth was filled with the dead, it seemed cooler here, just a bit darker though it was only early afternoon.

Braya hated it here. She was alive and she wanted to remain that way. She didn't want any more of her family in this place—not for a long time.

Her father came here every day after he ate. No one disturbed him while he stood before the stone. Braya didn't know if he spoke to the stone that was all that was left of his son, or stared at the grave, or wept.

Pulling on her belt and girding up her loins, she approached silently and placed her palm on his forearm. "Father?"

He turned his hooded face to her. She could see the alarm in his glassy gray eyes.

She offered him a tender smile. "Forgive me for disturbing you."

"'Tis quite all right," he assured her in a soft, mild tone, soothed by her smile. "I was seeking Ragenald's counsel regarding the scoundrel Bennett, and his men."

Good, Braya thought, then he hadn't yet made his final decision. "And has he given it?"

His broad chest fell from his long, deep sigh. "Alas, he has not."

She looked down at the stone. She missed her brother. Raggie was the only person in her life who fed her desire to fight as well as any man. She was a reiver, as good at thieving and fighting as the other men, better than Galien. She never apologized to him for it, and she never would. She'd worked hard—she still did—practicing at being the best. She was three and ten when Ragenald died. Since then, no one in her family, direct or distant, praised or rewarded her for her skill. In fact, all of the men at the games, or the ones she'd raided with, scorned her just for being there with them, whether she'd helped save their miserable lives or not. "I would offer mine," she said, lifting her eyes to her father's.

He stared at her with indulgence filling his gaze and nodded.

"I would beg you to truly listen, Father, for one day I may be standing here over *your* grave. Or mayhap, 'twill be mine or Galien's if we attack the castle."

"With the help of our kinsmen, we can triumph over them," he said, sounding indulgent now, as well.

"I do not doubt our victory. 'Tis what happens after that which concerns me." She didn't have much time to convince him before he sent her away, or Galien arrived. "We will lose a powerful ally. Aye, 'tis more peaceful now in the summer months, but what about when we need to raid more frequently? What will the other reivers do when they learn our protection is gone?" He looked like he might try to answer, so she quickly continued. "Father, we have known Robert Adams since I was a child, before he became a border guard. Do you truly believe he would look you in the eyes and lie? Or that he would kill any one of our lads if they were innocent? What if he and Sir Torin are innocent?"

He shook his head. "How will we know?"

"I do not know yet, but if Sir Torin is guilty then let us bring his head to the fallen lads' fathers. Let the knight's blood be enough before we lose more, Father. A war with the warden will cost us too much."

"If he is guilty, I shall send Galien into their midst. I—"

What? Galien? Braya pushed away from her father. "You would send him over me? Why?"

He had no answer, so she provided him with more direct questions. "Am I not a better fighter than Galien?"

"You have shown yourself a worthy opponent against him and the rest of our kinsmen at the games," he allowed. "But the stranger felled four men—"

"Proving that 'twill take cunning, *not* strength to take him down," she countered.

He stared at her and, for an agonizing moment, she feared he would dismiss her and her concerns. Then, he dipped his gaze to his first son's grave. "Aye," he finally said, lifting his gaze to her. "You are the most clever of my children."

"We do not want to lose you, Father."

His gaze went soft as he pulled her in for a quick embrace. "Let me ponder my decision. I will inform everyone of it in the morn."

She nodded, pressed against his strong chest. "I know you will do the right thing, for you have proven yourself wise."

He kissed the top of her head. "Thank you, my dear. 'Twould seem then that you take after me in more than just your sword arm."

What was that? A compliment? Was he calling her wise, or strong?

"Now go," he said as he gave her a little push away, scattering her thoughts, "for I must speak with your brother."

She wasn't sure which brother he meant since Galien was making his way over. She passed him on her way out of the cemetery without a word when he cast her a questioning look.

She finished the rest of her morning chores, pondering her father's words and finding herself smiling for most of the morning. After that, she enjoyed some conversation at the riverbank with her cousins, Lucy and Millie. The topic was, of course, apples—poor, pregnant Millie's passion for them, and the scarcity of them being found during raids.

When they exhausted the topic of the red, crunchy fruit, their conversation switched to the presumably English knight who had claimed to kill four Hetheringtons with no help from anyone else.

"Is he handsome or hideous? Millie asked, rubbing her swollen belly from where she sat on a small rock and dipped her toes in the river.

Lucy laughed softly behind her fingertips.

The girls were coy and ladylike, appealing to a part of Braya she missed when she was raiding, or besting the men. She had even changed into her stay and skirts while she was with them. She'd known the two her whole life and loved them like sisters. Millie was married to Will Noble and was expecting their first babe any day now.

Braya didn't want there to be fighting and bloodshed when Millie was delivering her babe.

"He is not unpleasing to the eye," she told them, stretched across a large rock. Her eyes were closed against the sun. Her thoughts filled with the memory of him looking at her when the warden had given her no notice.

In contrast to his dark golden brows flaring upward, his wintery green eyes were large and dipped downward on the outer corners. Together, they made his gaze sultrier, more alluring. His soft, silken curls were like a halo of chestnut and gold around his head. "He is arrogant and unrepentant."

"What will your father decide?" Millie asked with worry lacing her voice.

"I think he will do the best thing for all, and that is to take revenge on Sir Torin and count the misdeed settled."

"But what if you are correct," Lucy put to her. "What if our cousins robbed Carlisle's soldiers? What if Sir Torin was just protecting them as he and Mr. Adams claim?"

Braya knew that was a possibility. She wondered how she could discover the truth. She couldn't think of anything and opened her eyes to turn her gaze toward home. What if the warden's newest guard was innocent of murder? What should they do then? There was no law against it, but all reivers looked down upon killing innocent men. Her family would lose all support. "I cannot let my father gather the Hetheringtons for a battle at Carlisle. They will never believe the knight's tale."

She remained with her friends for another hour spent worrying. When she'd had enough, she returned home for her sword and her bow and quiver of arrows, and set off on her own across the shallow river for a little hunting.

Distracted by chasing hares, she traveled farther on foot than she had intended and almost stumbled into a small, sunlit clearing within the thicket. Alone in the clearing was a most breathtaking horse. A kind of horse Braya had never seen before.

Keeping just beyond the tree line, she barely breathed, afraid she might be dreaming this magnificent being. It was huge. Braya thought if she stood beside it, her head would barely reach the top of the creature's back. It was white with splotches of rich chestnut brown from its nose to its behind. Its long, opulent mane and thick flowing tail were pure white—as were the tufts of hoary hair covering its hooves.

Braya left the cover of the trees and walked slowly toward the horse. It was saddled. To whom did it belong? She didn't care. She'd like to take it. Oh, to ride such a magnificent animal!

She inched closer and held out her hand just as the horse turned its regal head and stared off to her right.

Braya lowered her hand and followed its gaze to a man standing alone on the other side of the glade. Sir Torin Gray! He hadn't seen her!

She reached for her sword. She could sneak up on him and...what was he doing bending to smell a flower? He brought his fingers to the blossom and lifted it closer. He closed his eyes and breathed as if the fragrance were bringing him back to life. Free of his hood, his sun-kissed curls fell loosely around his face, accentuating the strong cut of his slightly bearded jaw. The sight of him beguiled Braya senseless.

What in the blazes was the matter with her? This man had killed her cousins. Unless he had a good reason, he was an enemy.

The horse blew out a loud breath and neighed.

The knight's eyes opened and went directly to his mount...and to Braya standing beside it. He lifted his hand over his left shoulder and clasped the hilt of his blade beneath his mantle. In an instant, he went from glorious in the late sunlight, to graceful and deadly.

She wasn't sure she could fight him with a knife. If he truly had taken down four men on his own, she didn't want to try. She released her hilt and held up her hands.

"Miss Hetherington," he said, pulling his sword from its sheath anyway. He looked around for anyone else. "You are alone?"

Her spine stiffened. What would he try if he thought she was? "No," she lied. "My group is close by. My brother is likely searching for me right now."

He did his best to conceal his amusement, but she caught the slight curl of his full mouth. He didn't believe her. "Well, he shall find you in safe hands."

Braya tried to slow her thrashing heart. It was making her feel lightheaded. What should she do? What was he going to do? Why was she standing around doing nothing? She'd killed before, but those men were trying to kill her during a raid. This was different. What if this man had just been in the wrong place at a bad time? What if he had told the truth and he'd come upon five men attacking the border guards? She'd still prefer that he died rather than any of her kinsmen, but she didn't want it done if he was innocent of murder. She pushed her mantle aside and touched the hilt of her sword again. His gaze immediately followed. "What are you doing so far from the castle, Gray?" she asked.

He kept his eyes on her hand. "I was having a look around, trying to get to know Cumberland. I wandered off too far." He finally lifted his gaze to hers. She wished he hadn't. His eyes were mesmerizing and...melancholy. They drew her into a place she did not wish to go. "Please, call me Torin."

He came a bit closer, tempting Braya to step back. He was too close to shoot with an arrow. Did she want to pretend she couldn't fight? So often men had misjudged her, as Sir Torin was doing by re-sheathing his sword. Most of her opponents bore scars from her blades for it. What had the other soldiers told him about her? No matter. If he tried anything, she'd castrate him faster than he could blink.

"How about you, Miss Hetherington?" he asked. His voice was like the song of a siren, beguiling, with a subtle undercurrent of something melodious. "What are you...and your group doing so far from the border?"

How far was she from home? She thought about it and drew in a small bit of her bottom lip between her teeth. "We were hunting. We wandered off too far, as well."

His gaze deepened on her. She looked away from the power of it. The power to render her breathless, helpless, and reckless. She had things to discover about him, and if he needed killing to prevent an all-out war, she might even be the one who had to do it. She wouldn't let the chance to find out the truth escape her because the knight was handsome. She kept her fingers at her hilt just the same.

"Do you always stop to smell flowers?"

"Sadly, not always," he replied. He moved closer until his nearness made her blood feel warm as it rushed through her veins. He was close enough to run him through—or to kiss her if he bent down.

She could end everything now. Her father wouldn't have to decide. Her extended family would not be called to gather, and there would be no war with the warden.

He reached out his hand and, for a moment, Braya thought he was reaching for her. Her heart banged in her ears.

"I see you have met Avalon," he said, scratching between the horse's ears.

"Avalon," she repeated, liking the sound of it. "That—" she paused to let her heart slow down. "That is a lovely name. What does it mean?" What in damnation was she doing growing breathless over him, asking meaningless questions about his horse when she had so many other things to find out?

"'Tis a place where a legendary king was taken to recover from his wounds after fighting his enemy. 'Tis sometimes called the island of apples."

"The island of apples?" she said with a soft laugh. She couldn't help it, for it felt as if a thousand dragonflies just flew across her belly. Still, she kept her fingers at her hilt. "How wonderful." Which legendary king was taken there? She wanted to hear more. She shouldn't. She should ask what she wanted to ask, and then return home and tell her father what happened.

But golden light spilled around him, making him appear almost otherworldly.

"Have you ever been to Avalon?" She couldn't help but want to know. Perhaps he would tell her the way. She would ask him the more important question when the moment was right. It was still early enough not to be missed at home. She often went off alone. Besides, she liked the tale, and she liked the sound of Sir Torin's voice telling it.

He shook his head and his hair fell into his eyes. He plunged his fingers through it and cleared it away. He looked more like something from her dreams than a skillful killer. "'Tis said to be a magical place that produces all things of itself. Fields have no need of the plough. Nature provides everything and people live there a hundred years or more."

Her eyes opened wider, causing his gaze on her to go warm. "Do you believe 'tis a real place?"

"No," he said, his slight smile fading as he dropped his arm to his side. "But I like the idea of it."

Aye. So did Braya. No fighting. No hunger. But he was correct. It wasn't real. "Tell me what happened with my kin at the tavern. I must know the truth."

He knit his brow and slipped his shadowed gaze from his horse to her. "I already told your father what happened."

"Tell it to me, please, Sir."

What more did she need? He'd admitted to killing her kin; whether he had been trying to save Carlisle's soldiers or not, he had killed them. He was her family's enemy. She should kill him and run. How would she prove anything to her father if she had their enemy in her hands and did nothing but swoon over him?

"Sit and eat with me here," he invited her, "and I will repeat to you what you heard me say in the great hall."

She shook her head and realized that her fingers were nowhere near her hilt. "My brother—"

"Is nowhere near. You are alone," he told her, looking at her calmly in the face. "You have nothing to fear from me."

She doubted it. Though he was comforting, there was something innately dangerous about him.

"If I did," she answered, fighting not to be affected by his rakishly tousled hair falling around his face like a nimbus, "you would not find me so easily overcome."

His jaw tightened as if he were keeping his words from leaving his mouth. She thought she might have caught something dark pass across his features. A challenge, perhaps? He said nothing.

"All right," she allowed and moved aside when he reached out again, this time for a large bag tied to Avalon's saddle.

She knew it was a bad decision to stay when he untied his mantle and spread it out in the grass and offered her a seat. But when he sat close and opened the bag of food and six ripe, red apples fell across her lap, she thought of Millie and reconsidered.

CHAPTER THREE

TORIN STUDIED BRAYA Hetherington while she watched Avalon grazing close by. He didn't want to think about how she appeared as delicate as a veil in her flowing mantle and skirts, or which shimmered more in the sunlight—her hair or her eyes. Or that she was English.

What was she doing here with him?

He'd had a feeling the reivers wouldn't simply forget about their kin dying at his hands. Had they sent her to kill him? Why hadn't she already tried? What would he do if she did? He hoped they hadn't sent her. He'd hate to have to hurt a woman. He'd always avoided it in the past.

He was surprised she had agreed to stay. She was odd, showing little fear of being alone in the forest with a strange man.

"What brings you to Carlisle?" she asked.

He couldn't tell her the truth. That he was going to take the castle for King Robert the Bruce. "I had planned on just traveling through. I do not like staying in one place overlong."

Her expression hardened a bit, but she nodded, as if she felt the same way. "And now that you are part of the defender's border guards, will you be staying in Carlisle?"

He couldn't wait to leave it five breaths after he had stepped foot in England.

He offered her a well-practiced smile. "Perhaps."

He wasn't sure if he liked the way she looked at him. It was more of an examination—a thorough one, carried out by striking, strategic eyes, as blue as the vast summer sky. It made him want to fall in—toss aside his good sense and stay a little while longer.

He blinked his gaze away from her and looked around at the trees. He felt at home in them. Safe until...

"Tell me what happened last night at the tavern." Braya's silky voice pulled him back.

He told her the same story he had told in Bennett's great hall. She asked a few questions, which he answered without hesitation. "I hadn't known they were reivers, or friends to the warden," he added, telling her what he sensed she wanted to hear. "'Twas dark and I saw that they were about to kill their opponents."

"And you would rush to the aid of soldiers," she said a bit stiffly.

"I rushed to the aid of three attacked by five," he corrected. "I did not like the odds."

"Ah, then you are a man of fairness?"

He crooked one corner of his mouth and then popped a grape into it. She was about to try to trap him into something. He could see it in her bright, eager gaze. He wanted to give her her way—just to find out how good she was at being dangerous. "Aye, I try to be fair."

"And you believe 'twas fair to attack four men knowing you have the skill of six? Why did you kill them all? What were you trying to prove? Something to the soldiers, mayhap?"

Hell. For a moment, he simply stared at her, realizing she was deadly, indeed. He'd let himself be fooled by what he saw. She was clever—too clever. The passion painting her voice tempted him to remain silent, lest he say the wrong thing and give himself away.

"They all came at me at once." It wasn't untrue. "They would have killed me."

"You killed four men—at once?" She gave him a doubtful look.

He nodded and pushed more food in front of her. "I have been fighting for a very long time."

"Oh? And what is your age?"

"A score and seven," he told her. "And you?"

"A score and two."

"Unwed?" he asked.

She nodded, and Torin watched with delight as a crimson blush stole across her cheekbones. "No man will have me."

He almost choked on his bread. Did she jest? What the hell kind of fool wouldn't have her? "Why? What is wrong with you?" he asked with suspicion clouding his thoughts.

"They do not like the fact that I can fight better than they can."

It was difficult not to smile at her the way every other man had this morn in the great hall.

"I was told," he said softly, watching her pick at a hunk of black bread and bring it to her mouth, "you were one of the reivers' fiercest warriors." And he shouldn't forget it. Who else would they send after him but their best?

As if to prove him a fool to believe such a tale, her smiled widened, along with her eyes and pure joy filled her radiant expression. "Do you believe it, my lord?"

It was difficult not to be affected by her. What he'd been told of her was true. What he saw with his eyes made him doubt it. She looked more like an angel than a warrior.

He nodded. He believed it. She piqued his curiosity. Not many things did anymore. "It must be true if some men are afraid of you."

"Some?" The teasing quirk of her lips beckoned him to test her.

"Aye, some," he said, letting her know he wasn't one of them, though he wouldn't underestimate her.

They stared at each other across the ringing silence. The longer he looked, the harder it was to look away.

"Tell me," she finally said, "what else were you told by your friends?"

"My friends?" He took a swig of wine from his pouch and realized whom she meant, then offered the pouch to her. "I do not trouble myself with friends." He watched her while she took a drink. "But Sir John is afraid of you."

She nodded, handing him back the pouch. "Aye, he should be. Once, he made the error of thinking I was weak, and tried to force himself upon me."

Torin wasn't surprised to hear of the vile nature of the English, even ones dressed as knights. "And what happened?" he asked, biting into an apple.

Her eyes danced like cornflowers in the summer breeze. "I'm certain he bears the mark of my blade, but I have no interest in seeing for myself."

Torin smiled. "You gained his respect through fear."

"He left me no other choice," she told him and continued picking at her bread.

"I did not know. Now I do." He tried to sound impassive, but his voice was low and rough. He'd grown up an orphan, and then a servant, then, a soldier. He was quite used to seeing men forcing their wills on women. It was one of his strongest memories he had of his mother.

John Linnington would be one of the first Torin killed when the time came.

He looked down at the food he'd packed, spread out between them. He hadn't seen her eat any of it, yet most was gone. Four apples? More than half the bread and the cheese? Had he eaten so much? He would admit she distracted him, but would he forget eating?

He quickly noted the bulges beneath her mantle. She must have slits in the fabric so she could reach the pouches tied to her belt along with her sword. She was stealing his food. He had the urge to laugh. He bit the inside of his lip instead. Perhaps her kin needed it.

"When did Sir John do this?"

"He has not been the only one," she told him. "Most of the men in the garrison have learned a hard lesson at the tip of my blade, if you must know the truth. There are but a few who have not."

"Their names?" Torin asked her quietly, sounding only slightly interested. "The ones who have not."

She gave them, including Rob Adams. "I'm acquainted with all the men. I have spent much time in the castle with my father over the years he and Lord Bennett have been friends."

Aye, they were friends, Torin remembered. Mayhap he could find out more. "What is their friendship based on?"

"We have a mutual enemy."

"Oh? Who?"

"The Scots," she told him. "We helped keep them away when they attacked Carlisle five years ago and, in exchange, the defender offers us his protection against the other reivers."

So, the Scot's defeat against Carlisle was due to help from the reivers. Torin was going to have to make certain Bennett didn't receive their help again. "Your father must have found great insult by being thrown out of Carlisle."

"He did." She looked away. There was more she wasn't telling him.

"He is planning something." It was an obvious assessment, though she appeared uneasy when she heard him speak it. "Were you sent to kill me, Miss Hetherington?"

He decided she was just as alluring frowning as she was smiling.

"No, my lord, I was not. I wandered off too far and happened on Avalon." She shifted on his mantle in the grass and avoided his gaze. She pushed a lock of her loose flaxen hair behind her ear, reached for a grape, and then shifted again.

He waited until she stopped moving. But she was also finished speaking. Her silence told him plenty. Something was being planned against him, or against Bennett and the entire garrison. "I must warn you, Miss Hetherington," he said in a low, quiet voice and moved an inch closer to her, "many have tried to kill me and have failed. Whoever comes will die and I will feel like hell because you will hate me for it."

She went from pink to pale so quickly he thought she might turn green next. "What if..." She stopped and drew in a deep breath then began again. "What if 'tis me who comes in the morn?"

He gave her a doleful look and pushed out a ragged sigh. "Ah, I hope 'tis not you."

She arched her brow at him. "Are you saying you would kill me?"

"Would you kill me?" He realized how foolish their questions were. They hardly knew each other. Why would either of them hesitate to kill the other if they had to?

She did not answer. Nor did he.

"I do not find you ordinary or dull," he told her instead.

"And you find others so?"

"Aye. All of them. I know them. I have seen them in the faces and actions of others. They are all the same. But you seem different." His gaze captured hers for a moment before she looked away. "Perhaps I'm mistaken."

"Perhaps," she countered softly, "you assume too much, too quickly."

He didn't. He knew he was correct about her. There was something refreshing and different about Braya Hetherington. He was beginning to believe what he'd heard about her being a fierce warrior. He'd heard of women warriors before. Songs were still sung on the other side of Hadrian's Wall about fearsome Pictish queens. Something about Braya reminded him of the nine sisters of Avalon and made him want to smile at her—not for the first time today.

This wasn't the time to go soft on someone. It hadn't happened since little Florie Moffat when he was seven and lasted for three years after that. Just a few years after fleeing the massacre of his family, Torin had returned from visiting the village of Pitlochry with Jonathon and found Florie's dead body along with most of the other children he'd come to care for. They had been killed by the English when they found the orphans' camp.

Going soft hurt, so he never let it happen again. It worked out much better for him to draw others in while remaining distant.

It could be her coming to kill him in the morning. He needed to win her today so that he wouldn't need to kill her tomorrow.

"Forgive me," he atoned. "And forgive me for killing your kin."

He started to rise but the slightest touch of her fingertips on his knee stopped him. "All right, I forgive you," she granted, her voice a soulful melody to his ears.

Who else's forgiveness did he seek and would never find?

"But I fear 'twill not change anything," she said on a soft whisper. "'Twill be worse now."

Torin wished he hadn't met her. She was caught in the middle of his battle and would likely end up a casualty. He'd already saved one lass, young Miss Julianna Feathers, from the hell he'd unleashed on her home in Berwick. He wasn't completely wretched.

But Braya Hetherington was different. She wasn't helpless. He had to sever the Hetheringtons' friendship with Bennett so she would not fight against the king's army when they came to Carlisle again. He might meet her on the field.

He almost shook his head at the notion of it.

He would do what he could. In the meantime, he could keep abreast of what the reivers were doing through her. He would have to spend more time with her—that is, if they had any time before her kin struck back.

"Then let us enjoy the afternoon, for 'twill likely be the last time we spend together." Saying it left a sour taste on his tongue.

"I hope that is not true," she said, then turned scarlet as if she hadn't meant to speak the words out loud.

He wanted to laugh. He almost did. What was this spell she was weaving over him to make him forget she was an enemy, a hater of Scots? She could have stabbed him four times already and he would have been too slow and distracted by her to stop her.

"Tell me, Torin," she said a few moments later, as sweetly as the scented breeze. "Why do you bear the name Gray? 'Tis a name of a border family in the eastern Marches."

"Gray is not my true name," he told her. "I took it as a boy after lying in the grass and staring up at the sky. I felt a kinship with the clouds."

Her expression softened on him. "What is your true name?" she asked, no longer bothering to pretend interest in eating.

"I do not remember." He only remembered Florie and the other children telling him it was Scottish and to stop using it. So he had. Some nights, he wasn't certain if Torin was his true name. Had he made it up when he was a child?

He knew when her face went pale that he'd said too much. Living along the border, she wasn't immune to the horrors of war.

"What age were you orphaned?" she asked him.

"Five."

Instantly, her huge sapphire eyes filled with tears. "We do not have to speak of this," she said.

He didn't know why he had told her anything. He didn't want to relive a single moment of his life. "What about you?" he asked. "What is life like for a reiver?"

"'Tis simple. We guard and protect everything we own, or we lose it. If we do not raid, we do not eat. The land is unsuitable for arable farming. Our livestock keep us alive and every other reiver who does not belong to our kin would try to take it. King Edward does not care about us, nor does the King of Scots, so we live outside the law. We have our own laws that are respected and even followed by some wardens. We owe no allegiance to anyone but ourselves."

"And to the warden for offering his protection against the other reivers," Torin reminded her.

She studied him for a moment with curious eyes. "You sound as if you are troubled by such an alliance."

"Only because I have put it in jeopardy," he answered, but it was more than that. His task was to take Carlisle from within. He couldn't have outside forces getting involved.

He would likely need to betray Braya. He'd betrayed other people's trusts a thousand times in the past. He planned on doing so to Bennett at some point in the future. It was how he'd become so successful. If he were called on to betray Miss Hetherington, he would.

"I should be getting back home," she said, dragging him from his dark thoughts. She was up on her feet in one motion. He was up in two.

"Let me see you halfway home." It wasn't that he didn't want to leave her, though if he thought about it for a moment too long, he might admit that she was compelling and amusing.

"I can take care of myself," she assured him, flashing her dimple. She moved and her hips jiggled beneath her mantle.

He looked down at the food that was left and smiled. It was all gone. He picked up the pouch and handed it to her. "You will likely be needing this more than I."

He knew what she had taken and that she was going to return on foot. The pouch would help her carry the food stuffed into God knows what beneath her mantle. "Will I see you again, Miss Hetherington?"

She turned to him and stopped. Her dimple faded and her eyes grew large and regretful. "You might."

CHAPTER FOUR

Braya returned to her village after supper and met Galien on the way to his small cottage a short distance from their parents' house. "'Tis almost dark. Where have you been, Braya?"

"I was hunting," she replied, pushing her way past him.

"Oh?" he asked, catching up easily. "What did you kill?"

She pushed the right side of her mantle away from her hip and revealed the heavy pouch tied to her belt. "Apples, bread, cheese, and grapes."

She opened the door and left him standing at the entrance of the cottage, gaping after her. She hoped he wouldn't follow, but, of course, he did. Her heart beat even faster. Galien wouldn't listen, and he might convince her father not to listen either. She felt a bit lightheaded and unsteady on her feet. She had to tell her father the truth about where she had spent her day, how she had gotten the food. Mostly, she had to tell him about Sir Torin Gray.

She found Rowley Hetherington in the kitchen, sitting on a stool by the fire. His wife was standing behind him and working her fingers into his shoulders.

"Braya," her mother was the first to greet her. "You are late for supper. You will explain why, and then you may eat the food I have set aside for you on the table."

"Thank you, Mother. Forgive me for being late. I—"

"Braya has food," her brother blurted out. "Apples, and bread, cheese, and grapes!"

Braya turned to stare open-mouthed at him. She wished she could hit him over the head with something. It worried her that he couldn't command control over his tongue. Where would it leave her family when her father was gone?

Still glaring at him, she revealed the pouch, and then untied it.

When she dumped the contents onto the table, her father left his stool and came to stand at her side. "Where did you come upon this?"

She had to tell him because she hated lying to him. She respected him and admired his leadership. He had never been reckless, nor had he ever put his pride before the safety of the family. He had to know how Sir Torin felt before he made his decision. She wished her brother wasn't here, but there was nothing she could do about it.

"While I was out hunting, I came upon a man in the forest." She looked up into her father's gaze. "By the time I realized 'twas Sir Torin Gray—"

Both he and Galien stared at her, their mouths hanging open. Braya fought to steady her voice when she hastily continued. This wasn't the time in her life to go weak. She'd never let anything make her falter. This was no different. "We spoke, Father. He asked my forgiveness for killing our kin, but he insists they were about to kill the warden's men."

"You were alone with this murderer?" Galien demanded, looking stunned.

"Did he lay a hand on you?" her father growled.

"If he had," she gave them both an incredulous look, "do you think I would have come away without blood on my clothes? Do you not know me? He did not touch me. He gave me food to eat and I stole the rest."

Her father stared at her for a moment, his shrewd gaze piercing in the low light. "You are brave, Daughter." His low, gravelly voice was sweet in her ears. "Sometimes to the point of foolishness."

Her smile faded.

"But being alone in the damned forest with the killer of our relatives is by far the most foolish thing you have ever done." He held up his palm to stop her when she parted her lips to defend herself. "What were you thinking? That you would try to find out the truth, alone with him?" His eyes on her widened. "Did you?"

"I do not know. Perhaps. Aye."

"Which is it, Braya? Is he guilty? Did you try to kill him? 'Twas *your* suggestion we kill him to avenge the lads. But no." His voice dipped low, along with his brows. "You said he fed you. What happened?"

"We spoke, Father," she repeated to him and straightened her shoulders.

"What did you speak about?"

"I told you, he asked my forgiveness for killing my cousins. When I asked him why he killed them all, he explained that they had come at him at once. At once, Father." She waited a moment, letting her words sink in. "He is either extremely skilled, or the warden's men lied and helped him kill all the lads. But why would Mr. Adams admit to killing someone if they were going to deceive us?" She spoke quickly while Galien took in everything she said. "I do not believe we were deceived. I believe Sir Torin is a very skilled fighter. But he does not wish to fight us." She didn't tell her father how confident he was that he would kill anyone who came against him. Or that it still sent a chill up her spine because he made her believe he could do it. "He told me he was troubled because he had put our alliance with the warden in jeopardy."

Her father narrowed his eyes on her. "You believe he was telling the truth?"

"He had no reason not to," she answered softly.

"Father," Galien interjected. "Are we going to take the word of a stranger who claims our boys tried to kill the border guards?"

Oh, Braya could not believe how blind and unfair her brother was. "And Mr. Adams?" she asked him. "Since when has he lied to us? You saw how angry he was that our lads had attacked him."

His eyes smoldered with anger as his gaze found hers. "It seems you forget that five of our cousins are dead. Five, Braya. Are you not loyal to your family?"

"I am, Galien," she said through clenched teeth. "I'm concerned for the rest of us if we fight the warden and his men. Gather all the Hetheringtons you want, but when the battle is over and everyone returns to their homesteads far away, we will be left here with no extra protection from other reivers. Remember we are no friends with the Armstrongs. We will lose the support of the other wardens. We could lose everything…everyone. And for what? Pride? Revenge?"

Galien's face grew redder, making his eyes shine like burning flames. "Our family must be—"

"Galien!" Rowley Hetherington roared out the thunderous command, draining the color from his son's face. "She is correct. Sir Torin has asked for forgiveness. If he and Adams ask it of me, I will grant it."

Galien looked about to speak, but his father held up his hand. "I will not sacrifice more of you. You will do as I say and let this punishment go unfulfilled if 'tis what I wish. Do you understand?"

Galien reluctantly nodded, then stormed out of the cottage.

Braya's father turned to her without sparing a glance after her brother. "Send word to Mr. Adams tomorrow. Invite him and Sir Torin to meet me in the town hall in two days. Tell them," he instructed, his steely eyes hard and merciless. "If they do not come, I will bring battle to Carlisle and every one of them will die."

Braya sighed. Both sides believed themselves to be unbeatable. She was a bit more sensible. Everyone was beatable, even the most renowned leader, a raider for over twenty years. Her father was strong and experienced, but she wasn't sure if that was enough to triumph over a young man, who, if he had spoken the truth, had killed four men at once.

Galien's brute force could possibly take Torin down, but what if it didn't? She didn't want to watch another brother die. What if her father brought war to the fortress and Torin killed four more of her family members at once—before even more of them perished?

What could she do to stop it? The answer wasn't killing Torin. It was getting him to ask the forgiveness of her family. "I will do as you ask, Father."

"Hmm." He picked up an apple and examined it. "What changed your mind about him, Braya?"

Now? Now he saw fit to ask her opinion on something? "He was orphaned by the Scots at the tender age of five. He had a difficult time. You can see it in his eyes. But somehow, I do not know, perhaps God shows him favor, but he survived and he became a very skilled fighter, one whom the Earl of Rothbury recommends. And yet…"

"And yet?" her mother repeated in the same quiet tone.

"When I found him, he was smelling a flower. When I spoke to him, I found him to be genuine."

"We shall see," her father said, then set his gaze on the table. "For now, I must decide what to do with this food."

"There is not much," Braya noted without being asked, "but I would like two apples for Millie, please."

He handed them to her without quarrel and then placed the other two into separate pouches. He did the same with the grapes, bread, and cheese. He would hand them out tomorrow to whatever families needed it most.

When he was done, he took his wife's hand and bid Braya goodnight.

After a supper of cooled rabbit stew, Braya cleaned up and left the cottage to deliver Millie's apples.

Her friend walked with her in the moonlight to the tree-lined riverbank, unafraid of attack. Her family still had the protection of the border guards. If reivers attacked, they'd meet the defender's soldiers first. Braya didn't want anything to change.

They sat together on a large rock and dipped their toes in the water.

"I'm still unsure if he did not plan out the entire thing to make himself appear the hero to the guards," Braya confessed to her friend. "If that is the case," she said, shaking her head hopelessly, "then he is truly ruthless and deadly."

"Well, what do you feel in your belly?" Millie asked and then took a bite out of her apple.

"He is charming." Braya smiled before she could stop herself. "His countenance is perfectly crafted and his tongue is as smooth as a serpent's. But I believed him when he asked for my forgiveness. I believe he is innocent of murder. Do not ask me why, because I cannot tell you."

Millie curled her arm around Braya's waist and pulled her close. "I trust you, Braya. If you believe him, then so do I. But will he agree to your father's condition of seeking forgiveness in the town hall?"

"I will have to make him."

"But how? What if..." Millie stopped and cast Braya a nervous glance. "What if he demands a kiss?"

A kiss? Would she grant him his desire? He would be the first. "I...I'm not certain what I would do."

Millie giggled. Braya joined her.

"Every time he came nearer to me today," she said, sobering, "my heart beat madly in my chest and my head felt light. I do not know if I would push him away."

"All the more reason you must make him come to the town hall,"

Millie insisted, chewing her apple. "If there is something between you, he cannot be an enemy."

Was there something between them? They had met twice. The second time, they ate together and opened up a little to each other. Did it mean anything? Of course not. The moment he saw her fight, he would recoil with hurt pride. "There is nothing between us," she promised her friend. "He is handsome and he seems to want peace. 'Tis beguiling. That is all."

She stayed with Millie for a little while longer and then returned home and went to her small room at the far end of the house. She undressed down to her chemise and climbed onto her straw mattress. She closed her eyes to sleep, but thoughts and images of Torin invaded her mind. What kind of man was he behind his restrained smiles and thoughtful gazes? A man who knew stories about legendary kings and magic islands and who had named himself after the clouds. He wasn't what she had expected. In Carlisle's great hall, he had seemed arrogant, but today he had been calm and quietly confident.

Would Torin come and humble himself before her father and the families of the victims? It was a beginning. More than she had this morning. This morning, she had wanted Torin Gray dead. Now, she thought it would be nice to see him again tomorrow.

She closed her eyes and finally fell asleep thinking about a man who smelled flowers and rode a horse called Avalon.

CHAPTER FIVE

TORIN RAKED HIS fingers through his hair and pulled it all into a thin strip of leather behind his head. He didn't like it falling into his face while he practiced. He closed his eyes and tilted up his face to the new dawn.

He was glad the night was over. For with it had come dreams of Braya Hetherington. Dreams of kissing her, laughing with her, of desires that were unfamiliar and unwanted. He had a duty to see to, a promise to a wee lad to keep.

He rolled up the sleeves of his léine and adjusted the belt on his hips. Was it already a bit tighter? It wouldn't surprise him. The food served in the great hall was rich and filled with things that made a man fat and lazy. That was why he found himself on the practice field in the inner ward, alone with the crowing roosters.

Later, he would invite Sir John and the others to practice with him so he could discover how well was their defense. He didn't put much hope in a good fight when he finally took down Carlisle.

He'd returned back to the castle late last night and most of the men had been asleep at their posts, open and vulnerable to attack. It had pleased him.

But not as much as what he'd heard Braya say about him earlier.

...my heart beat madly in my chest and my head felt light. I do not know if I would push him away.

She liked him. She trusted him. It was all he needed for victory.

He had followed her home last night. If her father was about to make some momentous decision, Torin wanted to know about it early, if possible, to better plan his defense. Also, it was good to know where the reivers lived.

From his position in the trees, he'd watched the huge younger man from the great hall, whom Torin assumed was her brother, storm out of the cottage. Torin wondered if she had told her family where she'd been and with whom, and this was their reaction.

Not long after that, the front door had opened and Braya stepped into the twilight. She'd worn her hood far over her face, but he'd known it was her. He'd followed her slight frame and agile steps to another lass' house, and then shamelessly followed them and listened to what they had said.

He'd learned that her father wanted a public apology. It was better than wanting a fight.

What if he demands a kiss? Her friend, who was heavy with child, had asked.

A kiss. Torin had thought of it more than once, and was not opposed to the idea. Oddly enough, Miss Hetherington hadn't sounded put off by the thought of it either.

It was exactly as it should be—if he were going to take her down.

Could he have her? Did he want her? She thought he wanted peace. He wanted war. An all-out, bloody battle. And he intended to win it.

I'm still unsure if he planned out the entire thing to make himself appear the hero to the guards.

Hell, she was intelligent and clever. He would have to use caution around her. She might be the one who stood in the way. What would he do if she was?

He had successfully infiltrated the castle. Now, he had three weeks to plan his attack. Three weeks until King Robert and his men arrived, whether Torin had prepared the way or not. He could do it. He would see them all dead, including the Hetheringtons if he had to. He wouldn't let a lass stop him.

A rooster crowed again as he swung his heavy sword over his head. He brought it down in a chopping blow that spewed dirt around him. He jabbed it into one of the English soldiers who'd invaded his childhood home. He couldn't remember their faces. He didn't need to. They were all guilty.

He parried a swipe from the man who'd struck his older brother. With an effortless curl of his wrist, he flipped his hilt over and caught it again, ramming his long blade into the ghost of the English bastard that killed his father. He pulled it free and plunged it forward, in an arc of devastation that removed two heads at once. He heard his younger brother crying. Or was it his mother? His mother. *Look what we have here, a tender little pigeon,* he remembered an Englishman saying, and then lifting his mother and carrying her away. Torin stepped forward and swept his blade over his head, hacking it through his unseen enemies, laying waste to every last one—until he stood alone amid the carnage, having done what he could not do as a child. But nothing changed. It never changed.

He could go back in time and kill them all, but there would still be nothing left when it was over. He would never gain back his kin.

He would never have a family.

He straightened, drew in a deep breath that flared his nostrils, and balanced his legs again. Let the men sleep. Let them grow idle and unprepared for fighting. The defender had no defense. Carlisle was prime for the taking.

He turned at the sound of horse's hooves clapping the ground behind him and looked up to see Braya seated upon a black horse and smiling down at him. She was alone.

The thought of her coming to kill him did not seem so farfetched, even though he knew why she had come. But why alone? Did she travel alone so far from her home often? Or had her father changed his mind and sent her? He kept his sword in his hand.

Hell, he didn't want to hurt her. How had she gained his consideration? He hadn't known her for a full day! She was deadly as an enemy, striking like a snake.

She tempted him to get bitten, to swoop in like a falcon and take her as prey.

"Miss Hetherington, 'tis nice to see you this morn."

"You as well, Sir Torin," she replied. "You are a fierce and precise warrior. I would like to see some more."

How was it possible to forget how beautiful she was until he saw her again? He did his best not to let her appearance affect him, but it was more than her natural beauty that stopped his breath. It was the slight tilt of her chin, the strength in her eyes, and the confidence in whatever the hell she knew she possessed that straightened her spine.

She made his head reel and his ghosts scatter.

His gaze dipped to her pale braid draping her humble bosom. Was her heart beating madly now? "Perhaps we could practice together," he offered.

She shrugged her shoulder and dipped her chin toward it, as if she did not care. "Perhaps."

He looked around, suddenly aware that she, a reiver, had entered the inner ward without being stopped. "How did you gain entrance?"

"The east wall," she told him. "There is rarely anyone patrolling it and none guarding the walkway."

He nodded. "Aye, I have noticed that." What else did she know about the castle defenses? He should spend time with her and find out.

"So, 'tis morn." He looked up at her on her horse and let his gaze go just a bit soft on her. Though it wasn't difficult. "Has your father sent you to kill me?"

"No," she said, swinging one leg over her saddle and dismounting. "I'm here to speak you."

"Oh? About what?" he asked, pretending ignorance.

She landed like a graceful cat on her booted feet. Her legs were encased in breeches. She wore a snug jack with no sleeves and a sky blue mantle. She moved toward him, addling his senses. "Were you sincere in your apology last eve, my lord?"

"Aye," he said, knowing her father's conditions. Also knowing what she had said last night about making him agree if she had to. He wondered how she would go about convincing him.

"Will you stand before my father and ask his forgiveness?"

He stared at her, thinking about bending his head to hers and kissing her. Would she try to stab him in his nether region? In the heart, mayhap? Would he want to kiss her again and again, for the remainder of his days? He clasped his hands behind his back to keep himself from becoming too tempted and pulling her into his arms. "You ask much of me, lady."

"Oh?" she asked in a clipped tone, shattering his hopes of her begging him to help. "Are you so filled with pride that you cannot tell a few fathers that you are sorry for taking their sons from them?"

He almost rolled his eyes, but smiled at her instead. "Very well. If 'tis so important to you, I will do it."

Had he given in too soon? When she smiled, looking so relieved he thought she might have swooned for a moment, he was glad he had given in to her.

"'Tis important to me. My father will bring war here if you refuse."

Carlisle at war with a handful of reivers could be ideal for Torin's plans.

"I do not want to lose my father or brother if they fight you," she added quietly, honestly, like a hammer to his defenses. If he fought the reivers, he would likely take more of her kin from her.

Was he losing his damned mind?

"And Mr. Adams?" she asked, looking around. "He has been a friend to my father in the past. Do you think he will go with you?"

It was as if he couldn't stop his own tongue. "I will see what I can do," he promised and held out his hand to her. He didn't want to think about meeting her on the battlefield as Bennett's enemy or his ally. "That is not all, is it? You did not ride all the way here alone just to ask me a simple question. Stay for breakfast with me and let me escort you home later."

"I should not."

He nodded and smiled in agreement, keeping his hand out to her. "Aye, and I should not ask. But I am. Stay."

Her blue eyes seared into him, searching—hell, he could almost feel her peering around in the shadows, looking beneath this surface and that. He almost looked away, unwilling to give anything of himself to anyone, lest he lose them—and more of himself. But he let her search, almost daring her to look into the cold, dank darkness and not shrivel up and run.

"All right," she said, finally fitting her small hand into his. "I will. But on one condition."

He sighed inwardly. This family and their conditions! "Very well, what is it?"

"That you practice with me first."

He should have expected her to want to test him, feel him out—as he'd planned on doing with the other guards later. She was brave, throwing herself into the fray with him to learn how he fought since she might have to be the one who protected her family from him if they came here.

Or, this was her way of stabbing him to death without anyone even bearing witness.

"Of course" He stepped away from her, releasing her hand.

He held up his blade, ready to know for sure if she could kill him.

She did the same with the blade that had been hanging from her hip.

He smiled at her one more time, appreciating her readiness and willingness to fight him. He expected her to be a good fighter, but she was quite small at 5' 4" mayhap and delicately fashioned. How much trouble could she be?

She came at him so fast he almost didn't have time to block. He stopped a swift slice of her blade just before it would have rid him of his left arm. She took the opportunity to disappear from his view. He barely moved and she was already behind him. She'd had the slightest advantage after watching him practice and seeing how he moved. He'd had no way of knowing how fast she was until she was on him—literally strapped to his back with her legs wrapped around his waist and one hand closed over his forehead.

How was this happening? How was she in a position to kill him? And how had she arrived there so quickly?

He didn't pause and wait to see if she would do it or not, but reached around himself and tried to grab her. He saw her bringing her blade up to his neck and grasped her wrist. A harsh twist and her sword fell to the ground.

Taking hold of both her arms, he dragged her around to face him. Her legs were still coiled tightly around his waist. She stared at him, her breath coming as hard as his.

He could feel her heart beating *madly* in her chest. Could she feel his doing the same? He should peel her off him, but every nerve ending in his body was alive and on fire. Awakened with a need that was purely physical and deeply moving at the same time.

She stared at him with wide, shining eyes and breathed hard against him. He wanted to take her face in his hands and kiss her, breathe her, win her. He realized this was a fancy brought to life by all his reading. He wasn't here to *win* some woman! He was here to rip the last place of defense out from under Edward's feet and to kill as many English as he could, but her thighs were strong and tight around him. He didn't want her to let go. He wanted more than this spirited hellcat's mouth. He wanted to push her up against the nearest wall, pull her breeches down around her knees, and take her until their worlds changed.

She unwrapped her legs and slid down his body, stirring him to life. He clenched his jaw. She blushed and looked away as her feet hit the ground. "I would call that a draw," she said softly, stepping away.

He smiled, and then he laughed and reluctantly let her go. "You are very fast."

"I have to be," she replied over her shoulder while she walked away from him.

True. She did, he thought, catching up to her. "You are also very brave."

"But?"

He stared at her while they walked toward the keep. "But what?"

She turned to look up at him. A soft smile lifted her lips but there was dreadful anticipation in her eyes. "What else were you going to say?"

He thought about what other compliments he could offer her. "You are clever. You call me fierce, but you nearly had my throat five breaths in."

She stopped walking and squinted up at him as the sun came up in full glory. "You have no harsh criticism?"

He shook his head, and then remembered that men didn't want to marry her because she fought so well. Fools. "No, Miss Hetherington. I'm the best I know, and you almost killed me."

Her smile grew until it made him want to kiss her again. "Thank you."

"You act as if you do not hear praises often."

"I do not," she said and continued walking.

"Surely your father tells you."

She shook her head. "It makes Galien brood."

"Who is Galien?"

"My brother," she said, entering the keep with him. "My other brother, Ragenald, used to praise me."

"Why did he stop?"

"The Bruce's army killed him at Bannockburn."

He looked away. She had good reason to hate his kind. Her entire family did, evidently. It had to be why they'd aided Bennett when the Scots had invaded five years ago. "You were close to him?"

"Aye, he—" She stopped speaking and looked around.

Torin turned to see what silenced her. Every man in the stronghold who was finally awake and walking around, ready to start their day, had stopped what he was doing to stare at her.

"Does this happen every time you come here?" he asked Braya.

"Sometimes," she said, settling her hand over the hilt of her blade. "When I'm here without my father and Galien."

Torin's blood boiled. His sudden urge to protect her was so unexpected and unfamiliar that, for a moment, it was almost worrisome.

She didn't need protection—unless she was alone in a military stronghold filled with English soldiers.

Hell, he was supposed to wait until a certain amount of time passed before he could start killing. But Torin reached up for his blade. If these bastards needed convincing that she wasn't alone, he'd happily oblige.

"Miss Hetherington!" They both turned at the sound of Bennett's voice. He walked toward them, pausing very slightly when Braya faced him.

Bennett wore a long tunic with hose underneath. There were at least four blades of various lengths dangling from his belt. His dark hair dangled to his shoulders and was tied back at his graying temples. He sported a long scar across the bridge of his nose and below his eye, to his cheek. He might appear fearsome to some, but Torin hadn't seen him practicing yet, and a good fighter needed to practice every day.

"I was not expecting to see you here," Bennett said, keeping his gaze on Braya. He walked past Torin and moved to take Braya's arm. "I can take her from here."

"I'm not here to see you." She pulled her arm out of his reach, not afraid of him either.

"Oh?" Bennett asked. "Who are you here to see then?"

"Sir Torin," she advised him boldly.

The warden slid his gaze to him, looking at him for the first time. Torin was supposed to be making friends with him, not making him jealous of a woman he could never have.

Well, there was nothing to be done of it now. He offered Bennett a rueful smile and placed his hand on Braya's back to escort her back out of the keep. "We will speak of it later, my lord. I promised Miss Hetherington something to fill her belly. Since it does not look as if the castle is a safe place for Rowley Hetherington's daughter to eat, we will have to find someplace else to go."

"We will speak of it now, Knight," Bennett demanded, reaching out to stop Torin from moving. "I do not care if you both eat or not. Why are you meeting here alone? What is going on between you?"

Torin wanted to take out his dagger and swipe it across Bennett's throat rather than be questioned by him. Would Braya help him fight when the warden's men came after him? No. It was too soon. They wouldn't get out alive. There were too many men. He needed to wait until the Scots were standing at the doors as planned.

Torin didn't care if the warden knew the truth. It could work toward his advantage. "Her father requests that Rob Adams and I stand before him and ask for forgiveness for killing his family."

"Plead forgiveness from reivers! Ridiculous! They are beneath us!" Bennett closed his eyes and tossed back his head with laughter. He didn't see Braya's quick hand free her dagger and jab it at him.

Torin caught her and pulled back her outstretched arms just as

Bennett quit laughing and opened his eyes to look at them.

"Her father has promised to bring war to Carlisle if Adams and I do not go to him," Torin told him.

How much easier would it be to take the castle after the reivers were done with it? He could incite them to war with each other and his duty would be half-done. But he would have to fight against them—against her.

"I do not think 'twould be wise to engage in battle with the reivers when the Scots are possibly coming here."

Bennett furrowed his dark brows and cast him a worried look. "Have you heard something?"

"Same as you," Torin assured him, barely concealing his growl. "They have taken every other stronghold. How long do you think 'twill be before they come here?"

"Aye, you are correct," Bennett thankfully said after thinking about it. "You will go to their village with Adams. Do as her father says."

Torin nodded, dreading that he might have just sealed his men's fate when they arrived. How many reivers could Hetherington call upon? Bennett knew he needed their help. He was willing to do anything for it.

"Now," Torin told him, leaning in a bit closer, "if you will notice the men staring at your guest." He gave the defender a moment to look around. "If I'm to beg a man's forgiveness for something I think was right to do—if I must do that to avoid a war, I promise you, I will not tolerate any man tossing my hard work away because he could not keep his hands to himself."

Bennett smiled at him, not giving a damn about his threat against the men. He rested his dark gaze on Torin first, and then on Braya. "I will make certain the men understand she is not to be touched." His smile widened into a smirk. "Of course, that rule applies to you as well."

Torin stared at him for a moment, thinking about carrying her to the nearest glade and lying with her in the grass. "Of course," he answered, and then left the castle with her at his side.

CHAPTER SIX

"Y OUR FATHER MUST command a powerful army of men for Bennett to be so afraid to lose them," Sir Torin remarked on their way out of the bailey.

They rode their horses, she upon her stallion, Archer, and he upon Avalon.

"We can gather a thousand men," Braya told him, and then flicked her horse's reins and galloped away, not caring about armies or Bennett or fighting. She'd sparred with Torin and had nearly beaten him, and he hadn't scorned her. He'd complimented her!

She hadn't beaten him though. If it had been a real fight, he would have killed her. She wasn't big and muscular like the men. Strength was not her weapon. Speed was. She was as quick as lightning. He was quicker, stopping her from getting her blade close to his neck. And then...then he'd turned her around and...she thought of his strong body trapped within her legs and felt some kind of primeval desire she hadn't known she possessed. She hadn't wanted to release him. She'd wanted to kiss him. Millie would have cheered if she'd done it. Lucy would have turned every shade of red until she needed a fan.

Braya had felt his muscles tighten as she dismounted him. He was hard all over. He'd wanted to touch her. She had felt it in the heat of his gaze, his shallow breath against her face.

He hadn't. She was glad. He wasn't like the others.

If that weren't enough, he'd easily agreed to apologize to her father and had promised to try to get Mr. Adams to do so. Everything would be well—because of Sir Torin.

They thought the sun would remain, but the skies grew overcast as soon as they left the walls of the castle. They didn't turn back but let their horses fly across the moors.

They rode southeast, toward Carleton, staying clear of Hetherington territory in the northwest.

One of the things every reiver prized was a fast horse. Many times, the ability to escape quickly meant life over death. Avalon was mesmerizing to watch. She appeared and sounded surprisingly light on her hairy hooves; poor Archer couldn't keep up, though he gave her a good run. They reached a tavern with a stable hand just before Braya would have had to stop for Archer's sake.

Her family knew most of the families in Carleton, like the Bells, who owned the tavern, so Braya felt confident to rest for a bit and eat.

"You do not worry that a thief will try to steal Avalon?" she asked and sat with him at a small, stained table beside a great hearth that offered too much heat for so warm a day.

"No," he told her and glanced up at Yda, the serving girl approaching the table. "She will not allow herself to be taken. Any thief who touched her would not be a thief for long. Not a good one without any fingers." He smiled and Yda giggled above them.

"Greetin's, Braya." The serving girl's cheeks were so red Braya thought she had rubbed some kind of flower on them to make them so. But it was just Torin and his large, soulful eyes and shapely mouth. "Who is your companion?" she asked, feigning coyness behind hooded lids.

"Sir Torin Gray," Braya told her, wishing proper decorum didn't dictate that she had to answer.

He flicked his gaze to Yda then graced Braya with a slanted grin that made her catch her breath. "I'm hungry, so bring me plenty of whatever Miss Hetherington is having."

"What if she were havin' frog legs and pig innards?" Yda asked, resting one hand on her hip.

Torin rubbed his flat belly. "I would say, double my portion."

Braya laughed and Yda stomped away, having failed at her attempt to seduce him.

"You are not having frog legs and pig innards, are you?" Torin asked her, leaning in with the slightest sign of a more genuine smile seen first in his eyes.

She shook her head. "Porridge and dates."

His full mouth relaxed and curled. A shaft of light came through a nearby window and fell on his silvery-green eyes. He dipped his head to shield his eyes beneath the soft curls of burnished bronze and gold that had come loose from a tie behind his head.

Braya did not blame Yda for fawning over him. He was perfectly crafted, but Braya wanted to know what kind of man had grown from being orphaned at five. He smiled easily, though she had caught sight of something he was hiding—something that lurked in the fathoms of his eyes and darkened his soul.

What was it? She saw it in him while he was practicing. He'd moved like a wild beast, tearing and killing in a mad lust for blood. Why had she allowed him to attract her, touch her, tempt her to spend more time with him than she should? Who was he? A mild-tempered man who was good with his sword? Or someone far more dangerous? What was she doing here with him, wanting to know more about him? Who taught him to fight? Had he loved? Did he have a wife now?

"You are very kind to offer your apology to my family," she said, feeling as if the room and the other four tables in it were spinning slowly.

He turned from looking out the window at the darkening skies and studied her. She wanted to ask him what he had been thinking about.

"Do not compliment me for something I do solely to please you, Miss Hetherington."

Why would he do something solely to please her? It didn't please her to think his apology wasn't sincere, but her insides still went warm over it.

"Whatever the reason, you have my thanks," she said. "And you have my thanks also for stopping me from stabbing the warden earlier. I'm trying to avoid a war, not start one."

"You are a skilled fighter," he said, making her knees go weak. "And yet you want peace."

"I do not want to lose any more of my—" She almost said family and cringed in her skin.

He had lost all of his. He had to understand.

He slipped his gaze back to the window and grew silent. Just when she thought he might not speak to her again for the entire afternoon, his deep, rich voice fell across her ears.

"I will do what I can to help."

She offered him her warmest smile and then laughed when his belly made a loud rumbling sound.

"You do not like Bennett," he said, still smiling when her laughter subsided.

"You sound surprised." She quirked her brow at him and then waited while Yda returned with their breakfast—with an extra helping for Torin, and set down their plates.

"I am. I thought your family had a bond with him."

"My family is loyal to no one but Hetheringtons," she told him over warm bowls of porridge and dates. "You must see that after my cousins attacked the warden's men. They were foolish. We need the warden as much as he needs us. We help the border guards keep out the Irvines and the Carruthers'—even the Scots if they come back. He keeps the Armstrongs and the Elliots from gathering their armies against us on this side of the border. 'Tis a good partnership, but there is no loyalty other than to family."

He stared at her, considering her words, and then he nodded and they continued to eat for a while longer.

"Who taught you how to fight?" she asked him, wanting to know more about him.

His spoon paused halfway up. He looked down at it, shielding his gaze from her behind his dark lashes. She had noticed this same reaction whenever she had asked him about his past. He didn't enjoy speaking of it, which only made her want to know more.

"I became part of the garrison at Till Castle when I was three and ten, but I became one of the governor's fiercest men, and he became a friend of mine."

"His stronghold was taken down five years ago by the Scots," Braya said, proving she knew what was going on outside of her own backyard. "Shortly before they lost to us."

"Aye," he agreed. "I was there when the Scots killed him. They were fearless and savage, but I had learned how to be those things as well. Once more though, they killed someone I cared about. I vowed to kill as many Scots as I could before I died."

She nodded, and then looked away, guarding her gaze from his sight lest he see someone he didn't like; a heart that bled for too many, a fool led by her feelings. They were the words of men who had raided with her.

"You sound like Galien."

He laughed softly, more at himself than at her. "I do not know him, but I get the feeling that was not a compliment."

"I do not wish to insult you, my lord," she told him truthfully. She was a woman reiver, a warrior, and he had not insulted her once.

"I can bear it, my lady," he replied with a glint of warmth and amusement in his gaze. "I promise."

She smiled at him. She couldn't help herself. She wanted to get to know him and, so far, she liked almost everything she knew. Almost. "He enjoys fighting and killing his enemies."

"What is wrong with that?

Her heart sank, thinking he was another bloodthirsty, prideful fool. "You do not believe there is something wrong when you *enjoy* killing?"

"That depends on who is dying."

She was taken aback by his cold response and began to rise to leave.

His hand reaching for her across the table stopped her. "Do not go. Please."

"We are too different," she insisted. "I fight to eat—"

"The sound of my mother screaming tore me from my sleep."

What? What was he saying? His mother. Was he telling her how his mother had died to prove some people deserved to die?

"I sat up and rubbed my eyes," he continued in a soulless voice. "Someone was there in the darkness and yanked me from my bed to the cold rushes. I called out. She screamed again. My heart felt as if it would burst with terror. They brought me to her just in time to see another man shove a long blade into my father's belly until it came out the other side of him. Then they lit the house on fire. I do not know if they killed my two brothers."

"Oh, Torin, no!" Braya sank back onto the bench. "I did not mean to..." Her voice trailed off into a cough she produced to stop the sob wanting to escape her lips. "Forgive me." She reached for his hand and covered it with hers as a rush of tears fell from her eyes. She did not argue with him about whether he was entitled or not, to feel the way he did about certain men. She hadn't lost her entire family to the Scots. "I did not realize how terrible it must have been for you."

He looked at her and, for a heartbreaking instant, he didn't seem to know where he was. As if he were still there, dropped off into his past by her so he could remember again what had happened.

Then his gaze cleared and he looked at his covered, trembling hand and her tears that had fallen around it. "No," he said in a soft, smoky baritone. "I do not know why I shared such gruesome thoughts with you. 'Tis I who should ask forgiveness." He slipped his hand free. "You are easy to speak with."

She smiled. She believed that he didn't open up to many. She liked that he'd opened up to her.

Thunder cracked across the charcoal sky. Startled, Yda dropped a jug of ale.

Torin rose from the bench. "I need to see to Avalon. She does not like thunder."

"I will come with you," Braya said and followed him out of the tavern.

They hadn't walked more than three steps when the skies opened and poured down on them. Braya didn't mind. In fact, she loved the rain. It cleansed and nourished. It was cold, though, and she hurried toward Torin when he held open his cloak for her to take refuge under.

They ran together, laughing beneath his hood as they entered the stable. Torin grew serious immediately when he found that Avalon was not where he had left her.

"Has someone taken her?" Braya asked him as they ran back out into the rain.

"No. She must have become frightened and took off."

He called the horse's name, once, and then again. His voice, though loud and strong, was drowned out by the wind and more thunder.

He whistled and the sharp sound pierced the wind.

Braya's heart began to speed up as the realization that beautiful Avalon had run away. Would she return?

Torin kept whistling and searching for her until they were both dripping wet.

"Has she done this before?" she asked him while they headed for the trees.

"Once or twice."

"But she came back," Braya pointed out, hoping to comfort him. Was he distressed? She couldn't tell.

"No, I had to find her."

"Oh." Braya's heart drummed hard and fast. They had to find her. "Avalon!" she called out.

They searched for another quarter of an hour, calling out, wiping the rain from their eyes, and searching the forest for her.

"Let us split up," she finally suggested. He nodded and then caught sight of something over her shoulder. He blinked his large green eyes and Braya couldn't tell if what fell from his eyes was rain or tears.

He stepped around her and Braya turned to see his massive horse standing within the trees. Her long, dripping wet mane looked more gray than white as it cascaded over her wide, terrified eyes. She trembled and moved deeper into the trees when she saw them.

"Come, lady." He reached out his hand. "I'm here. You are safe."

Braya stayed where she was while he moved forward, speaking softly to Avalon. She watched him hold up both hands when the horse reared back her head and bit at the air. Avalon was warning him not to come any closer. He didn't let her fear stop him but continued to speak to her.

When he reached her, he lifted his hand to her nose. She pushed back and snapped at him. Braya's heart broke and raced together. Avalon was so afraid she couldn't recognize him. He didn't give up and, finally, the horse let him touch her nose with one hand, and then her cheeks with both. She swung her huge head toward him and nuzzled it close to him. He risked his handsome face by pressing it to Avalon's.

Braya thought about what kind of man he must be to have earned the trust of such an animal. He was patient and, after a little more coaxing, he led her toward Braya.

A man stepping out of the trees between them stopped him. "That's a nice horse, Brother." He held up his wet sword. "You will hand it over to me, and the gel—"

He stopped talking when Braya smashed the hilt of a dagger into the back of his head. He folded to the ground, leaving her facing Torin. He smiled and stepped over the thief and continued on.

"Where did you get her?" Braya asked him while he dried Avalon and laid down fresh hay back at the tavern's stable.

"I had been traveling two years ago and came upon a gypsy with a gloriously beautiful horse, and a cruel whip."

"Oh, no!" Braya whispered, horrified and understanding Avalon a little better.

"I almost killed him one night," he continued, remembering. "I had wanted to free her. She'd been skin and bones. Pulling his carriage for however long...I thought she was on the brink of death. I wanted her to run, untethered for whatever short amount of time she had left—free. But I had to free her from the carriage first. As you can imagine, she did not want hands on her, so I had a difficult time freeing her." He smiled at Avalon and petted her. "I finally managed and she hurried off, as fast as she could go. I thought I would never see her again. But she returned to me two nights later in a moonlit vale and has remained with me ever since."

Braya smiled. She didn't mind standing in the hay, feeding Avalon and Archer carrots while Torin told her stories of the Isle of Avalon and a king called Arthur.

"How do you know these tales?"

Torin went to stand at the window. The rain had stopped and the clouds had disappeared. He stared out into the sunlight. "I read about them."

Braya wasn't sure she heard him correctly. Why would a guard have any need of reading? "You can read?"

"Aye. I learned how while I lived at Till Castle." He turned away from the sun and smiled at her. "I can write, too."

"You use your time well," she said with admiration lacing her voice. Such skills were difficult and took many months, even years to achieve. She shook her head, marveling at him, and forgot the horses as she moved toward him. "Did the governor force you to learn?"

"No," he told her, watching her move, turning her bones to liquid. "I wanted to read so that I could find the story of Avalon."

"You are a very determined man."

He smiled. It was well practiced and didn't reach his eyes. Braya thought he didn't like this compliment. Why not? Who was he? She understood why he wanted to be a soldier of the king and help triumph over the Scots, but there was so much more to him than that. Who raised him? Where had he spent his latest years, the ones after the Scots took down Till Castle until now? There was so much more she wanted to learn about him. So much she felt she *needed* to know.

He was different. That was a good thing. Wasn't it?

CHAPTER SEVEN

T HEY STOPPED OUTSIDE the city, both of them mounted and ready to part ways.

Torin knew he should bid her good day and let her go home, but he didn't want to. He wanted to spend the afternoon with her...the night. What the hell was the matter with him? He was supposed to be making friends with the guards, with Bennett himself, finding out the garrison's weaknesses, the list went on—and here he was, wanting to make an English lass smile for the rest of the day.

"I was thinking of riding to Wetheral for some supplies," he said, trying to settle down an impatient and mayhap a tad jealous Avalon between his thighs. He didn't need any supplies in Wetheral, but he wanted to spend more time with her. "I would enjoy your company."

Braya smiled, which pleased him—which also made him scowl.

"What does a village have that a city does not?" she put to him.

"A waterfall.

Her eyes widened and sparked with interest. "I know one that is closer." But then she looked off into the distance, toward her village, and shook her head. "We have spent too much time together already." She breathed out a wilting sigh, as if this were the last thing she wanted to hear herself say. Then, vanquishing the melancholy that had overtaken her, she smiled again, flashing her dimple and making him doubt everything he believed.

The English deserved to die. But no. Not her. He didn't want her around for any fighting. They weren't on the same side.

"I had a lovely day with you, Sir Torin. Thank you."

He smiled at her. He didn't want to. He wanted to turn and go. Avalon wanted him to go as well.

She could have killed him this morn. She had moved her arm slowly, so he could stop her. "I will be here tomorrow—tonight," he added under his breath.

She laughed and he grew enchanted by her dimple, the sight of her, the sound of her.

"Farewell," she said, sobering.

She left him looking after her, wanting to charge Avalon forward and bring Braya back.

"Ye wouldna budge, would ye?" he asked his horse while he turned for the keep. He didn't wait for any answer. He knew what it would be. "What are ye jealous of anyway? I dinna feel anythin' fer her."

But what did he know of feeling anything for anyone? He hadn't cared for anyone since he was seven. He honestly didn't want to care now. It was too distracting. It could get him killed. What kind of charms did Braya possess to scatter his thoughts? There could never be anything between them. His secret was too great. His past was too dark and his heart was too consumed by the darkness to make a lass happy.

He had to stay with his plan and not deviate, keep his thoughts on what he'd come here to do. Bring war. He'd been driven by a single desire since he was a young lad. Use the skills he'd learned to kill them all, take them down, make them pay.

"'Twill be over soon," he told his horse. "And then..."

What? What would he do? Where would he go? After Carlisle, there were no more strongholds to take down. Mayhap he could settle down somewhere…with…someone. He almost laughed at himself and his foolish musings. It was too late for love and a family, though it was something a deep part of him had always desired. Why was he allowing Miss Hetherington to stir that desire? He had his family, he reminded himself, and reached under his cloak to touch his fingers to his brooch. He had Avalon. It was enough.

He didn't know why he had shared anything about his life with her. No one had ever tempted him to be so honest. He wasn't sure yet if it had done him any good. His skill was in making the other person tell all their secrets while he kept his own hidden. But he felt at ease with her from the moment he sat with her yesterday in the woods, and today in the tavern. When she had risen to leave, angry about his stance on killing, he hadn't wanted her to go, so he'd told her a little about that day.

But he hadn't shared his true self with her, or with anyone else. He was a boy, ashamed and filled with guilt for running away, for escaping when his brothers had not. For not killing those soldiers. He wanted others to see a confident, in-control soldier, not an emotional, scarred child whose purpose in still living was to avenge his family.

He rode Avalon over the stone bridge and through the large outer gatehouse. He noted the time of day and how many men were looking out over the ramparts for any sign of enemies from the north.

He greeted some of the soldiers on his way to the stables, where he handed over Avalon's reins to a stable hand with a warning not to touch her.

"I understand I'm to plead the forgiveness of Rowley Hetherington."

Torin turned on his way toward the keep and saw Rob Adams coming up behind him. He was coming from the practice field in the inner ward. He wore a sleeveless léine tucked into his belt. His arms glistened with sweat. He'd been practicing.

Torin almost smiled and stopped to wait for him to catch up. "And the father of the man you killed."

"Why are we apologizing for defending ourselves?"

Looking at him, Torin couldn't help but wonder how many battles Adams had been in. He was even missing an earlobe. "Rowley Hetherington has promised to bring war here if we do not do as he asks."

"He is no fool," Adams huffed. "There are only two things that would make him bring war: his daughter being hurt or his wife being hurt. Otherwise, he is all bark and little bite."

"I thought you were friends."

"So did I, and then his family tried to rob and kill me."

Torin liked his confidence and eagerness to fight. Pity he fought on the wrong side. Adams was skilled enough to kill a reiver while he was weary and drunk. Torin would be careful not to form any kind of attachment to him, since he was going to kill him at some point in the future.

Better to know now how he fought. Torin thought about it and pulled his curls back to tie them again. He hadn't had a good, hard practice with someone skilled in months. Braya was a skilled, interesting opponent but he wanted to kiss the hell out of her, not defeat her. "Let us speak while we spar," he offered. "Or do you need to rest?"

Adams narrowed his dark eyes on Torin and then smiled, proving he was missing a tooth on the right side on his mouth. "No, I do not need to rest. I was hoping to see you on the field today."

"I was out here just before sunrise," Torin told him as they walked together across the yard. A handful of men were practicing.

"Had I known you were here, I would have joined you for some sport." Adams ripped his long sword from its sheath. "But better later than not at all."

Torin pulled his sword free from over his shoulder. Practicing with him would give Adams an advantage, as well. Torin didn't care. He would practice with everyone in this damned castle until they thought they knew his every move, and he would still win.

"I do not recognize the accents of your speech," Adams remarked and swiped at the air with his blade to loosen up his arm. "From where do you hail?"

So, Adams was familiar with many different types of speech, meaning he moved around a lot. He was likely a mercenary. The most dangerous kind of man. For his loyalty belonged to his purse alone. "Bamburgh," Torin told him, ready to give an account of his entire false background if necessary. Bamburgh was close to the Scottish border in the east, so if his tone sometimes sounded more like the Scots, it was understandable.

He circled Adams once and opened his mouth to say more, but Adams had other questions.

"How did you know about my friendship with Hetherington?"

"His daughter told me," Torin said, readying his sword.

"Aye, I heard Miss Hetherington was here this morn," Adams braced his feet and held up his blade. "I did not know you spent time with her." He came forward with a long swing that made the air in front of Torin's face whistle.

"We parted just before you found me," Torin told him, straightening his arched back. He swung his blade, narrowly avoiding Adams' knees, then curved his wrist and found an open spot in the soldier's defense. He held the cold steel of his blade to his opponent's groin.

Adams gave him the win. They pushed off each other and readied for the next round.

"So you spent the morning somewhere with her," Adams remarked, hefting his sword over his head to block a crushing blow from Torin, "and returned without a wound."

She'd given Adams' name as one of the men who had not harassed her.

"Once she realized I had no intentions on molesting her," Torin told him, "she was quite pleasant."

Their swords met and crossed between them. Adams pushed against him and looked him straight in the eye. "She is not taken seriously and may be the downfall of this castle."

What the hell did that mean? Torin parried a sweeping blow to his hip and smashed his blade down hard on Adams', almost knocking the hilt from the soldier's hands. "How is she a threat to this castle?" He jabbed and swung and pushed Adams back with an onslaught of heavy blows.

Adams fought back valiantly but finally, he jabbed when he should have blocked and closed his eyes when Torin pushed the tip of his blade against his throat.

Torin took the second win and swung around on his feet to walk away and catch his breath—and to think about what Adams had said. Had he missed something? Braya didn't want war.

"She hates the warden." Adams told him when he returned a few moments later. "And she should. If Bennett had his way, he would..." He stopped and shook his head, unable to finish what he meant to say. "He's never made it a secret that he desires her, though he looks down upon her fighting and does not believe she is dangerous. If he touches her, I fear she will not hesitate to cause him the most grievous pain."

Torin touched his groin and swallowed hard.

"The instant Rowley Hetherington heard what Bennett had dared to do to his daughter...well, there would be no threat of war. They would just come. Do you know how many of them there are? So many," he said, answering his own question, "that I did not recognize the five who robbed us, and I have been here for twelve years. Bennett will die. Carlisle would fall and 'twould bring the Hetheringtons, especially Braya, to the attention of King Edward."

Aye, Adams was correct. She hated Bennett. Torin should have seen it. She'd kept it from him, but the warden hadn't acknowledged her the morning she was here with her kin. This morn, she would not let him even touch her. Torin had already stopped her from swiping at Bennett with her blade once today.

It was a threat to his plans, as well. As far as the reivers were concerned, he was an English soldier of Carlisle. They would slaughter the garrison, and he couldn't fight off a thousand men on his own. Hell, he needed to keep Braya safe from Bennett's foolish touch. He needed to make certain Adams' fears did not come to pass. He had to think. Who could he enlist to fight alongside him if a thousand men arrived?

"Why do you care so much about her life?" he asked Adams. Was the soldier in love with her? No. Torin did not see passion in his eyes, nor did he hear it in the older man's voice. "Let me guess. You saved her life."

"In truth, she saved mine."

"You are the most skilled warrior here," Torin said, smiling doubtfully. She was a slight wisp of a woman. How could she save a warrior like Adams? But he remembered how she'd practiced with him. If she'd had another instant, she could have cut Torin's throat.

"What does skill matter when you are smashed in the head with the hilt of a sword and knocked out? I owe her much and, besides, she reminds me of my sister." Adams explained with a shrug, as if it meant little to him. The pain in his eyes said otherwise. "I have not seen her in six years."

How long had it been since Torin had seen his brothers? Twenty-two years. Were they dead? They had to be dead. The English had burned down their cottage. Had they taken his brothers with them or let them die in the flames? It didn't matter. Chances were, they had died later.

But he hadn't.

"Bennett will not touch her," Torin assured him, blinking back to the present. "He is too afraid of losing the reivers' support, and I hope to remind him how much he needs it. I also have made him a bit frightened of my sword."

Adams eyed him curiously. "You would protect her from him?"

"Aye," Torin told him, preparing to fight once again, "would you not?"

"Aye."

They practiced a little more, with less talking, until Sir John appeared and informed Torin that the warden wanted to see him in his private solar.

On the way back to the keep, Torin thought about Rob Adams. He wasn't like the other soldiers. He was clever and experienced, and he clearly practiced every day, for he fought well against Torin. He cared about Braya, which was likely why she thought he was a friend to her father, though Adams hadn't denied that he was.

He would make it a point to see Adams later and finish their conversation.

But presently, he had to find the solar.

Thankfully, he had a good sense of direction, a result of his years spent living in the forest, and from the many castles he'd lived in since Till.

He knocked on the heavy wood and wrought iron door on the second landing and was called to enter.

"Ah, Gray," Bennett said, barely looking up from a table where he was inspecting an unrolled map. "You have finally returned from your outing with Miss Hetherington. How was it?"

"Informative," Torin told him, looking around as he stepped inside.

Bennett wanted Braya. Though the thought of it fired up his insides, Torin had to keep it in mind when dealing with him. If Torin were seen as a competitor for her affections, he would be tossed out on his arse.

"Oh?" Bennett looked up. "How so?"

Let him think Torin was interested in her only for information. It would make Torin useful to the warden.

"Rowley Hetherington was insulted by his treatment here yesterday. That, coupled with five of his family members dying at our hands, four of them at mine, has tempted him to consider going to war with Carlisle. I'm responsible for my part in this. Hetherington wants an apology. He will get one. Rob Adams has agreed also. He may expect something from you as well."

"Me?" Bennett scowled.

"You threw him and his children out on their arses. You know him better than I. Do you think he is the kind of man who will let that sort of thing go?"

Bennett's scowl deepened and he looked away. "No. But I will not apologize to him."

Oh, hell, what was he about to do? He wasn't here for peace. He was the Shadow, the war-bringer. But it wasn't time yet. He had time to settle in and plan the attack. The king wouldn't appreciate having a thousand reivers waiting when he got here. There was no other choice. For now, peace had to be maintained.

"Nor should you," Torin finally said. "Do something better."

"Like?"

"Invite some of them here for drinks, perhaps some music. Make them feel valued if you want to save whatever is between you."

"I do not think 'tis necessary," Bennett complained. "His anger will fizzle to nothing soon enough."

Torin shrugged his shoulders. "Well, I think I speak for Adams as well when I say we love a good fight. But Miss Hetherington informs me that her father can gather a thousand men and, from what I have seen of your garrison, this castle would not last a day against a thousand reivers. And then there are the Scots. I did not wish to alarm Miss Hetherington this morning, but the reason I came here was because I had heard the Scots might attack Carlisle this winter."

Bennett walked around his table. The look of concern already on his face grew deeper. "Where did you hear this? How reliable was the source?"

"My source is a foot soldier in Robert the Bruce's army. The bastard means to come here and take England's last stronghold. I swore to fight every Scot I could. 'Tis why I'm here. I want to help you fight the Scots, not the reivers."

Bennett moved closer and studied him with narrowed, searching eyes. Torin remained still and without a trace of guile under his scrutiny.

"Tell me, did you truly kill those four reivers with no help from my men?"

"I had to act quickly or we would have all died. They would have stolen my horse."

"Hmm, quickly. Aye," Bennett said, stepping away. "You would have to be quick to kill four men before mine could help."

"I knew what had to be done and I did it," Torin replied with a tepid smile. "I'm sure you would do no less."

"Of course." Bennett pinched his chin between his thumb and index finger and walked back around to his table. "You have given me important information about the Scots. Try to find out more."

Torin lowered his head and concealed the shadow of a satisfied smirk. He was in. Now, he just needed a reason to strike up a friendship with the warden.

"Do the same with Miss Hetherington and report everything back to me," he ordered and then waved his hand at him. "You may go."

Torin moved toward the door and stopped at the large shelf of books against the rear wall of the solar. Bennett read. "May I have a look?" he heard himself ask, already reaching for a volume by Monmouth.

"Do you read, Sir Torin?" Bennett asked, surprised, curious.

Torin smiled, finding what he needed. "Aye, perhaps we could discuss Monmouth over some wine, when you have a moment or two."

"After our last meal tonight," Bennett said, with a trace of exuberance in his voice that wasn't there before. "I will have time then."

"I look forward to it."

"Aye," the warden beamed. "So do I."

CHAPTER EIGHT

B RAYA WALKED ALONG the riverbank close to her home just after
noon and listened to the birds calling from tree to tree. She'd
been working since morning but still had much to do, thanks to Galien
taking up so much of her time questioning her about Sir Torin and
how much time she spent with him. She had told him that she was
trying to keep peace. Sir Torin regretted what he'd done. She'd told
her brother the knight wasn't so terrible. He was only trying to protect
Carlisle's guards that night.

But talking to Galien was useless. He wanted revenge. Braya was
worried about him going after Torin. Should she warn the knight? No!
That would be like preparing him. Galien might not stand a chance.
She had to speak with her father about it. He was going to have to step
in if Galien did not accept his decision.

She didn't want to think of any of it now. She'd slipped away from
her chores so that she could think clearly about…things. Not her rash
brother, or preparing meals, washing clothes, or hanging them to dry.

She would return before she was missed. Now, she simply wanted
to think and walk.

She wore her skirts and pulled them up over her ankles while she leaped over rocks and puddles of water, eager to be away from her village.

She'd regretted her decision not to accompany Torin to Wetheral yesterday five breaths after she'd declined.

She'd enjoyed her day with him so much that she was having a hard time keeping her mind off him and on her family last night when her uncle, Roger, and his wife, Cecily, showed up for an unexpected visit.

Thoughtfully, they had brought with them black bread and three different kinds of pie. There had been enough stew to go around and, after supper, they ate pie and talked about their lives. It seemed the Robsons were causing trouble for Uncle Roger. Braya's father promised to come to his aid with at least sixty men. His one condition was Uncle Roger had to do the same if he was needed for fighting.

Braya hadn't wanted to hear talk about her family in battle against Carlisle. Especially over something Torin Gray had done. She had excused herself and gone to bed, only to dream of him, his smile, his voice telling her…that his mother was screaming and seeing his father dying at the hands of the Scots.

She had wanted to go to him when he told her. She'd wanted to comfort him. He needed comforting. She could see it in his soulful, smoldering eyes. He'd seen much in his life. He'd most likely done much. It took a certain kind of heart to kill one, let alone four at once. She'd watched him practice and it thrilled her and frightened her at the same time. He looked wild yet precise, as if he were fighting living men, cutting down every one of them. His movements were graceful yet savage, a feast for her eyes. Was she falling for one of the warden's men? One who'd killed her cousins?

He'd agreed to apologize. He'd agreed to speak to Rob Adams. If they both apologized, they would avoid war.

She smiled and looked up when she came to the end of the tree line…and saw him sitting upon Avalon in the clearing. Her heart skipped so hard it made her want to cough. He looked like some legendary hero on his great warhorse. His shoulders were straight and wide, his hair painted gold by the sun. His thigh, draping Avalon's side, was long and muscular. She could hear her own breath, feel her blood flowing through her veins.

As if he could hear her breathing as well, he turned. When he saw her, his smile lit his eyes from within. She blushed and dipped her chin for just a moment, liking that he found her presence enjoyable. She found his presence just as pleasing.

"Miss Hetherington," he greeted and moved closer on his magnificent steed.

"Sir Torin," she said, looking up again, "What are you doing here?"

He stopped and swung his leg over his saddle and slipped his booted feet to the ground.

She looked behind her to see if Galien was there. The movement made her dizzy—or was it the rushing of her blood through her veins at the sight of the man she had dreamed of all night?

"I wanted to give you this." He handed her a parchment.

She took it from him and looked at it. It bore the warden's seal. "What is it?"

"'Tis an invitation from the defender to you and ten of your closest family members to dine and dance in Carlisle's great hall tonight. 'Tis meant as a show of peace."

A show of peace. Aye. This was what she wanted. Torin and Rob Adams were going to apologize and there would be no fighting. The warden had insulted her father and was now offering a show of peace.

"Did you have something to do with this?" she asked, continuing her walk along the banks.

"Just a bit, perhaps," he admitted, letting go of Avalon's reins. Catching up to Braya, he walked beside her. "I do not want to fight you or your family."

"Why not?" She didn't know why she asked him. She had a feeling she knew what his answer would be.

"Because I do not want to hurt or kill any of you," he told her in a low voice.

He was arrogant and thoughtful and he made her head spin. "Thank you," she managed. "And please do not worry about hurting or killing any of us. You will not."

She ignored the slant of his mouth and stuffed the parchment into a pocket hidden in the folds of her mantle.

"How did you know where I lived?" And what was he still doing here? He'd delivered the warden's invitation, but he was strolling with her as if he had nothing else to do all day.

"I asked Bennett. He directed me in which way to go."

She laughed and slanted her eyes at him. "Pity you did not say Mr. Adams or Sir John. They have been here. The warden has not."

"Oh, well, …he…I…ehm…"

She took a good amount of pleasure in watching him squirm.

"I followed you last night—just up to this point," he hastened to explain when she frowned at him. "That is why I was unsure of which way to go."

"What do you mean you followed me?"

Was this normal behavior for a man?

"I wanted to make sure you arrived home safely. I know you can fight well," he said, holding up his hands in surrender when she turned a glare on him. "But I do not know how many you can fight at once if you were attacked in the dark."

She blinked and his jaw grew rigid. "I do not need a guardian, my lord."

"I know," he told her, a deep guttural sound from the center of his chest. "I do not need to be one."

They walked for a little while longer. She didn't mind. No, she liked being here with him. She wouldn't question it as she walked further from home. "Never mind all that." She waved her hand across her face, dismissing their previous conversation. "Tell me about yourself. Where did you spend your years after the raid on Till Castle?"

"In…ehm…in Rothbury."

Heavens, but his brows were furrowed now. Why did he find such discomfort in speaking about his past?

She would take no mercy on him. She was beginning to feel as if he weren't telling her the truth—about Rothbury, at least.

"Who is lord there?" she asked and looked toward the winding river to her right.

"William Stone," he answered without hesitation, "Very loyal to the throne."

She nodded. "I'm surprised the Scots have not raided there yet."

"Hmm," he muttered and kept walking.

"Where are you going?" She stopped and looked over her shoulder at Avalon grazing in the grass, then back at the knight.

"I was following you," he announced a bit shyly.

"You are in front of me," she pointed out.

His face broke into a wide grin that nearly dropped her to her knees.

"I should be getting back to the castle and my duties," he said, growing serious again. For a moment, he looked so torn and undecided that Braya thought he would not move again…ever.

"Stay," she heard herself whisper. She was only certain she'd said it by the way his stormy green eyes roved over her. "I was hoping you could stay."

His gaze held her still. "I could if you ask."

She laughed again and watched his gaze go soft and his breath falter. "I just did! Would you have me beg?"

He nodded, his smile deepening to a playful grin. "Aye, I would."

She crossed her arms over her chest and shook her head. She tried not to laugh again and pretended to be indignant. "I will not beg. Go home now. I will wave farewell to your back!"

He tossed his head back with a short, mocking laugh. "You would pine for me. I think you would…"

She turned away lest he look into her eyes and see that she *had* been pining for him, holding her breath still, lest he see her tremble when she inhaled.

His laughter and his voice faded. "I meant no insult. I do not truly think you would—"

She returned her gaze to his and searched it, then smiled, wanting to keep things light. "What?"

"Pine for me."

Why wouldn't he think she would pine for him? He was mysterious and charming, fit, and a skilled fighter. She was sure many women had pined for him.

"I would never pine for you," she told him and kept walking. She knew she didn't sound convincing. She didn't care.

"Ah, you have cut me to the quick, my lady."

She smiled, looking up at him, and then they both laughed. "So then," she asked. "You are staying?"

"Aye," he answered, bumping his shoulder into hers as they walked. "For as long as you will allow."

He made her heart do flips and somersaults. She didn't want to blush or giggle like some smitten milkmaid. She was a reiver for goodness' sake. It was time she—

"Are you hungry?" His gently lilting voice caressed her. "We could sit."

She couldn't help herself from giving in to the urge to look at him again. She fell into the extraordinary depth of his eyes, where shadows masked his purpose. "Do you always carry food with you?"

He nodded. "I'm hungry often."

She nodded too. "So am I." She smiled softly and looked away. "Very well, let us sit. There is a small, quiet area just around that bend." She watched him return to Avalon and retrieve his saddlebag.

He seemed pleased enough, judging by the crinkles at the outer edges of his eyes when he returned to her. She liked when she made him smile, believing that he didn't do it often. He moved toward the bend and she followed, looking behind her for Galien and finding only Avalon.

"Come," Torin urged, leading the way.

What was she doing? She knew little about him for certain, save that he could kill more than four members of her family. And also—she thought about his horse—he didn't trample over flowers, but let them bloom.

They came to the small inlet, tucked away in the trees along the bank. She'd been here before. She knew it was a beautiful place with a private little beach bathed in sunlight that came from the break in the trees. It didn't have a waterfall, but she thought he would like it.

"'Tis beautiful here," he told her, his voice filled with awe. He looked around and drank in the vision of dragonflies dancing over the sun-dappled surface of the water, and various colored rocks and boulders woven between tall reeds.

She smiled, happy to have pleased him, though it scared the hell out of her. She couldn't be falling in love with him. What would her family think? Galien was already angry about the amount of time they spent together.

They removed their cloaks and spread them out on the pebbly sand. Torin sat beside her and unpacked more apples, figs, cheese, dried meat, oatcakes and honey, some carrots that Braya suspected were for Avalon, and more black bread.

Braya couldn't help but think about how many people she could feed. "You cannot possibly eat all this and look the way—" She nearly swallowed her tongue to stop her words. So? He was fit. Did that mean she had to melt all over him?

He bit off a slice of dried mutton and ate. She broke off a piece of oatcake and dipped it into honey. She closed her eyes and lavished in the sweet ambrosia. Honey was available only to the wealthy. She would eat no more but bring the rest home to her family, along with those apples, figs, and whatever else she could carry.

"What is that brooch?" she asked, narrowing her eyes on the shiny bronze insect pinned to his léine. "A bee?"

"A moth," he told her. "I wear it every day."

"Oh? I have not noticed it until now. 'Tis quite unusual. Where did you get it?"

He paused for just a moment and his gaze went to another place, someplace dark and terribly vexing. "I took it from my home as 'twas burning. I suspect 'twas my mother's."

Her heart raced, staring into his haunted gaze as it returned to the present.

"Oh," she said quietly. She didn't realize she reached out to touch the brooch until he covered her hand with his.

He was protective of it. "What happened...after? Who took care of you, my lord?"

He pulled away, letting go of her hand. "I'm not your lord."

She'd gone too far. She knew he didn't like speaking about his past and she had pushed. She was sorry.

She returned to her oatcake and ate, keeping her eyes on the water.

"Braya." His voice sounded so tormented to her ears that she nearly turned and pulled him into her arms. "I cannot change it."

CHAPTER NINE

TORIN HAD MADE up a dozen different pasts in case anyone had ever asked him about his. Very few ever had. He thought he might be able to speak about it with Braya. He found that a part of him wanted to tell her, as if confessing his soul to her would somehow free him from the shackles of guilt and leashed rage.

But nothing could ever do that, and he betrayed his own heart by allowing himself to have feelings for an English woman. He was a Scot. He was here to bring war. She would never forgive him for lying to her…if she lived through it.

He couldn't change what had been set into motion. King Robert was coming. What could Torin do to save her? What could he do to keep from meeting her on the battlefield? He didn't think he could kill her, and if he doubted it for one instant and she didn't, he'd be dead. He felt lightheaded from the realization that the one who made him want to live was the only one who could kill him.

"I know you cannot change it," she said on the softest of whispers, not understanding what was beginning to eat away at him. "But it hurts you when you hide how you feel. You must speak of it."

Her voice filled his ears like a soothing melody, luring him like no one else had before her.

"Sometimes you look as if..." She began to turn away. Her loose waves swayed and lifted around her face in the breeze.

His heart thudded hard in his ears. He touched his fingers to a tendril caressing her cheek. "As if?"

"As if..." She looked at him again with fearless abandon to face what she saw. "...you are filled with darkness and there is but a single part of you left that burns with light."

He searched her eyes. How could she see into his heart and describe it exactly?

His eyes stung and his vision blurred. For an instant, he wasn't sure what to make of it. When it dawned on him, he was too stunned to look away. Nothing had ever made him weep. Nothing since that day. He relived it always, and every time it made his heart darker. But now...tears? What the hell was happening to him? He brushed his hand down his face. Had he been pretending to be English for so long that he was turning into one of them? He'd seen many English soldiers weeping for their lives before he killed them. Was he forgetting who he was? Commander Torin "Shadow" Gray. He'd been slashing throats for almost a decade, avenging his parents, his brothers, his friends, himself.

It wasn't enough.

"Forgive me," Braya whispered, shattering his defenses with two words no one had ever spoken to him before. "I did not mean to—"

"You want to know my demons, lady?"

"Aye," she answered without hesitation. She squared her shoulders and set her chin. "I do."

"Do you think you can take them on?" He wanted to smile—to grin at her. Was she so confident? Hadn't she come to the castle alone to see him? "What makes you think you can?"

"Because I lost Ragenald. He was more than my brother. He was my friend, and the only man in my life who believed in me."

Torin raked his fingers through his hair. He hated that he had demons in the first place, and that Braya had them, too. He thought it admirable that she thought she could face his. In fact, he thought it the bravest act anyone had ever shown him.

"After my family was killed," he said with solemn determination to give her what she wanted and to find out if she was correct. Would this help him? "I was terrified to live."

And ashamed. But he didn't tell her that. He couldn't. Some demons were too dark and deeply hidden.

"I escaped and ran and did not stop for two days. Hunger finally forced me to stop, but I did not eat for another day. I slept. I dreamed of terrible things and woke up alone and afraid. I tried to steal a dried fish from a vendor but he chased me until another boy caught my arm and pulled me into the shadows. He was older than me—like my brother. He took my hand and told me to go with him."

"What was his name?" she asked.

"What does it matter?" *Jonathon.* "We ran out of the town and disappeared into the forest. That was where I lived with a band of other orphans for the next five years. I learned how to survive, how to steal, swindle, and fight.

"I was ten when the Scots raided our camp and killed everyone. I had been away thieving in one of the surrounding villages. I was not there with the others. I had escaped death yet again." Were these his words, his voice he heard coming from his lips? Why was he telling her about his life when he had never spoken of it before? Just because she had asked? He wasn't ready to give his heart over again. He didn't think he ever would. He would lose her and finally go mad.

"After that, I lived on my own for another three years, fighting everything, it seemed, to survive."

He pulled in a deep breath and shook his head. "I do not feel any better."

"You…" She looked shaken. As a matter of fact, her hands shook as they rose to swipe tears away from her flushed cheeks. "You have never played. You had no chance to be a child."

"What?" What the hell was she talking about and why was she standing up and walking toward the water? When she kicked off her shoes, hiked up her skirts, and entered the shallow current, he bolted to his feet and followed.

"Are we going swimming then?" He smiled, pulling off his boots.

"No, but you will be getting wet." She backed away and kicked a cold spray of water at him.

He laughed, a bit shocked, and dripping wet. "What are you doing, Braya?" He kicked back.

She turned and bolted across the calf-high water, laughing and teasing him as she went. He chased her, bending to scoop up water in his hands to shovel it at her.

She responded by soaking him—being the more experienced of the two, in splashing.

When he reached for her to stop her, he missed at first. But then he grasped her elbow and pulled her back, into his arms. She laughed, falling into them, but sobered when he caught her gaze in the stillness of his own.

"You continue to bewitch me, lady." He didn't think about her pulling out a dagger and pointing it at his groin. He didn't think she would stop him when he bent his head to hers and planted a series of slow, sensual kisses over her lips. He was correct. She didn't stop him.

He pulled her in closer, reveling in the shape of her body pressed to his. She smelled of the morning sun and…cattle. He breathed her in deeper, liking that she was not afraid to help with the livestock she'd helped rob. He crooked one arm around her waist and cupped her nape in the other hand, tilting back her head.

He wasn't any more skilled in the art of kissing than she. He didn't care. It didn't stop him from kissing her senseless, until she went weak in his arms and he felt too weak to stand.

She raked her hands through his hair. He wanted to remove her clothes. But no. He wouldn't do that to her. If he left her with a child and she died...he broke their kiss and opened his eyes slowly to look into hers.

"Let us dry off before we head back," she suggested, smiling dreamily at him.

"Aye." It wasn't what he wanted. He doubted it was what she wanted either. But it was best, and best she didn't know why.

He let her go with great reluctance and watched her hurry over the stones, back to their cloaks.

"You did a good thing by talking your father into accepting my apology, though you were quite bold in your assumption that I would offer it." He smiled, sitting next to her. "Sometimes peace is better than fighting."

Her startling blue eyes delved deeper into him than anything he'd ever felt before. What if she found him buried beneath his shame and yanked him out by the collar and exposed him to all the world?

"But sometimes," he continued, fighting to remain strong, "war comes anyway."

She said nothing but bolted forward and pressed her palms on each side of his face. "I do not want to lose anyone I care about. Not anyone, Torin."

He curled his fingers around her creamy throat and pulled her forward for a kiss. He knew he shouldn't, but hell, he didn't give a damn about any of the reasons—not when the pout of her lips made them even more plump, more delectable. When the sound of her voice saying his name made it finally sound right to his ears.

But no! An alarm sounded in his head. She is English! She doesn't know you are a Scot! She doesn't know that you knowingly led her cousins to their deaths.

He groaned along the seam of her mouth, agonizing over things he'd never given a moment's thought to before. Why was she any different? He'd deceived hundreds, including Bennett last eve while they drank together and laughed, and planned the celebration to reconcile the leader of the Hetheringtons with the warden.

"Braya..."

"Torin," Her breath fell like sweet wine across his lips, "what is it that troubles you so?"

He shook his head and moved away from her a bit. "I...would not have you think me a brute by taking leave to kiss you whenever the mood strikes me—which would be often, I fear."

She smiled, almost doing him in. "I have not objected, my lord."

That was another thing. He wasn't a damned knight. He was a warrior, a cold-hearted killer. He planned on killing every guard in Carlisle Castle, possibly Bennett himself, and if it weren't for Braya, most likely her family.

His belly knotted with pain, but he ignored it. He wasn't born to have a woman, a family, peace. Everything about him was a lie and, soon, Braya would find out. When King Robert came, the Hetheringtons were going to stand with Bennett. Hell, Torin was making sure of it now. He rose up, tugging at his hair, his collar.

But what else could he do? Not attend the town hall meeting to give his apology? Fight them now?

He looked at her sitting on his cloak, her beautiful face tilted toward his, waiting for him to finish speaking. He would rather put it off and fight them later. He needed time to think of a way to save her.

"Braya, I'm not the—"

Avalon came hurtling toward them from out of the trees and stopped when she came to Torin.

Someone called Braya's name. It was a woman's voice echoing through the trees.

"That is my cousin, Lucy!" she said, bounding from the ground and hurrying for her shoes. She called out to her. "Here, Lucy!" She picked up her cloak and whirled it around her shoulders.

"Braya, 'tis Galien," Lucy told her anxiously when she rounded the bend on her horse and fixed her stunned gaze on Avalon first, and then Torin pulling on his boots. "He looks for you."

"Damnation!" Braya swore and started toward her. She needed to go. Now. The last thing she wanted was for her brother to find her with Torin. Galien wanted revenge for their cousins. Until Torin made his public apology, and her father and the others accepted it, he wasn't safe around Galien.

She stopped and turned back to look at the food piled on Torin's cloak, and then at him. She blushed and smiled, proving the food meant much to her family. "I must go. My brother is rash."

He nodded, not wanting her to leave. "Take the food."

She shook her head but he insisted, and after gathering the food into the saddlebag, he tied it to Lucy's saddle.

"Perhaps I will see you tonight at the celebration," she said, smiling at him as she leaped up into Lucy's saddle with her.

"Perhaps," Torin agreed, hoping he would.

They were about to depart when they heard the sound of another horse trotting around the bend.

Torin heard Braya swear above his head. It was her brother Galien. He approached on a large brown horse. His dark hair was pulled back, making the angles of his face seem harsher. His shoulders were as wide as a sunset. It was clear from his hard, murderous stare that he'd rather see Torin dead than alive.

"Sir Torin Gray," he called out, coming forward. "I should kill you where you stand for showing your face so close to Hetherington land after what you have done."

Avalon drew near to Torin, and when the brown horse reached them, she reared back her head, opened her jaws, and brought her teeth down snapping.

Braya's brother took a moment to calm his horse after it had nearly lost part of its nose, and then set his murderous glare on Avalon.

Torin stepped in front of his horse, blocking Hetherington from making any move against her. Almost instantly, Braya was there with him.

"Galien, what is the meaning of this?" Her voice snapped across the air like a whip. "Why were you looking for me?"

"I thought you might be alone with him again," Braya's brother flung at her. His accusation and his tone inferred that something vile and wicked had occurred. "What is going on between you? What were you doing?"

"We were…" Torin paused and quirked his mouth. "…playing."

For a moment, Galien Hetherington appeared too stunned to react. But then his eyes began to blaze and he reached for his sword.

"You killed four of our cousins."

"I was defending three guards who your cousins attacked and, still, I will come to ask forgiveness from your father and theirs at your town hall tomorrow."

"You cannot kill him, Galien," Braya declared with her hand on her hips. Torin had to fight the urge to pull her into his arms. "Take your hand from your sword before you bring shame to our family."

"'Tis you who will bring shame to our family with your secret meetings with this murderer."

"This was no secret meeting, Galien," she defended. "Sir Torin was bringing an invitation to us from the warden." She pulled the folded note from her pocket and handed it to him.

"An invitation to what?"

"A celebration," she told him. "A peace offering."

Her brother took the parchment and tore it in half then tossed it away. Braya cast Torin a nervous glance. He remained still and calm.

"Get on my horse, Braya," her brother demanded.

"I will leave with Lucy, Galien," Braya told him and turned her back on him before he had time to utter anything else.

Torin turned from watching her leave and let his smile settle on her brother. He could let insults roll off his back to avoid killing a man, especially if that man was Braya's brother. He wasn't bothered by the thought of Galien thinking he'd frightened Torin or anything of the sort. He knew what he was capable of and he wanted to keep it away from any of the Hetheringtons.

"Good day, Mr. Hetherington," Torin tilted his head at him and then leaped up onto his saddle. "I hope to see you at the town hall tomorrow."

He trotted off, and then rode out of the trees and back toward Carlisle.

He knew what he was feeling wasn't normal. He cared about what she wanted. She didn't want him to fight with her brother, and he hadn't. He went back to the castle reluctantly—because he had to. He had a duty to Robert, King of Scots. He should be there now, preparing it for the Scot's army. He knew where the weapons were stored. He should be there, destroying what he could. He'd begun his friendship with Bennett last eve, getting the warden to trust his advice and seek peace with the reivers. Because it was what she wanted.

He was pitiful.

And he was worried.

"I DO NOT like or trust him." Galien pressed his palms on the kitchen table in his father's house. "I do not believe his story about our lads. Something does not sit right with me."

"Son, they tried to kill the guards. Rob Adams would not lie to me." His father leaned back in his chair and looked up at him standing over him.

"You put so much trust in him then?"

"Aye, I do. I have known him long. He has entrusted me with many things. Things he has sealed away, barricaded behind an iron gate." He sat forward and took a swig from his cup. He drew his hand over his bare head and closed his eyes for a moment. "He does not want them ever revealed. He would not lie to protect a stranger. Besides, I told you. I have made up my mind. I want peace. I do not want to lose any more children."

Galien knew he would never get his father to move on this. It frustrated the hell out of him that his father could be as stubborn as a bull. But when Rowley Hetherington rubbed his head, it usually meant the topic was over.

"Very well, Father. You want peace. You trust Adams. Fine. But do you trust Gray with Braya? They are together all the time." He didn't realize he had raised his voice, or that he had swung his arms. "I just left them together yet again!"

His father stood up and rested his callused palms on the table and stared at him with smoky gray eyes that could compel an ancient Norseman to run himself through rather than face him.

"Your sister needs a man who will take her mind off fighting. You will leave her future up to me. As for Gray, I will have his apology. 'Tis the least we can give to the lads' families. Do you understand, Galien? Do you understand!" he shouted when his son would have spoken.

Galien nodded. There was nothing to be done about Sir Torin Gray. But he was certain the man was lying.

CHAPTER TEN

BRAYA ENTERED CARLISLE keep with Millie and Lucy at her sides and her parents behind her. Galien plodded along belligerently behind them with Will Noble, angry that he'd been ordered to attend by his father.

Lively songs, played on pipes and lutes by talented musicians, filled the great hall, and Braya's spirits. She smiled and pointed to a juggler, and then to a man garbed in colorful clothes standing on the shoulders of an identical looking man. She gasped at their acrobatics and was surprised that the warden had gone to such measures for her family.

Torin had had something to do with this. A peace offering. Torin was coming to the town hall tomorrow to apologize. He was a soldier who wanted peace. Her heart raced at the thought of seeing him.

She looked around, lifting her hand to the thick braid draping her shoulder. She wore her best kirtle and overgown. They were both fashioned in soft wool, dyed to match the color of the sea. Her kirtle fit close to her body and a bit off the shoulders and it had long, fitted sleeves that ended just over her knuckles. The top half of her sleeveless overgown fit like a bodice, tight around her waist and into full, flowing folds of wool with silver thread stitched in delicate patterns.

She loved her breeches and boots, but she didn't mind donning more feminine attire when the occasion called for it.

Lucy hadn't stopped talking about Sir Torin the entire way home this afternoon. She'd used words like smoldering and resigned, charming and serious. Braya agreed with all her friend's descriptions, but she had seen more. She had seen him laugh, heard him soothe his horse. There was something about him...not the memories shrouded in darkness, but the light, the gentle, quietness of him that attracted her immensely. She'd never felt anything like it before.

She found him standing with the warden and Mr. Adams before a large tapestry on the northern wall. Golden light from the hearth and the candles danced around him, casting splashes of copper and bronze through his hair and through the hair on his face. The pommel, hilt, and guard of his sword jutted out over left shoulder. He wore his breeches and boots beneath a soldier's tabard of red and blue—the same as all the border guards wore. But he was nothing like anyone else. He looked like a statue of some war-god that had come to life to create a whirlwind.

His eyes had already found her, stopped her from moving, her blood from flowing.

"Braya," Lucy whispered close, tugging her along. "Come now, you're holding everyone up."

Braya smiled and held up her foot behind her, pretending her skirts were snagged. "Onward," she called out merrily when she "repaired" it.

She couldn't bear to look at him after what she had just done. How much of a fool was she for Torin Gray? She moved her feet. One after the other. Steadily.

"Ah, Hetherington!" The warden came forward and held out his arm to her father. "You have my thanks for coming." He offered a quick, polite greeting to her mother and the others.

"Your invitation," said her father with a practiced smile, "did not say what this celebration is for."

"Why, 'tis for you," the warden explained. "For the Hetheringtons. For their help in the past…"

Braya stopped listening. This was Bennett's apology for throwing them out on their arses. Her father would accept because he was wise.

Her feet hurt, stuffed into tiny shoes. She wanted to sit down. Her belly rumbled. She wanted—

"Pardon me."

Torin's voice rode across her ears like drums as he closed the distance between them. Ah, he was coming to get her out of here and into a chair. She did her best not to smile too brightly at him.

"Sir Torin Gray," her father ground out. "I expect to see you at the town hall tomorrow."

"Aye, you will see me there, Mr. Hetherington. But right now, I think this woman," he turned toward Millie, "should be sitting. Allow me to show her to her seat."

"Her husband can do that," Braya's father said with a smile that seemed a bit more genuine than the one he'd offered the warden. "You can show the rest of us though."

"Of course!" the warden cried out. "Sir Torin will show you all to your seats, where you will eat, drink, and enjoy the night!'

Torin nodded and pointed Will and Millie in the direction of a cushioned chair at the end of the enormous trestle table set up in the hall.

Braya tried to get his attention as he led her family to the front of the table and invited them to sit in the first ten places at the right and left of the head. He didn't look at her for longer than a breath before he moved on.

Her father sat in the first place to the right, her mother beside him. Galien sat in the first place on the left, and Braya's uncle sat beside him. Braya would like to sit as far away from the warden as possible, but she wanted to be close to her mother if fighting broke out, so she sat next to her. She also didn't want to sit among the soldiers, even the ones who had wives. Lucy slipped into the seat to her right and the two smiled at each other.

She looked over Lucy's shoulder and watched Torin make his way to the end of the table, check on Millie and Will, and then move around to the other side and take a seat in one of the few that remained on the other side.

He'd chosen to sit far from her when he knew there were two extra places for her family members since he'd given Millie a special seat. Did he ignore her for her father's sake? She didn't care for it at all and decided to do the same to him.

"What is this?" the warden pouted as he approached his chair at the head of the table and saw Galien sitting at his left. "Old friend, I was hoping I might enjoy the company of your daughter at my left. I'm certain young Galien would not mind exchanging seats."

He didn't give a damn about insulting and mortifying her brother.

"I will stay where I'm sitting, my lord," Braya said, unable to keep her anger from sharpening her tone.

He cast an innocent look at her father and then at her. "Have I done something to offend you?"

He hadn't, but she knew he wanted to. Still, she couldn't say how she truly felt without risking the fragile pact her family had with him.

She shook her head.

He smiled and she looked down at the table. It was decorated in fresh, white linens. There were bouquets of flowers, jugs of ale and wine, and enough food to feed everyone in her village for a pair of weeks. Shame she would enjoy none of it.

"Then I invite you to sit with me," she heard him say on a sickly sweet voice.

She couldn't help her gaze flicking to Torin when she stood up. He looked like he was about to spring to his feet and stop her, but he didn't. She was glad. She didn't want any fighting.

Would Torin fight for her?

She passed Galien on his way to her seat. He said nothing. She glared at the warden for embarrassing him and ruining the night.

"Warden?" her father sat forward in his seat and eyed his host. "Now, you will do me the same courtesy, I hope."

"Of course," Bennett agreed, dragging his satisfied gaze from Braya to her father.

"Tonight," the leader of the Hetheringtons said, "I would like to know the man who is to kneel before me tomorrow. I would know the measure of his sincerity. Bring Sir Torin up and seat him beside my daughter that I might ask him some questions. And put Mr. Adams beside him. We have things to discuss, also."

Braya stared at her father slack-jawed. Sit Torin beside her? What was this? Did she dare smile at her father? Peer down the long bench and see if Torin was coming?

"Of course," the warden said with a stiff smile and called for Torin. "Come share some words with Rowley Hetherington."

Oh! Braya wanted to kiss her father! She almost couldn't conceal her smile when she turned to see him coming. She knew that what she was beginning to feel for him was more than simple attraction. It was hard to take her eyes off him and the sway of his hips beneath his belted tabard. She fought to keep from looking at the beauty of his profile haloed in sun-bleached curls, his furrowed brows above steely eyes when he turned to look at her. She almost couldn't swallow.

"So, tell me, Miss Hetherington," the voice to her right raked across her ears. She clenched her jaw and listened to the rest of what the warden had to say, realizing he wasn't going to leave her alone for a moment to talk to Torin. "What do you think of the man who killed four of your cousins?"

She turned away from Torin and set her icy gaze on her host. So, he was going to be more than a pest then. He was going straight for the jugular, was he?

"Does it matter what I think of him when 'tis my father who will decide what is to be done? And if it matters, then I would like to know to whom?" She tilted her head at him. "You?"

He opened his mouth to reply.

"Surely," she continued, cutting him off, "*you* do not trouble yourself with what *I* think." She arched a golden brow at him and finished woodenly. "And if you do, then let me be blunt. You have no reason to trouble yourself over me."

She turned and greeted the man who'd slipped into his seat beside her. "Good eve, Sir Torin. 'Tis nice to see you again." She looked over his shoulder at Mr. Adams and greeted him as well. She was fond of Mr. Adams. He'd always been kind to her and her family.

"Miss Hetherington." Torin smiled, and she wanted to breathe a sigh of relief. He was here. And it made the night better. He greeted her parents and her brother and even smiled at poor Lucy stuck with sitting with Galien.

After her parents greeted Mr. Adams and thanked him for coming to the town hall tomorrow, they shared their smiles with him, which boded well.

"Sir Torin." Her father turned to him next. "I hear the food here is quite good."

Braya held her hand to her mouth to conceal her smile. Her father was referring to the food Torin had given her to take back to the village. She'd told her father that she didn't think the warden knew about it. She didn't think Lord Bennett would be pleased to know one of his newest guards was giving away his food.

"The apples are especially good," Torin replied and gave her leg beneath the table a soft bump.

He touched her many more times while they ate, brushing his pinkie over hers on the table, his thigh against hers, beneath it. He didn't need to touch her. She could feel him near her, like a charge of heat, setting her nerve endings up in flames.

"Now that you are all together," said the warden, bringing their attention to him, "why do you not tell us what happened at the tavern."

Mr. Adams started talking first. His story matched with what Torin had told her.

"I had no idea they were Hetheringtons," Mr. Adams told her father. "You know I would have done anything in my power not to kill anyone had I known."

Braya's father nodded and drew out a long sigh from deep within his chest. "There is not much else I would ask you, Sir Torin. I trust Rob Adams is telling me the truth. In that case, you must be telling the truth as well."

Galien balled up his fists and looked about to speak but, thankfully, he held his tongue.

The warden tried to make conversation with Braya, but she answered everything with as few words as possible until finally he turned his attention to others at the table.

Torin barely spoke to her directly, but he shared slight, intimate smiles with her when others were too caught up in their own conversations to pay them any notice.

He made her heartbeat quicken and her belly flip. A dozen times, she wanted to turn and look at him without hiding it from her family or the warden. But she kept her eyes mostly on her plate and on her mother.

When supper was over, the musicians picked up their instruments and played, and many left the table to either dance or stretch their legs and mingle.

Braya left the table with Lucy and the two of them went to check on Millie at the other end.

Braya felt Torin's eyes on her while she laughed and danced with Will Noble and Rob Adams. He remained close to her but he did not ask her to dance. When she had finally had enough of being ignored, she strode up to him. "What is wrong with you? Do I displease you now?"

His eyes pored over her, but he offered no other reaction, save to say, "Nothing about you displeases me, Braya. But the warden is jealous."

"So? Let him be. He is nothing to me!"

"He can station me at any of the borders," he explained quietly, quickly, and left the conclusion to her. "The less he knows, the better."

"Aye," she agreed, understanding now why he had barely spoken to her all night. "But I miss speaking freely with you."

She was close enough for him to brush his hand against hers, to let his thumb linger and then trace her knuckles. "Aye," he said, moving a bit closer, as if he could not stay away. "I find I miss speaking with you as well."

She wanted him to kiss her, to take her in his arms and tell her...what? That he cared for her? That he would do anything to keep peace with her father?

"Meet me in the inner ward," he said in a deep, hushed voice that went straight to her head, "near the northern stairs—"

"My lord!" someone shouted. Sir John Linnington pushed his bloodied way toward the warden. "'Tis the Armstrongs, my lord. They are outside. They are raiding Carlisle!"

CHAPTER ELEVEN

Torin ripped his sword from its sheath and turned to look at the men's wives, Millie, the musicians, everyone who didn't know how to fight. Torin and the men were going to have to protect them all.

Hell. The castle was under attack.

The first thing he had to do was make certain it was, in fact, the Armstrongs and not the Scots.

"Braya," he said, turning to her and handing her the hilt of his sword. "Protect your mother. Your brother has already left the great hall and I do not see your father."

"Where are you going?" she said, grasping his arms. "You have no weapon." She wasn't about to let him go outside without a sword.

"I will get one. I must go have a look and see what we are up against. Stay here. I will come back for you."

He wanted to kiss her but the bastard Bennett was still here, barking out orders.

"Go, Braya," he urged. "Keep Millie with you as well. Aye?"

She nodded and he broke away, then ran out of the great hall. Had they breached the outer wall? How many were there? He hoped they weren't Scots. Not yet. He wasn't ready. Ready for what? To face her with the truth? To leave her? To die or…he saw Rob Adams on the way out of the keep. "What do you know?"

"Same as you," Adams called out. Then, "You need a sword." He pulled one away from where several were leaning against the wall by the door and tossed it to him.

Torin thanked him and pushed open the heavy wooden door. The first thing to hit him was the refreshingly cool air. The second was the sound of the guards shouting questions and commands. Too many voices, not enough direction. He didn't concern himself with it. Not yet. Not if it was his men out there.

Sheathing his borrowed blade, he began running for the battlement stairs.

When he reached them, he took them two and three at a time and pulled a bow and a quiver full of arrows from where they hung on the wall. He knelt along the crenelated wall and realized there were six guards behind him, following him. He motioned them forward and to get ready to shoot. If the Scots were here early, he would kill the six and go on to kill as many more guards as he could. If they were Armstrongs, he would let them fight for a bit and take out some guards. Less for him to worry about later. He nocked his arrow and looked over the side. Armstrongs, dressed in breeches, jacks, and steel bonnets lined the hill just outside the outer wall.

He fired his arrow and hit an Armstrong on the other side. He fired two more and brought down two more men before he heard Bennett shouting in a clear voice below.

"To the walls! To the walls! They surround the castle!"

Torin's heart sank. The east wall! No one ever watched it! He didn't want to fight them yet, but if they were allowed to breach the wall, they could get to the keep…and Braya was in the keep. He raced down the stairs and almost ran Bennett down in an effort to get to Avalon. "Get your horse!" he told him. "Gather some of the men and meet me at the east wall!"

He didn't wait for a reply or for the warden to catch up but ran to the stable. Avalon rose up on her hind legs and pawed the air when she saw him. He released her and without bothering with a saddle, leaped upon her back and thundered out of the stable, clutching her snowy mane.

When he reached the east outer wall, he found Rob Adams alone and holding off at least fifteen men. Four were dead or close to it on the ground around him. Torin didn't dismount since some of the reivers were mounted, arriving inside the curtain wall by way of the unguarded gate.

It was as if the reivers knew about the east wall and the gate. Torin hadn't been here long enough to know if the Armstrongs were aware of the unmanned wall. But he was certain they could know nothing about the celebration tonight that would surely see almost all the castle guards in the keep and not on the walls. There was a traitor somewhere in the castle.

He didn't trouble himself about it now but ripped his sword free and rushed Avalon into the oncoming swarm of reivers. She moved with him, a warhorse made of pure muscle and fire, guided by the power of his thighs.

He swiped his blade across the throat of one man and blood splattered across his face like war paint. He hacked at the chest of another while keeping Avalon at a charging pace. He didn't slow or hesitate but cut down two more, felling them from their horses with one deadly swipe. A large, hairy brute bore down on him, lifting his axe, ready to remove Torin's left arm. But Torin moved with the skill of an efficient killer, slipping slightly to the right with Avalon beneath him. At the same time, he brought his right arm up and around and swung his sword, removing the brute's head from his shoulders.

He took down three more Armstrongs with masterful ease and morose satisfaction. He wasn't here to kill reivers and protect the

English, but every rider who approached met either flying, feathered arrows, deadly hooves, or huge chomping teeth before they got close to Torin, and when they did get close, they died.

But Avalon could not keep away five horses at once, in every direction…and Torin was having a hard time fighting off their riders. One stabbed at him from his left rear flank while another rider galloped in from the right and swiped his blade across Torin's throat. He leaned back almost flat on Avalon's back, avoiding them both.

But there was another sword coming from the right. It came down but was stopped inches from Torin's shoulder with a clang from a blocking blade that sent sparks scattering.

Rob Adams brought his sword around and killed the man in his saddle.

Torin smiled at him. Adams nodded and then they both continued fighting.

One of the Armstrongs could have killed him and it fired up Torin's anger well enough to hack the limbs from two more men before noticing a figure standing high upon the keep battlements. Braya. Her hair waved like a pennant behind her. She was watching him. Something leaped in his heart…or his belly. He couldn't tell which.

She turned suddenly to look behind her, as if someone had called her name. He watched in horror as she lifted his sword and disappeared beyond the wall.

The Armstrongs had breached the keep! How many were in? All at once, it felt as if he were falling back in time…when he found Florie, when he watched his father die and his house burn down with his family in it.

This time, he wasn't going to run.

He tugged on Avalon's mane and turned her toward the keep.

Now, he wouldn't hold back.

Now, he would treat the Armstrongs like a true enemy.

BRAYA TURNED FROM watching Torin fight and met Millie's wide, fearful eyes as someone pounded on the door. She had wanted to see what was going on outside and thought the battlements might be the safest place to go. She'd brought her mother and her two dearest friends to the top of the keep, where a heavy wooden door protected the upper battlements.

Could it be her father, Galien, Will? She didn't call out and held her finger to her lips to keep the others quiet.

"Open the door, lady," a voice she had never heard before called out and set her heart to pounding. "We saw you come up here with the others. Open the door or we will break it open ourselves. No one is coming to save you."

For a moment, her fear vanished and anger took its place. She tilted one edge of her lips in a disgusted smirk. She'd like to open the door and kill him for saying that to her. If she was alone, she might have. Although she had to admit, she did hope someone came to aid them. She could kill—just not more than one at a time.

How long would the door hold?

The man outside the door took an axe to it. Braya startled at the powerful thump and crack. She was thankful she'd been on more raids than she knew how to count. She was afraid, but she'd had men running at her before in the midst of worse chaos than this. She would not lose her command. But her family. She was afraid for them. She hurried to the other women and made certain they had the knives they'd taken from the table ready.

"If one of them comes near you—" Another crack of the wood under the strength of the axe sounded in all their ears. Lucy whimpered. Millie prayed softly under her breath and held her hand to her belly. May Hetherington held her knife at the ready and nodded. Braya thought she could almost hear her mother's heartbeat from here. "—do not hesitate to kill them," she continued.

She spun around as another axe joined in with the first. She was going to have to protect her family. She bit down hard to stop her teeth from chattering. There were at least two men outside the door. The metal landed once again and made it through the wood.

Braya lifted Torin's sword and knew it was too heavy for her to fight with it. But she could still use it. She'd have to come upon their assailant from behind and stab him. She hurried toward the door and waited behind it.

Her heart thrashed against her ribs, through her veins, making her feel a little ill. She looked across the rooftop at her mother. May Hetherington winked at her. Braya smiled, gathering strength from her mother as she always had.

If there was one, she'd kill him. If there were more, she'd kill them, too. She had to.

They were almost in. A few more strikes. She prayed and hoped they were too tired to move with any speed. They began kicking, and the look of horror on Millie and Lucy's faces told Braya the men were almost through. She readied the sword.

The door splintered and caved in and the first man stepped outside. Braya wasted no time and drove Torin's sword into his back, using all her body weight. She ripped a knife from a fold in her skirts and turned to swipe it at the next man before the first went down. She slashed his face then aimed it at his neck. He screamed and smashed her across the jaw with the back of his hand.

She flew off her feet and landed on her arse. Her knife went the other way. No! Her mother! She fought with everything she had in her not to close her eyes, not to surrender to the darkness and sleep. She had to save them!

Her assailant grasped his bloody face and then pulled her up by her hair and closed his fingers around her throat. She heard someone scream.

Millie. She looked into the gash going across his face, his eye, and pounded her fist into it. It angered him further and he tightened his grasp until she could no longer breathe.

She felt her fight begin to fail. No.

His fingers loosened, and then his hand fell away from her neck. She sucked in a deep, life-giving gulp of air and almost sank to the ground with him when his suddenly lifeless body was shoved away from her.

Torin stood in his place. His wide, terrified eyes were a startling emerald against his blood-covered face as he reached for her to hold her steady. "Braya!" he breathed, lifting his fingers to her bloody throat. "Are you hurt, my joy?"

She took a moment to look at the three dead bodies behind him and the knife in her assailant's back. She shook her head and then began to tremble. They would have killed her and the others.

He was there. He saved her. No one had ever saved her before.

Without another word, Torin began to draw her in. She wanted to go. If she didn't feel so weak, she would have flung herself into his embrace, but her mother and cousins were there to gather her in their arms.

Torin smiled slightly at her as she left his hands. She smiled back.

They heard more footsteps running up the stairs. Torin stepped on her first victim lying dead on the ground and yanked his sword free of the man's body, then pointed it at the door.

"May!" It was Braya's father and uncle. Just behind them was Will Noble. They rushed outside and into the arms of their family.

"We cannot stay here," Braya said after a moment and moved away to look over the wall.

"'Tis safe," Torin said, coming to stand beside her. "The Armstrongs lost a heavy number. The rest are retreating."

She turned to look at him. She'd watched him fighting down there, protecting the gate. He'd moved his sword as if it were a part of him, hacking away at their enemy as if they were not fighting back. She had never seen anyone move the way he had. He was a force unto himself. And then he had come for her, killing four at the door, including her assailant.

"You saved them," her father echoed her thoughts, moving toward them. "What can I do to thank you, Sir Torin?"

"Acknowledge that your daughter almost gave her life doing the same," Torin replied, and slanted his wintry gaze to her.

She did all she could not to leap into his arms.

Thankfully, he looked down into the ward, littered with the dead. "Where is your son?"

"Here."

Everyone turned at the sound of Galien's voice. He stood in the archway. His face was pale. His jack was bloody. "Are any of you hurt?"

"No, no, thank God," their father assured while Braya and her mother rushed to him.

After he assured his family that the blood was not his and he was well, their father gathered them toward the door. "We need to find the warden. Let us hope he still lives."

"Aye," Galien agreed quietly. When Braya moved to pass him, he took her hand and held it to his lips. "If anything would have befallen you or mother..." He paused, unable to continue.

"They are unharmed," said their father, "thanks to Sir Torin...and Braya."

"Aye, and Braya," her mother and her cousins all agreed.

Braya wondered how one of the best moments in her life could happen in the midst of so many bad ones.

As they hurried down the stairs, she said a silent prayer of thanks for her family's safety and for...him. He'd gone ahead and she watched him, hoping he would turn around and look at her the way he had on the battlements. As if his next breath and every one thereafter depended on seeing her. But he had reached the landing below and spoke to Mr. Adams while the older man wiped blood from his face.

"The great hall is safe," Torin called out to them and led the way inside. Braya and Galien took the rear.

Before Braya entered the hall, the warden came upon her. He took one look at the swelling purple bruise along her cheek and reached his hand out. "What's this? Who dared put a hand to you, Miss Hetherington?"

"A dead Armstrong," she replied, moving away to avoid his touch.

He smiled, not truly concerned about any man putting his hand to her. "As are the relatives he brought here with him tonight. The inner ward is littered with them. The Armstrongs have been defeated, I'm told, by the efforts of Mr. Adams and Stir Torin. 'Tis said the two held the eastern gate alone. Then again," he laughed, "we know how tales are enhanced."

"The tales are true," Braya told him woodenly. "They did hold the entire east end by themselves. I saw them."

She wanted to tell him he repulsed her, but why anger the old toad? The Armstrongs had proven tonight that they were a powerful enemy. They needed Bennett's army. Still, no one had expected the Armstrongs to be so bold as to raid the defender's stronghold.

"What will you do about this bold, unlawful family, my lord?" she demanded.

"I must wait and bring it up before the other wardens on the day of truce since the Armstrongs have family on Scottish land. But believe me, I will see that the Armstrongs pay for this." He breathed and seemed to move closer to her. He dipped his head and lifted a finger to her cheek again, touching her this time. "Especially for this, little pigeon."

CHAPTER TWELVE

BRAYA HETHERINGTON WAS not his woman.

Torin didn't want her to be, he thought as he led Avalon and another horse out of the stable and looked up at the morning sky. He didn't want a woman. He'd managed fine enough on his own his whole life. Besides, Braya was going to hate him when she discovered who he was and why he was truly here.

He searched the inner ward. Where the hell was Adams? They were due in Rowley Hetherington's town hall within the hour. Torin hated not being someplace when he was supposed to be. He'd even saddled Adams' horse to save time.

As they had a nasty habit of doing of late, his thoughts returned to Braya. He couldn't stay away from her. He'd even insisted on escorting her and her family home last eve after the attack. He hadn't wanted to leave her. He missed her now. It made him feel ill that he was allowing himself to feel a bond with someone. A lass. An English lass. An English lass who hated Scots. There didn't seem to be anything he could do to stop it. He hadn't been sure he wanted to stop it—until he thought he might be too late to the battlements last eve. He'd tried to get to her quickly, but the Armstrongs had tried to stop him. He'd had to hack and slice and stab his way through them. And he had, leaving dozens of dead behind.

When he'd reached her and found her struggling in the arms of a bloody bastard, Torin thought he might go mad with rage.

If he thought denying himself her attention all night because of Bennett had been hard, then resisting her because her family was watching had been the most difficult thing he'd ever accomplished.

He was glad he had though. He needed to keep a clear head. He was to meet the king's messenger tonight. He had both good news and bad. The good news was that, as of last eve, there were twenty-two less English soldiers in Carlisle. The bad news was that Carlisle was thick with reivers. The king's army should be prepared for possible heavy fighting.

He was bringing war.

What else would he tell the king? That something terrible was happening to his heart and he was seemingly, achingly helpless to stop it? And what was so terrible, the king might ask. Torin would like to be able to tell him that because of an English lass, he was having some second thoughts about things he'd never had second thoughts about before. Things like war.

Her family needed Bennett. What good would a Scottish defender do them after Bennett was replaced? Mayhap he should reconsider killing the warden and, instead, compel him to swear fealty to Robert. They could avoid much killing, especially if reivers joined the fight.

He'd gone mad. He'd showed no mercy in the past. He'd never let the lord of a stronghold live whether the lord wanted to swear fealty or not. Perhaps other commanders did it differently, and that was why there were so many seized lands still occupied by English converters. Torin didn't believe a man ever changed the way he saw his captor. Submission came from fear, and the instant that man had a chance to fight against his lord, he would. If the lord served Edward with his sword once, Torin killed him.

He had many demons. He had never believed he would be free of them. He still didn't. But as of late, he found himself doing things for peace—like asking for forgiveness, of all things! Or convincing Bennett to invite Braya's kin to the castle for a night of feasting and celebration...and a chance for Torin to see her again. Or killing his enemy's enemy for her.

He usually traveled alone. He was used to keeping his thoughts to himself. Never once in all his years since he was let out of the pit in Till Castle had he let anyone through the walls he'd erected around his heart.

He'd never felt lonely before, and if he had, he found a willing wench's bed to occupy and nothing more. If he ever needed an ear, he had God's and Avalon's. Whether either of them listened, he didn't know.

But now that he found himself at such odds and on unfamiliar ground, he wished there was someone who could speak back to him.

"Ah, you are ready," Rob Adams greeted when he entered the inner ward and found Torin leaning against Avalon's left shoulder, and his own horse, saddled and ready to go.

"And waiting," Torin replied with the flash of a wooden smile before pushing off his horse.

"I know I'm a bit late, but are you not sore?" Adams rubbed his shoulder. "My arms ache."

"I practice every day," Torin advised him and leaped onto his saddle.

"As do I," Adams defended, then shook his head and fit his boot into his stirrup. "I'm getting old."

Torin almost cast him a genuine smile. Hell no. Torin couldn't...wouldn't speak to Adams. Aye, he'd saved Torin's arse last eve but that didn't mean they were friends—not truly. But there was something Torin wanted to finish talking over with him.

"Have you given any thought to what we spoke about last eve, after the fight? You know the men better than I. Who would have gone over to the Armstrongs and informed them that Carlisle was ripe for raiding?"

"Why does it have to be someone in the castle?" Adams asked as they rode toward the outer gate.

Torin turned to Adams. "You think it was a Hetherington?"

Adams shrugged beneath his tabard while his horse matched Avalon's slow trot. "Could be. None of their own died."

"But Braya and her mother..." No. The men trying to get to the battlements had deadly intentions. None of the Hetheringtons would have risked such a danger to their women. But, then again, what better way to get revenge without being blamed for the deaths of Carlisle's men? "Would Rowley Hetherington put his wife and daughter at such risk?"

Adams shook his head without needing time to think on it. "No, he would not."

"You can say this for certain?"

"Aye, for certain."

"Can you say the same for his son?"

"I would like to," Adams answered solemnly. "He would not purposely put his family at risk, but he is rash and ill-tempered and he has been known to disregard consequences when his pride is at stake. Still, I do not believe he would endanger his mother and sister."

They rode on in silence until they reached the trees along the river. The water was cold but shallow enough to pass through without trouble.

"What should we do about it?" Adams asked, guiding his mount over slippery stones.

"There is nothing we can do," Torin told him, keeping a gentle hold on Avalon's reins and letting her walk at her own pace in the water. "But if he is responsible for what happened last eve, I will make certain he pays. And if he is responsible, then the Armstrongs likely had instructions on making certain you and I perished. You saw how angry he was when his father stated that he believed we were telling the truth. There is nothing more sinister than passion."

Adams tossed him a skeptical side-glance. "You believe passion is sinister? Does Miss Hetherington know that about you?"

"Why does it matter whether she does or does not?" Torin asked, doing his best to sound disinterested.

"Come now, Gray," Adams chuckled. "'Tis plain in your eyes when you set them upon her. You are fond of her. There's nothing to be ashamed of—"

"I'm not ashamed," Torin disputed stiffly.

Damn it, that wasn't the point he should be arguing.

"She is beautiful," Adams pointed out as if Torin hadn't noticed.

"So are a hundred other women," Torin countered.

For some reason, his words made Adams smile as if he were privy to something no one else was. The older man nodded. "But a hundred other women do not fight and kill with a sword and still believe in peace."

"She desires peace," Torin corrected him, "for her family's sake."

"And what is wrong with loyalty to one's family?" Adams asked him. "Are you not loyal to yours?"

"Of course I am," Torin told him, turning away. "Let us ride. At this pace, we will never get there." He didn't wait for a reply and he didn't see Adams' wide grin as he rode away.

It didn't take them much longer to arrive at the large glen dotted with sheep and thatched-roofed cottages. A group of people met them and led them to the stable first, promising that their horses would be well cared for.

"No one is to touch my horse," Torin warned them, knowing their natural inclination was to steal. "She will chomp off the fingers of any who do, showing me who ignored my warning." His eyes gleamed in the soft glow of a few lanterns. "If anyone thinks to take her, let me make myself perfectly clear. If there is anything that can cause me to toss everything to hell and make me take back what I say here today and kill whoever I need to kill, 'tis my horse."

After they swore not to touch her, the villagers led them toward a large structure built of stone and timber.

"You have them suitably frightened," Adams moved in close to tell him. "You sounded entirely serious."

Torin furrowed his brow at him. "I was," he said and followed them inside.

The walls of the town hall were covered in thick, masterfully craft-ed tapestries. Beeswax candles burned in two enormous wooden circular candleholders hanging from the ceiling. Beneath them, several rows of long, carved benches were set to face the front of the hall, where Rowley Hetherington sat with his wife and his ear inclined to a man leaning over his chair to speak to him.

Torin looked around the hall as more people crowded inside and quickly filled up all the benches. He found Braya quickly, as if his soul instinctively knew where to look. She was already seated on the third bench at the far right with her cousins, Millie and Lucy, and a handful of men. Torin squinted his eyes on them. Who were they?

He forgot them soon enough when Braya, finding him as well, smiled at him. His gaze dipped to her bruised neck and he felt his blood boil.

She lifted her fingers to her neck, making him realize where he was staring. He looked up at her mouth. He wanted to smile back.

She looked radiant with her long hair spilling over a white over-gown with gold stitching and a saffron kirtle beneath. But hell, she could have worn a sack from neck to toe and he would still want to smile at her.

Adams shoved his shoulder into him to get him moving. Torin hadn't realized they had been invited to sit on the front bench. He raked his fingers through his curls and stepped forward.

Somewhere along the front bench, a woman wept. Torin looked the other way.

Rowley Hetherington made the introductions, and after turning to face the fathers of their victims, the apologies were underway.

Torin had never asked to be forgiven for killing any of his victims so he had no idea what to expect. The lads' fathers, who were all fighters and brawlers, seemed to handle the mourning better than the dead lads' mothers, who wept and even cursed Torin and Adams for what they had done.

Torin tried not to give a damn, but that was easier when one killed a man and did not have to face his family. He realized he would never fit in here, just as he had not fit in anywhere else. It had always amused him when these mad desires crept up on him. They meant nothing, just some old remnants of when he was a child and had a family and a home, whether in Invergarry or in the forest.

He decided soon after he'd arrived at the Hetheringtons' town hall that he wanted to leave. He never expected Braya's father to stand up and tell all his kin that Torin had helped Braya save his wife and his nieces, including his niece or nephew yet to be born.

For this, the Hetherington leader had said, he owed Torin much.

Mayhap, Torin thought while he listened, the leader could keep his kin out of Bennett's fights and Torin would consider the debt paid. Ah, but it was not so easy. No matter if they fought the Scots or not, they…*she* would discover that he was one. A Scottish soldier. Their enemy. They would all end up looking at him the way Galien was looking at him now, seated in the front row with his uncles.

"Sir Torin," Braya's clear voice rang out amidst the soft clamor.

He turned in his seat and let his gaze feast on her.

"…is also the source of the extra food my father has shared with some of you."

"What extra food?" someone called out.

"Why was it not shared with *all* of us?" cried someone else, followed by more disgruntled murmurs.

How serious was this going to get? Torin thought and looked at the faces around him for the first time. Most were clean. All were thin—not overly so, but not one weighed a stone more than they should. Most, if anything, weighed less.

Braya had stolen food from him to bring to them. His gaze flicked back to her.

"There was not enough to distribute evenly to everyone," her father's voice overrode every other. "Or do you all think me so unfair?" He waited, his gaze raking over every row. No one spoke, save to assure him they believed the opposite.

Watching him, Torin was reminded of some of the great clan chiefs in Scotland.

"The most needy among us received a share," the leader told them all.

"I will bring more." Torin didn't know why he volunteered—and so hastily, but he didn't seem to have control of his mouth—or his thoughts. "There is plenty at the castle."

"If you are caught, you will lose your place in the guard," Adams warned him, his dark eyes somber. But then, his lips curled into a sinuous grin. "But I have not been caught yet so I do not see why you would be."

Torin stared at him for a moment, surprised to hear Adams say such a thing, and happy that he did. Another reason to hate Bennett; for filling his belly while his "friend's" kin went hungry.

"We can work together," Adams suggested. "And bring double the portion once a month."

Torin smiled but wrinkled his brow. "I was thinking more like once a week."

Everyone in earshot grew silent and waited with hopeful anticipation for him to continue.

Anything to bring suffering to the English soldiers. "You and I both know they could use less food and a lot more time on the practice field."

"Aye," Adams agreed. "But where will you tell them it has gone off to?"

"I will tell them I threw it away," Torin advised him, tossing up his hands. "That I fed it to the pigs or the horses. I do not care. And after last night, I do not *need* to care. The warden will not release either of us from our service to him."

Adams thought about it for a moment then nodded and turned to the villagers. "Food will be here every week. As much as we can provide."

Cheers went up, even from some of Torin's most formidable enemies, like Galien and the mothers of the lads.

Soon, cups of cool water were passed out and the doors of the hall were swung open, letting in fresh air and sunshine. The gathering was coming to an end.

Torin found Braya's gaze, and as much as he cursed the emotions she made him feel, he was thankful he was not beyond feeling them—for her sake. He wanted to please her, whether it be keeping peace or feeding her family; everything he did, it seemed he did for her. He'd never felt things like this before, but he wasn't at a loss about what was happening to him. He wasn't a fool. He suspected he might be losing what was left of his heart. He hadn't guarded against caring for her because he hadn't thought it was possible. He told himself it was the last thing he wanted in his life, but he wasn't certain that was true.

"To fuller bellies," Braya's father called out, lifting his cup when everyone had theirs.

Torin raised his cup. Aye, he could drink to that.

"To new and lasting friendships," Adams said next.

Torin smiled, more because it was expected of him than because he believed it. The cup felt a bit heavier.

"And to peace."

Braya's words pierced like arrows. His smile faded though he fought to keep it intact. It didn't matter what he wanted. He was bringing war. Soon, there would be nothing between them but hatred.

Chapter Thirteen

B RAYA SMILED AT one of her aunts but did not pause her steps on her way to Torin in the town hall. Many of her family had gone home, back to their daily duties. The meeting was over. There would be no fighting, but more food instead. It had been a great success. Braya wanted to thank the two men who had made it so.

She wanted more time with her knight, for that was what Sir Torin was—her knight, bringing what her family needed, what she needed. He was a man who was not unsettled by her skill. He hadn't tried to manhandle her, and she doubted it was because he was afraid of what she might do. He didn't seem to be frightened by much.

She wanted to speak to him and get to know him more.

"You must think him a true hero," Galien said, moving in front of her and blocking her path.

Braya looked toward heaven and let out a tight little sigh. "Who?" she asked with a cool smile. "Father? For being so wise and sound and for keeping those of us who still live first in his thoughts?"

"I keep us first in my thoughts, Braya," her brother argued quietly. "Five of us were killed. If there is no punishment for their deaths, others will think little of doing the same."

"And what respect will the border regiment gain if robbing and trying to kill them goes unpunished? Many times—like last eve for one—they have protected us. Our enemies fear them. Once that is gone, we will have great trouble."

"What do I care about respect for the border guards?" Galien snarled at her and shook his head. "I will forgive you for your lack of good judgment, Braya. You are smitten." He spoke the last word as if he wanted to spit it out of his mouth.

"Sir Torin is a good man, Galien," she argued, knowing what he insinuated. "I will not treat him like anything less because he was trying to stay alive that night and he happened to be able to fight better than our cousins."

Her brother looked as if he either wanted to say something else, or throttle her.

He made the wise choice by remaining quiet and walking away.

With her path cleared, she set her gaze on Sir Torin again. She found him engaged in a conversation, which he appeared to find pleasant enough, with her cousin, Louise.

Braya slowed her pace, spellbound while he plunged his fingers through the curls dangling over his eyes. Damnation, did Louise find him as irresistibly handsome as Braya did? She wondered what Louise was telling him. Her cousin giggled and Torin looked away. His gaze met Braya's.

Anyone bothering to look could clearly see his mouth softening, his eyes warming on her, drawing her closer.

"Louise," she said, reaching them. She offered them a pleasant smile. "I was hoping to have a word with our guest before he leaves for the castle."

"Of course," her cousin said and hurried off, looking a little disappointed.

Alone, Braya moved an inch closer to Torin so she could relish in the scent of him. "I wanted to thank you for promising to bring food. I know the risk you are taking—"

"'Tis no risk," Torin assured her.

"Well, either way, 'tis most kind. It means much to me and I wanted to thank you for it, and for coming to the battlements last eve."

She had almost breathed her last at the hands of an Armstrong, but Torin had arrived and saved her. Then he'd given her praise for saving them. She'd wanted to find him last night and fall into his arms, the way she'd wanted to on the battlements. Her father liked him, despite what Galien thought. Perhaps Torin would court her, marry her—

Would she want him? Of course. He was raw magnificence with a kind heart despite the life he'd suffered. He was fit and clever, and he would make an excellent reiver, if he ever wanted to become one that is.

"Lady."

He spoke and set hundreds of butterflies free in her belly. She liked that he called her lady when she was nothing more than a thief.

"I was hoping you might spend the afternoon with me."

She felt her face go flush. Lord, help her keep her composure and not let him see how happy she was. "I would like that," she told him in a quiet voice. "But I have chores."

His smile faded and he stepped back and dipped his head. "Forgive—"

"Meet me in an hour in the clearing where we met." Without another word, she turned away from him and left the town hall.

Outside, the warm breeze pushed her hair away from her face. She hurried home to start her daily chores so they would be over quicker. So she could be with him.

A little over an hour later, she rode Archer out of the stable and headed in the direction that would lead her to the small clearing.

TORIN LEFT AVALON on the other side of the clearing and watched Braya from behind the thick bramble.

For the first few moments while she waited for him, she paced the clearing, looking a bit worried. Was she doubting her good senses as he was? Why would she? She wasn't the one doing the deceiving and misleading. He hated himself for allowing her to get under his skin and make him care. But hell, he was helpless against it. Like a torrent, it washed over him, sapping him of reason and good judgment. Because of her, he spent the last hour thinking about what would become of her family, who were already hungry, after the Scots finished with Carlisle. War, even if they had no part in fighting it, was going to hurt them. Braya knew it.

If they did fight against the Scots—against him—and he killed any of them, he would be plagued by what their mothers would say to him.

Hell, the Hetheringtons weren't his dilemma to fret over. He was keeping his promise. He was doing his duty. Since when didn't his duty come first?

He gazed at her through the leaves while she studied the patches of beautiful common mallow flowers and then bent to bring one to her nose.

He smiled and stepped forward where she could see him.

She looked up from beneath her long lashes and smiled back. "They smell good," she said in her dulcet voice.

He moved closer to her, drawn by unseen tethers, and reached his hand out to her cheek. He wanted to kiss her. It was all he'd thought about since he kissed her last. He'd wanted to kiss her last eve when he feared he'd lost her. He wanted to ride into Armstrong territory and kill more of them. He cared for her. He wouldn't let it prick at him now. Not now.

He dipped his gaze to her neck, washed clean of blood but stained with red and purple bruises. "How is your throat, lady?"

"It pains me a little." She lifted her slender fingers to it. "Nothing I cannot bear. I'm grateful to be alive to feel it."

He looked into her eyes and saw that the spark of fire that usually lit her gaze had gone dark. Will Noble had told him what his wife shared with him. Braya had told Millie that she was about to die before Torin got there.

He ran his hand over her head and then cupped the back of it and pulled her into his tight and tender embrace. She went in willingly, yielding immediately to his touch. He wanted to comfort her from the memory of being at the edge of death. It wasn't the same as fighting to live. When the fight was over and one looked death in the face—when the cold, black emptiness of it overwhelmed, there was nothing more terrifying.

He held her until she pulled away just enough to look up at him.

Was that his heart pounding like a drum against both their chests? What the hell would she think of him that he would fall for a lass so quickly? Give in to her every want and desire?

"I owe you much," she whispered, lifting her hand to his cheek.

"You owe me nothing."

He let her lead his face down to hers and covered her mouth with his. She opened to him and he plunged his tongue inside her, letting a thread of fire lance down his back.

She parried his tongue in a dance that made him as tight as a bowstring. No one before her had ever made him feel like he could snap in two. He spread his splayed hand down her spine and cupped her backside.

When she closed her soft lips around his tongue as he withdrew it, he thought he might go mad with the need for her. He didn't stop kissing her, but tasted her and teased her, and breathed her in as if he would perish if he didn't.

He thought he would perish.

He wanted more of her and dipped his mouth to her throat. His kisses were gentle against her bruised skin. He wouldn't be too forward with her, as things might escalate too quickly and he wouldn't put her in a position of shame when he left.

Hell, he wasn't staying here. He could if he wished it after the Scots took Carlisle, but there was no future with Braya.

He might have to fight her.

She must have sensed his sudden unease for she withdrew slightly and smiled.

He basked in the sight of her red, puffy lips and flushed cheeks.

He had to find a way to resist her so that he would remain strong to his duty, strong to his promise. Make them pay. Make them all pay.

"I spotted some mulberry bushes not far from here," she said, letting him go slowly. Her arms slipping down his shoulders and away from him tempted him to reach for her and pull her back.

"Come, let us pick some." She broke away, tossed him a bright smile, and hurried off.

Torin watched her for a moment, his brows flaring upward at the edges, along with his lips. He took off after her through the bramble, listening to the sound of her laughter through the trees.

She was playful and deadly, and so damned alluring. She made him feel primal, instinctual. He wanted to chase her down, catch her, and take her against a tree. Or keep playing with her.

Mayhap, they could do both.

She stopped running when she came to Avalon and Archer basking in the shafts of sunlight.

"I tied him to a tree near the clearing," Torin heard her mutter as he caught up. She settled her gaze on Avalon's steady, sapient one. "Did she get loose and set Archer loose as well?"

"I did not tie her," he said, "and aye, she likely did untie Archer."

"What kind of horse is she?" Braya marveled then stepped closer to them and gasped. "They are eating the berries!"

She gave Avalon a little push and Torin reached out to pull her back before his horse chomped off Braya's fingers. But Avalon didn't try to bite her and Torin pulled her into his arms instead.

"She likes you," he told her, running his lips over her cheek. "She's a very intelligent horse."

"So she's the brain and you are the brawn," she said, giggling when he kissed her earlobe down to her neck.

"And you are the beauty," he whispered, snaking his arms around her.

"What a silver tongue you have, Sir Torin."

He ran the tip of it over her lips and groaned into her mouth when she opened to him. She coiled her arms around his neck as they fell to their knees onto the soft earth, kissing.

Nothing mattered to him in that moment but her. He wanted to tell her, while he kissed the breath from her, that he hadn't cared about anyone in so long, he wasn't sure he knew what to do. He wanted to tell her everything; even about the guilt and shame he carried with him. But he couldn't give that much of himself away. Not to her. And that was the pity of it. She was the one he wanted to tell.

He was afraid. Afraid of loving her and losing her—and the odds of losing her were very high. What would be left of him this time?

How could he find such passion with an English woman? How could he betray himself? Would he be haunted forever? When would it end?

He withdrew from their kiss and cupped her face in his hands. He didn't know what to say, so he pressed his forehead to hers and closed his eyes.

"Are you someone's husband, my lord?"

He opened his eyes and stared at her. "No. I'm not."

"Are you away from someone you love?"

She looked so apprehensive about his answer he had to smile at her. "I love no one, lady."

She didn't appear relieved so he kissed her hoping it would help. It didn't. She looked more miserable than he.

"I'm plagued by many things," he told her quietly and sank to his arse on the ground.

Braya followed. "Tell them to me."

He couldn't. How could he tell her who he was, *what* he was? Even if he wasn't deceiving her, how could he ever tell her how he had run away from his family that day? What would she think of him? Her family meant everything to her. He understood it. If he had not lost two families to the English, he would have felt the same way.

"I have lived most of my life for—" He stopped, realizing that this was the first time these words, in this order, had ever left his lips. He wasn't sure how he felt about it, or what it meant. All he knew was that he wanted to tell her *some things*, not all.

She moved closer to him, almost in his lap, and ran her fingers down the side of his face. She didn't say anything, and mayhap because of that he knew she could be trusted with what he wanted to tell her.

"For revenge," he went on, closing his eyes at her touch. "Every single thing I did or said had a purpose, and that purpose was revenge against the E—Scots. About a month ago, I was in Berwick and I overheard some of the Bruce's men talking about possibly riding here this winter, mayhap sooner. I came hoping to fight. But now I fear you will join the battle."

Her eyes were large, her face pale. "They are coming?"

He nodded, keeping his steady gaze on her. "I believe they are."

Her eyes immediately filled with tears. "I have never seen a Scottish soldier. I was too young to fight their war against the warden. My…father is older." Her tears fell to his hands that were holding hers. She let him go and swiped at her eyes. "When will your revenge be satisfied?" she asked softly.

"I do not know, Braya. But right now, you should be asking your father that question. Will he risk his entire family again by fighting the Scots over some pact he has with Bennett to keep enemy reivers awa—" Aye, right, then. It was not Galien who informed the Armstrongs.

Torin didn't think her eyes could get any bluer as the truth dawned on her as well. "The warden is working with the Armstrongs. He set up the attack."

Torin smiled at her cleverness.

"'Tis the perfect way to keep us beholden to him. Have our enemies strike. Show us how much we need him and his men. You," she corrected, "and Mr. Adams. Oh," she bristled. "How many other things has he lied to us about? How many other times did he *protect* us from enemies he brought to our doors? And all to make certain we fought on his side again if and when the Scots came back."

Aye, Torin thought, and now he might also have the Armstrongs on his side. He would have to do something about that. But for now, Braya was the only one on his mind.

"You have my sword, Braya. I swear." He had no trouble making the promise to her. He was here to kill Bennett, not fight the Scots with him. "But now more than ever, you need to convince your father that his debt to the warden is over. He must let go of his revenge and not stand with Bennett when the Scots come. Too many will die. The Scots are a formidable army."

Was it enough? He was glad it was Bennett who had brought the Armstrongs here. Braya's father was now less likely to fight for him. It had to be enough.

Hell, he should have refused to apologize and that would have caused dissention between the Hetheringtons and Bennett, but he had kept peace...for her.

"What about you?" she asked him, taking hold of his hands again.

"Will you fight this formidable army?"

"I must do what I came here to do," he told her, looking away.

"You ask my father to give up his revenge but you cling to yours," she accused, and rightly so. "And what about us having a Scottish warden? Whose side do you think he will take in a raid?"

"It will not matter if everyone is dead, Braya."

She shivered and he pulled her closer and closed his arms around her. "I do not mean to upset you. But I want you to leave Bennett's fights to Bennett."

"You need not worry about me," she whispered against his neck.

"I know," he smiled, loving her confidence, but wishing she didn't possess so much of it. "You can take care of yourself—"

"I'm guaranteed safety," she interrupted and pressed her lips to his, "with you at my side.

CHAPTER FOURTEEN

TORIN SAT ALONE beneath the moonlit sky, beside the river Eden just outside the city. Roger MacRae, one of the king's messengers, just left him carrying Torin's message beneath his mantle. Torin had written the king, as he had dozens of times in the past, giving him all the information he'd gathered so far about the stronghold. He knew exactly how many men resided in the garrison, and how many patrolled the borders. He knew how many weapons they possessed and he was learning how well they fought. Most of them were poorly trained and would be easy to take down.

If not for the Hetheringtons, Braya most especially, Torin's plans would not have changed. The Scot's army could be here by the last few days in July as planned, but so much had changed since he'd come here.

A few days ago there wasn't a woman in his life who was beginning to matter more than he cared to admit, for whom he feared he was willing to do anything.

Had he said enough, made her afraid enough to warn her father tonight? He hoped so. His army was coming. All he could do was postpone it a bit by asking the king for another sennight before the troops arrived. He would have no way of knowing if Robert would do as he'd asked, but the Bruce always had in the past. The king trusted him. Torin wouldn't let him down.

There wasn't much time. If the Hetheringtons insisted on fighting, Torin would have to take Braya away to keep her safe.

Where the hell would he take her and how would he fight if he was not here? No! He had to be here. He wanted to see the stronghold fall.

He looked out across the moon-dappled surface of the river. It was time he began preparing Carlisle for its fate. He would make certain the Hetheringtons did not fight.

Still, it wouldn't be long now until Braya knew the truth and this was over, the way it was destined to end. It should never have begun in the first place.

Why had he asked for another sennight? Why did he want to prolong this yet again?

He heard a sound and looked over his shoulder to find Rob Adams coming up behind him. What the hell was he doing awake and out here beyond the city? How long had he been skulking about?

"What are you doing here?" Torin asked him with a hard edge in his voice.

"I often come out when everyone else is asleep." Adams replied, as if he were repeating the weather. "I find it more peaceful."

Had he seen Torin speaking with MacRae? Torin was tempted to ask him. What if he had? Would Torin kill him if he started asking too many questions? "Aye."

"What are you doing out here?" he asked Torin and sat down next to him on the grass.

"Seeking peace," Torin answered and folded his arms across his knees. He kept his gaze on the water before him and said nothing else. Let Adams get the hint that Torin did not want to talk to anyone and let him leave.

He did neither.

"What do you seek peace about?" he asked annoyingly. "Is it Miss Hetherington?"

Torin gaped at him. Had he given Adams any reason to think he could be so bold? "I would rather not discuss my—"

"'Tis clear," the older man said, ignoring Torin's warning glare, even if he likely couldn't see it. "What plagues you about her? That she is the leader's daughter? That she is a skilled swordswoman? That she—?"

"Adams!" Torin held up his hands. "Enough! I have no intentions on sharing my feelings with anyone, about anyone. Do you understand?"

"Of course. You know I only meant to help with your dilemma."

Did Torin appear so poorly then? "I need no help with my—I do not have a dilemma."

"Of course not."

"Do you mock me?" Torin demanded, wishing there was no full moon so he didn't have to see Adams' mocking smile and he could at least pretend ignorance.

"Perhaps just a bit," the older man admitted. "Only a man as cocksure as you would deny his attraction to her."

"I'm not cocksure and I do not deny my attraction to her," Torin confessed quietly, without realizing how much of himself he was giving away.

Adams may have softened his smile. Torin couldn't be sure, nor did he care.

"I believe I know who alerted the Armstrongs to our weakened defense, and it was not Galien Hetherington," he said, changing the topic.

"Who was it then?"

"Bennett." Torin explained to him what he had inadvertently realized tonight. "Braya—Miss Hetherington agrees."

Adams nodded. "It makes sense that he would want to keep the Hetheringtons under control, especially after all that has happened. How do we prove it?"

Torin didn't care about proving it. Bennett, the defender, would be on his knees soon enough. "We?"

"Aye," Adams challenged. "We. I have not trusted him for many years."

"Then why work for him?" Torin asked in a low, gravelly voice.

"'Twas either this or become a reiver like the rest of my family," Adams answered.

Torin turned to set his eyes on him in the dim light. "What do you mean? Are you a Hetherington?"

"My mother was a Hetherington," Adams told him. "My father is a Forster. Bennett does not allow reivers to become guards so I changed my name, left my family, and came here many years ago."

Adams' family were reivers. That explained why he helped them. Why they considered each other friends, and why Adams had felt slighted by their attack.

Still, Torin would not be tempted to trust him with too much.

"You said Braya saved your life. What did she do?"

"She convinced me to forgive myself for something I did once."

Torin smiled. "And that saved your life?"

"Aye. What I did was quite terrible. I was ready to end my life over the guilt of it."

"Aye, I understand guilt," Torin agreed quietly.

They sat for a little while without speaking. That was fine with Torin.

"I'm half-Scot," Adams finally said, and then smiled at Torin's look of stunned disbelief. "My father, the Forster, is a Scot."

"Does Rowley know that?"

"He does," Adams laughed. "'Tis only Scot soldiers he hates."

Torin nodded. "Aye, I had forgotten."

What would Adams do if Torin told him the truth? He could use an ally on this side of the wall. The Scots weren't coming to harm the reivers. Mayhap he could help keep the Hetheringtons from fighting. "You have an interesting story, Adams."

"What about you, Gray? You said you hail from Bamburgh, aye?"

Torin thought about telling him the truth. He was a Scot. He was here to take down the stronghold. Either Adams joined him or he died. "Aye. Bamburgh."

"What of your family?"

Torin was prepared for these questions. He had to be. He had to have a past, else people wouldn't trust him and would turn on him. He didn't want to tell his own, so he had many made up and ready to tell. "My father was a blacksmith." He lifted his fingers and drew them faintly over the moth brooch pinned to his léine beneath his mantle. "My mother was as good as any mother, I would imagine."

"Oh?" the older—and proving to be wiser—man put to him. "Was she taken from you at a young age?"

Torin nodded his head. He hadn't mentioned anything about her dying, had he? "Aye, she was," he said, before he could stop himself. "As was everyone in my family, all taken from me in a moment."

"Oh, hell, Gray, my apologies." Adams' stricken voice echoed through the trees, across the water. "I had no idea."

"No apologies are necessary," Torin assured him quietly, glad that they were done speaking of it.

"How did it happen?"

Torin closed his eyes to stop them from burning. "Fire."

"God help you, lad," Adams lamented. "How did you survive?"

Torin rose up, brushed off his breeches, and turned back for the castle. "I ran."

"GALIEN," BRAYA SAID, with a warning lilt in her voice. "I would hear Father's voice on the matter."

"Soon," said her brother, sitting at their father's kitchen table. "Father's voice will be mine."

"Until then," growled Rowley Hetherington next to him, "my voice is mine and if you interrupt my thoughts on this matter again, mine will be the only male voice to be heard in this house for a long time to come!" he shouted, coming to a close.

His son closed his mouth and did not open it again.

"Now, Braya, tell me again why you and Sir Torin believe 'twas the warden who advised the Armstrongs to attack."

She patiently told her father—for the second time—everything she and Torin had spoken about tonight. "The warden wants us to think we need him—and…we do, but not as much as we have been made to believe. He is the one who needs us."

"'Tis ingenious really," her father muttered through his teeth. "The bastard."

"Father," Braya started as she reached across the table and touched his arm. She cut a worried glance to her mother sitting beside her. "He is the one who needs us because the Scots are returning."

Galien cast her a look of shock and fear. "How do you know this?"

"Sir Torin heard the Scots speaking of it when he was in Berwick last month."

"Father." Her brother turned fully on the bench to face him. "If this is true, we need to send out the call for our other brothers to gather."

"'Tis true," Braya interjected. It was time her voice started being heard. She disagreed with her brother and she was tired of being quiet about it. Her sword was worth more than silence. "But why should we fight for a man who deceives us with little regard if we, his guests, were taken against our wills or killed. I do not wish to risk my life or any of yours for him."

"You have no firm basis for your argument, Sister. We do not know for certain if the warden had anything to do with the Armstrongs. There is no proof. I do not want to take the word of a man I do not know. A man who killed four of my cousins, and stand by while the Scot's army decimates Carlisle and takes over. Where will we be then?"

No! She saw that Galien's words were making sense to her father. She shook her head. "Father, please, do not cast us into a war that will take more sons from their parents, more brothers from their sisters, more fathers, husbands. Do not, I *beg* you, send us to our deaths over the warden."

"Braya." Galien held up his hand. "'Tis not just for the warden, but for Carlisle and for Cumberland. We fought the Scots five years ago and won. We will win again."

"At what cost?" she demanded and looked again at her father.

"Leave me, both of you," he said and waved them away.

Braya rose and left the table, the kitchen, and kept on going out of the house. She didn't want to be around anyone. War was coming. Her family was most likely going to fight. Torin had called the Scots "a formidable army". What was best for her family? If they helped Bennett and he conquered the Scots again, things would remain the same. If they didn't help and he lost, the Scots would sit in Carlisle and everything would change.

Perhaps, in the long run, fighting wasn't a mistake.

She wished she were with Torin now. She looked toward the stable. She could have her horse ready in minutes. What more was there to do here but worry? Torin didn't want her to fight. How would she tell him that she might have to? She could fight. It was what she'd been training for, trying to prove her whole life. She was the Hetheringtons' best fighter. She won all the competitions at all the games and could beat almost any man she came against. If her family went to war with the Scots, she had no choice but to join them.

The more she thought about telling him, the more she wanted to go to him. They would think of something together. She thought more clearly when she was with him. She gave herself a dozen reasons why she needed to go…go saddle Archer and find him, kiss him as she'd kissed him yesterday. The memory of his mouth on hers, the taste of him, the scent of him…she almost laughed out loud hurrying toward the stable.

She couldn't wait to see him. To—

"Braya!" She turned to find Will Noble hurrying toward her. "'Tis Millie! I think the babe is coming!"

The babe! Oh, none of them thought of the babe and what kind of world they were bringing him or her into. "Mother!" she shouted toward the house. "Mother! 'Tis Millie!" There was no time to worry about her family now. Millie needed her.

BRAYA STEPPED OUT of Millie and Will's house and leaned against the doorframe. She breathed a deep breath and reveled in the cool, fresh, evening air. Early evening of the next day. Dear God, seventeen hours.

Poor Millie. It had been a difficult birth. Her babe was turned feet-first. Thank God the older women had come to take over. Braya's mother and her aunts, including Millie's mother, had known what special maneuvers to use to help little David come into the world.

Braya was glad she had been there to watch and learn, but it also scared the hell out of her and made her realize Millie was more courageous than she. She felt a bit shaken, stunned, and a bit sick to her stomach at what she'd just witnessed. It wasn't the first time she'd seen it but she'd never grown accustomed to it and she never would. It was the most violent, most savage experience of a woman's life.

With Millie and her babe safe in the hands of the older women, Braya left the house in need of a break and some air.

She closed her eyes against the cool wood and thought of her bed.

A soft touch along her temple pried open her eyes.

"Torin!" She startled seeing him. Was she dreaming? She smiled into his beautiful green eyes. "What are you doing here?"

"Your father told me where you were." His voice played across her ears like a familiar, soothing song.

"My father?" she laughed softly. "He likes you, I think."

She let him lead her away from Millie's door and toward her own.

"We spoke at length, your father and I," he told her as they walked. "He is a wise man."

"What did you speak about? The war?" Her heart thudded in her ears. She felt more awake. Had she dreamed it all? Were the Scots still coming?

"Aye, the war."

She felt a bit lightheaded and held on to his arm for support. "And?"

He crooked his arm and placed her hand inside his elbow, then covered it with his. "And he is still undecided."

She sighed and rested her head on his upper arm while they walked, keeping their pace slow. "Galien wants to fight, of course."

"Aye, I know. He sat with us."

She lifted her head off his arm and looked up at him. If she weren't standing so close that she could feel the heat from his body and count the number of hairs on his handsome face, she would have sworn he was a dream.

"What will we do, Torin? Millie just had a son and he will need his father."

"We will convince your father not to fight." His deep voice seeped through her to her bones. "Tomorrow. Tonight, you need to sleep. You have been awake for two days and will say things you will not remember when you wake up."

He smiled at her. All the hours with Millie and before that fell away along with all worries of war. "I would rather stay awake with you."

His smile deepened and his gaze on her warmed. "Do not tempt me to be thoughtless and whisk you away from your bed."

Oh, how she wanted to tempt him. She wanted to tempt him to carry her away to someplace secluded and serene, quiet and coz—she opened her eyes. Had she just fallen asleep?

She suspected she had when Torin swooped down and lifted her off her feet to cradle her in his arms.

She squeaked and then laughed with surprise. The last man to pick her up was a Milburn with malicious intentions. She had rid him of those intentions with a knife to the eye. "You do not have to carry me, my lord." She didn't mean it. Her legs had gone out from under her. *And* she didn't want him to put her down. He was strong and carried her as if she were but a breath of air. His arms were hard, but warm. They molded to her legs and back and pressed her close to his broad chest and tight belly with the fingers of one hand curled around her hip and the other, just below her breast.

She loved looking at him from this angle, his head a sensual slant over her, ready to plant the perfect kiss on her mouth.

Oh, why did she have to be so weary? She would beg him to take her beyond the trees—

"I will take you to your bed, lass."

She heard his voice as if he were hundreds of leagues away. No. She wanted to be closer to him!

Did he just call her lass?

CHAPTER FIFTEEN

ORIN LOOKED DOWN at Braya's sleeping face and felt his heart and his breath stall.

How was it that he cared so much for her? He'd done everything for peace between Bennett's men and her family and now, just a few short days after he stood before her family and apologized, he faced fighting them on an even larger battlefield. He'd known it was coming. He'd failed to keep possibly a thousand enemies away from the king's men…his men. He should have let the reivers and the border guards battle it out over five dead fools. Who gave a damn about them? He surely hadn't…until he had to meet their mothers and fathers.

Hell.

He reached her front door and knocked. He knew her father was inside. He'd left him not too long ago.

Rowley opened the door. The look of stunned disbelief on his face when he saw his daughter asleep in Torin's arms was so comical, Torin almost smiled at him.

"Come." He stepped aside and waved Torin in. "I'll show you to her bed."

Torin followed him inside. Galien stood at the entrance to the kitchen watching the spectacle, almost as shocked as their father.

Torin wondered what they were seeing that produced such a reaction. Her vulnerability? She was slight, but not weak or helpless.

He suddenly felt honored that she let herself be vulnerable to him.

Hell. He was in trouble.

He had never felt this way about anyone, not even Florie. Braya had his sword. He would kill for her. What did that mean for the Bruce and his men?

Torin followed her father to the other end of the house and a curtained wall. Her father pushed the curtain aside and Torin looked into the dimly lit, cozy little space where she slept.

He smiled at her humble life. What could he give her if he took her as his wife?

He set her down on her straw bed and lingered over her for an extra moment. He was thinking of her as his wife. What the hell was happening to him?

He had Bothwell Castle in Glasgow, or his smaller keep in Thornhill, both given to him by the Bruce.

"Did you speak to my wife?"

Torin pulled away from Braya and looked at her father. "My wife?"

"What?" the older man asked, confused. "Your wife?"

"No, no. I'm not wed." Torin knew he sounded like a fool. He felt like one. "Forgive me," he said with a soft chuckle as he stepped away from her room. "I did not hear what you said."

"Of course," her father nodded, eyeing him as if he'd just sprouted a third eye. "I asked if you spoke to my wife."

Torin knew his face went up in flames. Damn it all! He was a warrior who never lost a battle and he was blushing!

"Eh, no, I did not see or speak to her."

"I should go see to her. If she did not nap, she will be worse off than Braya."

Before Torin had a chance to say a word, Rowley Hetherington hurried to the front door, pulled his jack from a hook close by, and disappeared outside.

Alone with Galien Hetherington, Torin eyed the man while he went to the door. He didn't trust the reiver not to stab him in the back as he left.

"Gray."

Torin stopped and looked at him, waiting for whatever it was that Braya's brother wanted to say.

Not that Torin cared really. Galien made no secret that he didn't like him. Torin felt the same. Galien was rash and led by his emotions. Not a good trait to have in a leader. He would end up getting his entire family killed.

"What are your intentions for my sister?"

"I intend on keeping her alive."

"She can do that herself," her brother declared.

Torin was glad to hear Galien admit how skilled his sister was, even though he did not tell her so.

"And she has me and my father."

"And me," said Torin with a silent agonized breath. How could she have his sword if he was on the other side? He blinked and set his shimmering gaze on her brother. "But we will all fail against what is coming. 'Tis not your fight."

"If they win," Galien argued, but offered more quietly, "there will be a new warden and the reivers will be slaughtered."

"Only if you fight against them. Reivers have not been slaughtered elsewhere in Scotland, have they? Robert the Bruce does not give a damn about thieves."

Galien's dark eyes narrowed on him. "You speak as if you know these things for certain. As if...you know the Bruce. Do you?"

Hell! Torin tried his hardest not to react or instinctively look down the hall to where she slept. Someone usually figured him out. Normally, Torin killed whoever it was and hid the body. But this was

Braya's damned brother.

"I speak from experience. That is all."

Galien narrowed his eyes on him. "Where did you come from? I have asked others and no one has heard of you."

Torin wondered, for a fleeting moment, if he could get away with killing Galien and burying him. Or if all his plans were about to fail because of him.

"Have you traveled to Bamburgh then?" Torin challenged, then moved closer, tired of insinuations. "If you have a charge, then make it," he growled, all nonchalance and detachment abandoned. "You are a prideful fool. Do not talk your father and…possibly your sister into dying. I promise if the Scots do not make you answer for it, I will."

He raked his scathing stare over Galien once more, letting the promise sink in, and then left the house.

Damn it. He probably should have killed him. What if Galien shared his suspicions with his sister?

He made it back to the castle, practiced for an hour with Adams, and then retired to bed. He had much to think about besides Braya or her brother, like a plan of attack. Once the Scots were outside the walls, he would begin taking down Carlisle's guards. He might have to kill Adams, but he would do all he could to avoid it. Adams wasn't a full-blooded English and, besides, Torin liked him. He didn't like many.

Torin would make certain the Hetheringtons did not fight for Bennett. If he had to kill a few guardsmen before the Scots arrived and blame one of the Hetheringtons, like Galien, for instance, he would. Once Bennett accused Rowley's son, the leader of the reivers would withdraw his support. Torin would see to it. An extra sennight would give him the time he needed.

Of course, his plan could backfire if *too much* time passed and Braya's father was allowed the chance to call for war against Bennett. Torin would be in the same position he had been in days ago with two battles on his hands and only one he wanted to fight and win.

Hell, everything had to be perfect, or as close to perfect as possible. Too much could go terribly wrong. He hadn't planned on Bennett possibly having another thousand men on his side. King Robert wouldn't appreciate it either. If the Scots suffered another loss to Carlisle, the blow would be too great. He would have failed, and he could not allow that to happen.

Whether his decision to keep peace between the reivers and Bennett was right or wrong no longer matter. He had to continue moving forward. He had to take down this last stronghold or the guilt and shame of his life would never cease. He had to keep Braya safe, and not just Braya, but her family.

He fell asleep wondering how he had allowed himself to fall so hard for a lass that he would risk so damned much.

He awoke the next morning without an answer and an even bigger problem.

According to Adams, whom Torin found on his way to the great hall, Rowley Hetherington had been summoned to the castle. He was to come alone.

"Why was he sent for?" Torin asked, trying not to sound overly concerned.

"Bennett sent for him late last eve," Adams informed him, paying no heed to Torin's forced calm. "Or so I have heard. He is accusing a Hetherington of betraying the guards to the Armstrongs."

Torin looked down the candlelit hall toward the stairs leading up to Bennett's solar, and then walked around him and headed that way. Bastard. Why would he make an accusation when he was the one who had done it?

"Where are you going?"

"To find out what he is up to." Whatever it was, Torin would find out. He wouldn't let there be any surprises. He couldn't. He would keep Braya safe against any enemy. His dark, dusty heart depended on it.

When they reached the door to the solar and knocked, Bennett invited them in. Torin was not here to drink or sit. He was here to find out one thing. Still, he wouldn't do or say too much to make the defender suspect anything about him other than that he was bold and brash.

"Why have you sent for Rowley Hetherington? What has happened?"

Bennett eyed him beneath sullen, suspicious brows.

Torin squared his jaw and tilted his chin. Bennett wouldn't confront him. He was afraid of Torin, as he should be.

"We will need his men when the Scots come," Torin said, trying to divert Bennett's thoughts away from wherever they were heading. "Now is not the time to make him an enemy."

"We will have his men," Bennett finally promised with a curl of his thin lips. "He will have no choice but to send for them."

"Why not?"

"I'm going to tell him that I believe Miss Hetherington betrayed us to the Armstrongs."

Torin grew silent for a moment as shock settled in. What? This scum could not be serious!

"She hates us," he continued, ignoring Torin's pale face. "She stirs strife between us and her father—and worst of all when we need the reivers the most on our side. There is only one way to stop her from trying to cause a war between us."

No, no, Torin told himself. Bennett was speaking of Galien, not Braya. She sought peace.

He stared at Bennett with rage darkening his expression. "You know perfectly well 'twas not her who betrayed us to the Armstrongs."

Bennett shrugged his shoulders. "I said I was going to tell him I believed it. In truth, I do not know how they knew we were vulnerable. I must take Miss Hetherington as my wife and secure the promise we have with her family to fight with us when the Scots come to Carlisle."

Torin would have laughed but there was nothing humorous about this. He would kill Bennett before he ever came close to marrying Braya.

"She will never agree," Adams muttered. "Will you force a woman to your bed?"

"If 'twould guarantee our safety against the Scots, aye, I would," Bennett replied.

"Nothing will guarantee your safety against the Scots," Torin pointed out through clenched teeth. "They are wild and savage and if they are coming here, they are coming to kill *you*." If he could, Torin would kill him right now. But he wouldn't be able to hold the castle alone until the Scots got here. He had to wait. He wished he hadn't asked the Bruce for another sennight.

"With the reivers help, the Scots lost five years ago," Bennett said with a chuckle. "I will ensure we have their aid again by marring Braya Hetherington."

"She will kill you before the Scots ever get here," Adams pointed out with a sneer.

Bennett laughed, tempting Torin to leap over a small table that separated them and knock out his teeth. "I'm certain Hetherington will agree that this is best. I will continue to keep the Armstrongs and other warring reivers away from his family and I will have his protection against his hated enemy, the Scots. 'Tis a perfect plan."

Not if Torin killed him first. He balled his hands into fists and forced himself to remain still and try to look non-threatening. "That is good news, my lord. We can use the men. Now, if you will excuse me." He had to leave the solar before he ruined all his plans and killed Bennett where he stood. Torin was an excellent swordsmen, the best he knew, in fact. But even he could not fight all of Carlisle's guards alone.

He smiled and walked out without waiting for Bennett to reply. As soon as he was out of the solar, he closed his eyes and ground his jaw. The thought of Bennett forcing Braya to marry him was enough to make Torin risk it all. No, he told himself. She wasn't his. He had no right to act as if she were. He was going to have to change that. What did he mean to do? He didn't know, but he was not going to let Bennett near her ever again.

He soon realized that Adams was behind him. "Do not ask me where I'm going. 'Tis better for you if you do not know what I'm about to do."

"I already know," Adams drawled. "I'm coming with you."

He turned at once and held his hand up to stop Adams' advance. "I'm not—I will not be back until the Scots arrive."

The tall, older man nodded. "You will need someone at your back until you take her wherever you are taking her."

Torin looked him straight in the eye. "You will not try to stop me?"

"Why the hell do you think I would?" Adams asked him frankly. "I do not want Miss H—Braya with him."

Would he want Braya with Torin? "Her father will likely try to stop me."

Adams nodded. "You will have to convince him that you can keep her safe from the warden's treachery." He swung his thumb over his shoulder toward the keep. "And from fighting the Scots."

Aye, Torin thought, Adams understood. Torin didn't really want company but it never hurt to have another sword and, besides, he could use a bit of advice. Like, was it normal to ache in every muscle, every bone, his head?

"Very well, let us go."

After saddling their horses, they set out for the Hetheringtons' village. Torin was surprised Rowley hadn't yet arrived at Carlisle. He was glad though and thought nothing more of it as he and Adams rode toward the river and then through it.

"How serious are things between you and Braya?" Adams asked him as they went. "And do not try telling me they are not. 'Tis clear to see when you see her or even speak to her. Do you love her?"

How should he answer? With the truth? How could he love her when he was a deceitful fool—her enemy, who was tricking her into liking him? He felt a wee bit ill. He was pitiful and he needed help. "I have never been in love," he confessed. "Unless you count when I was seven."

Adams stared at him with a look of disbelief, and then his scarred, weathered face broke into a smile. "Do you jest, boy? You have never loved?"

Torin shook his head. "I do not know for certain if what I'm feeling for Braya is love, but I will not let Bennett have her."

"Nor will I, but I'm not in love with her. What do you *feel*?" Adams dug his fingers into his belly. "Here."

Torin clamped his jaw, but then loosened it. He would get no help being quiet on the matter. But would Adams help him? How did he feel about Torin being with her? "I feel twisted in knots, torn apart, hopeful and more hopeless than ever before."

Adams' smile widened, bringing Torin some relief. Adams had said that Braya reminded him of his sister. Torin did, in fact, feel as if he were confessing his heart to her older brother, Ragenald, and being given Ragenald's blessing.

They neared the village and spotted someone running toward them. It was a woman. Braya's cousin, Lucy. She was pale and her eyes appeared to be puffy and red from crying.

Torin's heart began to race.

"My lords!" she shouted, almost reaching them. "They took her! The Armstrongs took Braya!"

CHAPTER SIXTEEN

F OR A HORRIFYING instant, Torin was back in his mother's kitchen, watching...back in the forest, finding his friends. He felt the dark beast stirring, merciless, ruthless, determined to find and kill every enemy.

"Where is their village?" he asked Adams calmly from high atop Avalon's back.

"'Tis south of here," Adams replied, and then looked down at Lucy. "The men gave chase?"

She nodded.

"How long ago?"

"Less than an hour ago. Oh, will you find her?" She turned her gaze to Torin. "Will you bring her back?"

He nodded, and then he gave a slight tug to Avalon's left rein and took off. He didn't speak to Adams on the way south, but rode Avalon hard and fast until he saw signs of the Hetheringtons in the distance. They had stopped their advance. Why?

He pushed Avalon harder and she went with ease, her long snowy mane flowing out behind her as she passed Adams' horse.

When he reached the reivers, he spotted Rowley on his feet with other men, including Galien. He slid from Avalon's saddle before she came to a complete halt, let her go the way she wanted, and hurried to Braya's family.

"What is going on? Why have you stopped here?"

"Further ahead is the Armstrong's well-fortified village," her father informed him.

"What are you doing here?" Galien demanded, and then turned away when both his father and Torin cast him murderous glares.

"We do not know where they have taken Braya," her father continued. "If we rush in, who knows what they might do to her before we reach her."

Torin nodded and then leaned in. "I will get inside this well-fortified village and I will find her. I will bring her out and help you slaughter those who took her."

Her father stared at him. He could feel Galien's eyes on him as well.

"The warden," he continued, "has accused your daughter of conspiring with the Armstrongs against him and his guards and plans on forcing you to agree to let him marry her. That is why he summoned you to the castle."

"I will kill him," Rowley Hetherington vowed. "I suspect he has something to do with this."

"Aye. Perhaps he wants to give weight to his accusation by having her 'caught' with the Armstrongs."

Torin was relieved, as even Galien seemed convinced.

"Give me two hours to get inside and find her," Torin demanded. "Come in any time after that."

"Why does he get to go in alone?" Galien griped.

"I can find a way into any enemy stronghold," Torin told him directly. "I have done so many times. If the slightest thing goes awry, it could cost Braya her life. Please, trust me. I can get her back. We are wasting time."

Her brother gave him the slightest nod.

Her father stared him in the eye. Torin could feel the strength in the older man's gaze. He could see the hope there. "I will not fail her," he promised.

"How do you plan on doing this?" her father asked. "How will we know when you have found her?"

Torin reached out and patted his shoulder and finally smiled. "You will know."

"When Adams and his horse finally get here," he said as he moved away, "tell him not to follow me. And no one touches my horse!"

THE TIME FOR hesitation was over.

Thankfully, trees surrounded the village of Scorney—and Torin was at home in the trees. He knew how to climb them, to wait in them, to listen high atop everyone else without them knowing.

He looked around from where he sat on a thick branch. To the east was a great pasture dotted with sheep. To the north, dozens of cottages spilled down green hills.

The Armstrongs had much. Why the hell were they such a threat to the Hetheringtons? They didn't need to raid. Torin thought mayhap they received payment from Bennett to attack every so often just so the warden could defend the Hetheringtons.

After this, surely Braya's father would not fight for him.

Torin watched men hurrying toward a large house west of him. He didn't know who the leader was, but he suspected he lived in that house. He also suspected Braya was in there with him.

Knowing where to go now, Torin climbed down the tree and pulled up his hood. He went to the tavern, where he hoped to hear some gossip, something to help him get inside the house without being stopped. If their leader had just returned with a Hetherington, there would be talk of it.

"I never saw a woman fight the way she did. I tell you, at one point, I feared she might overtake John."

Torin moved closer to the small group of men standing toward the back of the tavern. The man he'd heard was speaking of Braya, no doubt.

"I do not understand why he insists on doing Lord Bennett's bidding and picking fights with these people," said another man.

"It does not matter if you understand or not," the first man argued. "He does what is best for the family."

Torin's ear picked up another conversation to his left. A woman's voice.

"The new cook should have been here by now."

Torin turned away from her and raked his gaze over the people in the tavern. He started for the door when he saw a tall, pudgy man enter. He wore a bag over his shoulder and an iron pan from his hip and looked around as if he were lost. The new cook.

Torin smiled and hurried toward him. "The cook?"

"Aye," the man smiled. "I—"

"Come," Torin snaked his arm around the cook's shoulder. "Let me get you to the house." He escorted the cook out the door, led him around to the back of the tavern and smashed him in the head with the hilt of his sword. His victim would only be out for an hour or less, plenty of time for Torin to do what needed to be done.

He unfastened the pan, adjusted his mantle to conceal his sword at his side as best he could, and carried the cooking utensil back inside. He headed toward the woman. It turned out that she was sitting with two other women at a table.

"Pardon me," he said after he cut across the tavern in three strides and pulled down his hood. His hair fell around his face in broad streaks of different shades of gold. "I seem to be lost. I'm the new cook."

The lasses stopped talking to one another and looked him over from the tips of his worn boots to the cooking pan dangling from his fist, upward to his broad, draped shoulders, and haloed head.

"Do you always carry your pan around in your hand?" one of the lasses asked, giggling behind her fingers.

He smiled indulgently. His eyes shone like sunlit fields of summer green, inviting and mysterious. "If I let it dangle from my hip, it gets in the way of my sword."

All three women giggled. Two blushed.

"Do you happen to know where I should go?"

They stopped smiling instantly and remembered their duty. "Aye! Follow us back to the house," one of them said, standing up. The others followed. "Elaine will bring you to the kitchen."

He bowed slightly and let them pass.

"Is that a sword at your side?" one of them asked.

"Aye, Miss," He gave her a curious look. "I mentioned it a moment ago."

"Aye, but I thought—" Her face went scarlet. "Never mind."

They left the tavern and headed for the large house. Torin smiled. "'Tis dangerous out there. I need to protect myself."

They agreed and told him of the wild woman their leader had captured from her bed. She had clawed and bit and kicked half the way here until Lord John had to strike her and knock her out.

Torin's blood boiled. He could barely keep his rage contained. His hands curled into fists at his sides.

"Is the wildcat in the house?" he asked as they reached it. 'Twas built well with two floors of stone and timber. "Should I keep my sword ready?"

"The guards will not let you in with your sword," one of them told him.

Torin didn't care. He would get another one.

"She is inside, but do not fear. She is locked away upstairs."

"I do not trust locks," he replied with a dubious grin that made his frosty emerald eyes go dark. "Locks have keys."

"Richard Bells is the only one with a key."

"And where is Richard Bells?" he asked as they entered the house.

They were met immediately by four guards who demanded Torin's sword, but not his pan. The thing was made from heavy wrought iron. It could likely do as much damage as a sword until it grew too heavy to wield.

"He is guarding her door," one of the lasses with ginger-colored hair falling around her shoulders told him while he handed over his sword. "Come. I will show you the kitchen and then to your room."

Ah, Elaine.

He smiled and followed her. He didn't have too much more time. He'd told the Hetheringtons to give him two hours. That time was fast approaching.

Still, it wasn't as if they would attack after two hours. Was it?

He saw the kitchen and did his best to show interest. Elaine took him to his room and reluctantly left when he showed her even less interest than the newly forged pots in the kitchen.

He waited a moment and then ran out and hurried down the hall. He searched for a moment for the stairs and upon finding them, climbed up them slowly.

Before he reached the top, he looked up and down the hall. He saw two men at the far southern end guarding a door. Which one was Richard Bells? No matter, he thought, climbing up the rest of the way.

The two guards saw him right away and drew their weapons.

Torin moved forward. He held up his hands, and then chuckled at the pan before his face. "I'm the new cook." He lowered the pan. "Elaine said the garderobe was up here."

"There is one below stairs. The small door to your left," one of the guards told him with a warning lacing his tone.

Both men were tall and broad of shoulder. Both were armed with swords. One of them had a key swaying from a string at his hip.

"You two look as if you have not had a proper meal in weeks."

"Months," the man who wasn't Richard corrected. "The last cook was terrible."

Torin grinned and held up his pan again. "I will remedy that."

The one who wasn't Richard smiled. Richard did not. Torin swung the pan at him and turned away from the blood that splattered across his face. He hit Richard's companion next, narrowly missing a swipe of the man's blade across his throat. When both men were down, he dropped the pan and pulled the key from Richard's string. He fit it into the lock.

He pushed open the door and saw her lying on a bed. Her mouth was bound, as were her wrists to the bed. Her ankles were bound to each other.

Torin's heart cried out in rage for her and in joy at finding her alive.

When she saw him, she let out a breath that made her shoulders sag with relief.

He moved quickly, pulling a knife he had hidden behind his back and untying her. He wanted to go on a rampage. He felt the fury building up in him and almost let it loose when he saw her swollen, purple jaw.

"Come then, Braya." He pulled her up and led her to the door pressed close to him so he could kiss her bruised face.

"How did you—"

"Later, love. We still need to get out of here."

Outside the room, he bent to take Richard's sword and then bent again to take his companion's. He gave one to Braya and then led her down the hall, to the stairs. They raced down and almost reached the front doors when two guards noticed them and hurried to stop their departure.

Torin was ready with a swipe to the first's belly and then a jab of his blade into the next guard's chest.

He pushed Braya behind him as more men hurried toward them, weapons raised.

They had to get outside. He had to let the others know to come.

He made quick work of three men, one of whom had his sword, which he retrieved. Braya took down two more.

Torin grabbed a torch from the wall and they hurried out of the house. He could hear men behind him. He took Braya's hand as he ran and tossed the torch on top of the tavern when they reached it. He ran inside and shouted, "Out! Everyone leave! 'Tis a fire!"

Everyone got out. Flames engulfed the roof. Smoke billowed upward and outward like a cloud over the village. It was becoming difficult to see but Armstrong guards were everywhere.

He stepped out into the crowd and began fighting the guards. Soon, he could hear the sounds of men attacking. The Hetheringtons were here. They knew the smoke was his sign. Good for them. He fought among them, at their sides, against their enemies. But he was too aware of Braya fighting for her life close by, so he took her hand and ran with her toward the edge of the village.

But she would not leave her family, and he admired her for it—more than she might ever know. He would save her from the manipulations of a powerful man, but he wouldn't drag her away from protecting her family. And he wanted to find John Armstrong.

He didn't have to wait.

"Where do you think you are going with my woman?"

He was a hulking brute with clipped yellow hair and a long scar across his chin. He wore breeches and a jack, and wielded a long sword and shield.

Nothing would help him.

Torin dropped Braya's hand and moved forward confidently. "I will fight you for her."

CHAPTER SEVENTEEN

I F TORIN LOST, Braya would kill them both.

She watched, afraid for Torin, for she'd fought this mountain of a man and he was strong. But Torin knew how to fight and he seemed eager to battle John Armstrong.

She swung her blade and ended the life of a man coming toward her with an axe. She saw Rob Adams hurrying toward her and let him embrace her when he reached her. Her father was there next, to hold and cherish her, and to witness the most savage warrior their eyes have ever seen.

Torin circled Armstrong like a predator sizing up its prey. His wore no expression on his face save for anger, dark and dangerous. He moved quickly, rushing in and then leaping back, slicing, swinging, jabbing, and, most impressively, dodging and deflecting deadly blows and combinations.

John Armstrong wasn't the leader because he was handsome. Because he was not that. But he was a skilled fighter, able to protect the Armstrongs of the western Marches. Could Torin beat him? He had better. She tilted her head. Mr. Adams did not look worried, but her father did.

It didn't take her long to realize that Torin was tiring the bulky leader in the sight of all his people. Armstrong couldn't keep up with his quick movements. The leader would swing something massive and miss, using up his power. He was growing weaker by the moment.

Her father must have realized the same thing because he called out, "Finish him!"

Torin ducked low, avoiding a blow to the head, and came up swinging his fists. One of them—the one which was wrapped around the hilt of his sword—hit Armstrong in the jaw.

The leader cried out in pain. Torin lifted his boot and kicked him onto his back, and then fell upon him. He held up his sword and looked ready to plunge it into the man who had kidnapped her.

"Torin, no!" Braya called out and ran to him. "We will never have peace with the Armstrongs if you kill him."

He turned to look at her as she dropped to her knees beside him.

"Please! Please, show him mercy!"

She wasn't sure he would, and it pricked at her heart. She knew Galien wouldn't show mercy. In this case, she didn't think her father would either. Men and their pride. What had been done, had been done to her! If she could show him mercy, why the hell couldn't they?

He lifted his sword. Her heart accelerated. He drove the blade into the ground and turned back to his prisoner while Braya's heart melted all over her ribs.

"You will tell the Hetheringtons who put you up to this," he demanded. "They will know the truth or you will die."

"Bennett," the leader cried out, clutching his face. "'Twas the warden."

Braya didn't want to believe Bennett would go this far, but he had. She knew her father would never support him after this. She was glad for it all.

"Let us leave this place," she called out to the others while she stood. She turned to Torin as he straightened and stepped over the

Armstrong leader. "Take me home."

She wanted to hold him, to kiss him. He'd shown mercy when he clearly wanted to kill their enemy. He'd listened to her and done what she'd asked. None of the other men ever listened to her.

Oh, to hell with it! She didn't care what her family thought. She threw her arms around her knight and fell against him, careful not to bump her bruised jaw. "Thank you, Torin. Thank you for coming for me."

"Come," he said in a comforting tone. "We have more to talk about. You will ride back with me on Avalon."

When she agreed, he turned to the villagers and Armstrong's guards, even Armstrong himself. "You will not fight on Bennett's side for any reason or I will come for each of you. As for the Hetheringtons, if you attack them again, you have me, Torin Gray, to worry about. I will not be merciful next time."

Her family had him. Was he going to settle down here then?

Braya wanted peace but she knew that, sometimes, some people only understood peace through fear. So let them fear Torin Gray. He'd come for her...how had he gained entrance to the village? She knew from past raids that it was almost impenetrable. How did he know where to find her? What other things did he want to speak with her about? She had many questions, but most of all, what had he said or done to quiet Galien?

They left the village and Torin called for his horse. His white and chestnut mare came from out of the trees and raced toward them. Braya thought Avalon was the most beautiful creature she had ever seen, but she wasn't sure she was ready to ride her.

"She will bite me," she said as the horse neared.

"I will make certain she does not," Torin assured her.

Without waiting for her reply, he lifted her up and helped her into the saddle. Avalon spun her head around and Braya was certain she was about to lose a piece of her leg, but Avalon did not bite her. For a moment, Braya had the urge to smile, proud of herself for avoiding Avalon's ire.

When Torin leaped up behind her, she finally felt safe.

"You will dine with us tonight," her father invited Torin when he mounted his horse and reached them. "We have things to discuss."

Torin shook his head. "If Bennett knows she's free, he will come for her. We cannot stay in your village."

"Then…" her father's voice dipped low, "where should she go?"

"She should stay with me."

Braya's heart sank and raced at the same time. "Just a moment. What is going on? What else has Bennett done?"

She noted the side-glance her father shot Torin and bristled between his thighs. "What has happened?"

"He wants to marry you."

She turned around to look in Torin's eyes and laughed. "I do not care what he wants. He will not have me."

"He went to great lengths to have you kidnapped, Braya. He wants your family's protection against the Scots." He turned to her father. "You should promise your allegiance to him. You do it so that he does not have to marry your daughter to have it. If he questions you further, tell him that I have taken her and that *I* plan on marrying her."

Braya turned around completely and gaped at him. "What are you saying?"

"I must keep him from having you."

"No." She shook her head. "I will not marry you for that reason."

"Now let me say something," her father exclaimed. "I did not give you my permission for this."

"He told me you would have no choice but to agree to a marriage," Torin argued with him—with them both. "He will not stop at this. I must take you somewhere."

"Where?" her father demanded.

"I do not know yet."

"Take her to Rothbury," Adams suggested. "To the earl. You were employed by him before. I'm sure he will take her in and 'tis far away enough to—"

"I do not wish to go to the Earl of Rothbury!" Braya insisted. "I will not run and hide from Bennett. I will—"

"Do you want us to fight the Scots?" her father asked.

She swallowed and shook her head.

"Then you will do as I say. We will discuss this further with your mother and decide what is best."

They were quiet for the rest of the ride home. Braya was afraid to turn around and look at Torin. Was he sincere? Would he marry her to keep her safe from Bennett? She would have been more receptive to appreciating him if she didn't suffer feelings for him. She wanted more than protection. She wanted him to feel something for her, something powerful and profound.

When the Armstrongs took her, she thought about Torin and about the kind of life she would like with him. She knew her family would come for her, but she had no idea what Torin would do. She hadn't been expecting him to sneak into the house, kill the guards, and rescue her before the afternoon meal.

She leaned back against his chest. He closed his arm around her tighter. Did he care for her? What would happen after he took her to Rothbury? Why the hell did Bennett think she would become his wife? The bastard had her kidnapped! She wanted to kill him the next time she saw him, which was likely why Torin wanted to get her out of Carlisle.

They made it back to the Hetherington holding and were greeted by her mother and Lucy and a dozen others.

Instead of things being spread by word of mouth, they alerted everyone to come to the town hall.

When everyone had arrived, Torin told them that he believed the Scots were coming soon. If the Hetheringtons fought with Bennett and lost, they would pay a heavy price. If they stayed out of it, even if it meant Bennett losing, the Scots would leave them alone.

"You do not have the supreme protection against your enemies that you thought you had," he told them. "The warden has been behind every raid and the last two attacks to frighten all of you. You," he pointed to her father, "can gather a thousand men and you would do it because you hate the Scots."

"Aye," her father agreed.

"You were easy prey," Torin told him and looked away before her father glowered at him.

Braya covered her mouth with her hand and smiled at her knight's boldness. But he was correct, and her father knew it.

"We will not be fighting for him," her father assured. "Though I do not know why I'm giving *you* my word."

"Because your daughter will not be able to stay away if she does not hear you say it."

Her father settled his loving gaze on hers, and she wiped her eyes yet again. "We will not fight should the Scots come."

She flung her arms around him and thanked him in his ear. When he let her go, she wanted to throw herself into Torin's arms next.

"Galien?" she asked her brother. "How about you?"

He scrunched his face at her. "I would never lend my sword to a bastard who had you kidnapped freshly out of your bed and then struck you."

She smiled at him, though with her wounded jaw, it pained her to do so, thankful for the millionth time that God had sent Torin, a man of peace, into their lives. Even her brother had stopped being so argumentative.

"I will bring her back to you," he vowed to her parents. "I will bring her to the place Adams suggested earlier."

They were going to Rothbury then, Braya thought. She would miss everyone terribly, but part of her was thrilled at the idea of a journey into Torin's past. What were his years like in Rothbury? What would it be like being alone with him every day while they—

"Robbie," her father said, turning to Mr. Adams. "I would like you to help escort my daughter to her safe haven."

"Of course," Mr. Adams said, amused by Torin's dark glare. Apparently, her knight wanted to be alone with her. She wanted it, too.

"Fine then," Torin brooded, turning for the doors. "We should go now."

Braya said her farewells through tears and promises to see her loved ones soon. It was the most difficult thing she'd ever had to do in her life. She made a vow to herself never to do it again. She was glad Torin was staying.

She met him outside a few moments later with Avalon, Archer, and Mr. Adams, ready to go. She knew what the warden had done was unforgivable, but Torin saw him as a threat worthy of his urgency. She hurried to Archer, gained her saddle, and turned her mount north.

An hour later, Torin still hadn't brought up marrying her. She was beginning to worry that he hadn't truly meant them. "Why did you come for me?" she asked him, keeping Archer close to Avalon, who didn't seem to mind at all.

Torin slanted his glance at her and shifted around in the saddle, making Avalon bob her head angrily. He stopped. "Because I was not about to let a man have you through kidnapping."

That was a pleasing response, but not a personal one. Would he let a man have her through other means? "Hmm," she murmured. She wished she hadn't questioned him. She wasn't prepared for his detached reply.

"What do you mean, *hmm*?" he asked—demanded really. "What would you have preferred me to say?"

She glared at him. "What do you mean by that? Do you think you are under some kind of spell and you cannot say what *you* wish to say? It must be what I want?"

"In truth, I do not know—"

"You said what you wanted the first time!"

He blinked as if she slapped him. She smiled at him. She hadn't realized she'd snapped at him. She didn't want him to think she was so affected by him.

"What did I say the first time?"

This time, she really did want to slap him. She managed to keep her smile intact while she spoke, "You came for me because you were not about to let a man have me through kidnapping."

He slanted his gaze toward Mr. Adams and said nothing.

Braya figured it was best this way. He would avoid getting poked with her sword if he kept his mouth shut. She stared at the treetops for a moment or two before her next question popped into her head. "How did you get through the guards in the village and into John Armstrong's house?"

"Aye," Mr. Adams agreed. "You have not told us that part. When I arrived and spoke to Braya's father about your promise to go in alone, find her, and get her the hell out, he told me you said you had done it before, many times."

Many times? Braya thought. When? As a child thief? A soldier for the Governor of Etal? When he was in Rothbury? There was so much about him she did not know.

"In the past..." he began and paused, then continued. "I have found myself in situations where I needed to get in and out of a place quickly."

"Why?" Mr. Adams asked.

"He was a child thief," Braya informed him.

"Oh," Adams said on a ghostly whisper.

"Come now," Torin said, sounding impatient, "there is no reason to grow solemn and gloomy over things that canna—*ot*." He coughed into his head. "Cannot be changed. We have a long way to ride. At least a day and a half. Let us not drag it out to feel like an eternity."

Braya agreed. Torin needed to do things that made him laugh once in a while. "The horses are well rested. Let us race them!"

He laughed then leaned over Avalon's wide neck and stroked her hoary mane. "Your horses would be shamed."

"Ha!" she shouted with a short laugh then grimaced at the pain from her bruised jaw. "If she is as fast as you are arrogant, then no doubt you are correct. But let us give it a go." She turned to Mr. Adams with a bright smile, refusing to let pain take her joy. "How about it, Mr. Adams? Are you with us?"

He nodded then flicked his horse's reins.

"I will give you both a head start," Torin called out.

Braya shook her head and rode closer to Mr. Adams. "Do not push your mount until the arrogant bastard catches up."

They both kept a slow pace and waited for him to finally move his arse and go after them. "You are going slow on purpose," he laughed, reaching them.

"Aye," she admitted. "I wanted to tell you that you need not play these silly games. I'm going to win. In fact, I will even reach Rothbury before you."

He threw back his head and laughed.

"Because if I do not win, you will take my hand in marriage as you told my father you would."

His laughter faded. "So you are my prize?"

She shook her head, keeping her horse at a slow pace. "Your responsibility. A saint or a shrew, depending on you. But yours if I lose."

He looked so undecided that, for a moment, she felt insulted. He wouldn't let her lose. "And if you win?" he finally asked quietly.

"If I win, you can forget I ever existed and go on with your life without me."

She met his steady green gaze head on and tilted her chin. She would be strong. She would—

He took off with a great heave from Avalon that left Braya and

Adams in a cloud of dust. Braya pushed Archer hard, but not too hard. She knew Torin wouldn't let her lose. She wanted to know what he truly felt about her. Was there anything between them that could become something bigger? Or was he just a kind, merciless knight who would do the same for anyone?

She thought for certain he would slow Avalon and let her win, but he raced with her and Mr. Adams across the valley and over Hadrian's Wall and laughed when she looked as if she might catch up.

She wished she had answers but she didn't really care about them right now. The wind whipping through her hair was fragranced with heather and other wildflowers. The sun was warm and full on her face. She felt free of the confines of duty, and raiding, and obeying. She felt seen, and heard. Finally.

She was with Torin. She liked being with him. She saw something in his eyes at times like innocence and purity. She thought it was perhaps so clear to see because it showed in the darkness that captured the rest of him. Could she get through? Could anyone? She thought he felt something for her. Perhaps he didn't want to, or he was afraid to. She didn't care. She wanted him in her life. If she had to steal his heart right out of those shadows, she would. She would appeal to the light and force him to decide.

But later.

She didn't care if Avalon seemed to fly over fields and flowers, or if Torin beat her to their destination, or if Adams beat poor Archer, too. She closed her eyes for a moment and let herself fly.

They stopped in a small tavern in the village of Gilsland for drinks for them and their horses. They didn't have to open their rations her mother had packed because Torin had coins and used them to buy them food.

"You beat me, my lord," Braya said playfully while she ate small bites. "You know what that means."

"No," he objected. "You said you must reach Rothbury first. That is the end of the race."

"No," she said after a moment. "Let us make it whoever enters Lord Rothbury's home first and then you will tell me if you want to marry me or forget me."

She stood up and left the table, and Torin and Mr. Adams looked after her.

Her smile faded as she went. What if Torin chose neither? What then?

CHAPTER EIGHTEEN

T HEY MADE CAMP that night on the northern outskirts of New-brough and sat awake under the stars. Adams rested against the trunk of an old oak tree, while Braya and Torin sat closer to the fire.

Torin thought about what he had told her father to tell Bennett. Torin had taken her away and was going to marry her. He'd said it. He was going to marry her—and now she wanted to know if he meant it. He understood the choices she was giving him and why he believed she was giving them to him. She wanted him to commit to something. At least, that was what Adams had told him.

What the hell did Torin know of love and of a lady's tender feelings? He would be a terrible husband! He'd thought he'd given her a good answer when she asked him why he'd come for her. But he was incorrect—again, according to Adams. He didn't know why he'd brought up marriage. She was turning him into a fool.

He would likely marry her if he could. Chances were, the choice would no longer be presented to him.

He didn't want to have this kind of nonsense clouding his thoughts, affecting his decisions, but he feared it was too late.

"What is Lord Rothbury's place like?" Adams asked, biting into an apple.

"He lives in Lismoor Castle," Torin answered. He had never been there. "'Tis a castle just like any other. I should pen a note to him tomorrow and have it sent on ahead so that he can be prepared for us."

"Is the earl wed?"

Torin looked at Braya and nodded. He hoped so. He hated deceiving her. He knew that the more lies he told her, the harder it would be for her to ever forgive him. Not that she would forgive him anyway.

"What is she like?" she asked in her quiet, honeyed voice.

It was difficult for him to keep his thoughts from trailing off to the delectable dip of her lower lip, the alluring curve of her jaw, a sweet, soft chin that was never haughty…her spun gold tresses falling around her face—around his fingers when he held her.

"She is perfect." He smiled at her, unable to help himself. "For the earl.

Hell, she was exquisite in the firelight…all the time, making his head spin in every direction. He stared at her purple jaw, feeling the same rage he'd felt while fighting Armstrong.

His life was broken, but he had always held himself together. Somehow. Until now. Until Braya shattered him into pieces at her feet. She had asked him to show mercy. She had no idea what it had cost him to do so. It had torn a great block of his defense asunder. Defense he needed. All he'd known his entire life was revenge. It had darkened his soul, turned him into something savage and hardhearted. It fit the life he led, not a life with her.

And yet, knowing her, caring for her, was making him want to be the kind of man worthy of her.

Hell, he should go to bed before he got into trouble.

He was a Scot. He was one of King Robert the Bruce's commanders. Did it matter who won the race? She wouldn't want him at the end of it, and he was sure he would never forget her.

He should have gone to bed, for they stayed awake too long, talking about their families and whom they had lost. Braya told them about Ragenald joining the English to fight at Bannockburn and never returning.

Torin told them about his brothers and the few vague memories he had of them. They were mostly bad memories, ones of terror on children's faces and crying, memories he prayed he could forget.

One or two others weren't so bad. He shared those. "I remember my older brother tripping me in the pigpen. My mother found us playing in the mud and tried to scold us while she laughed." He smiled thinking of it. He hadn't in years. "The babe of my family was only two when..." He paused as shadows passed across his eyes. Then he smiled again. "He was always on my mother's hip, even while she read to me. I think of the three of us, she loved him the most."

"Every mother is most reluctant to let her youngest go," Braya's voice soothed him from across the flames. He wanted to go to her and carry her away.

"That may be so," he laughed softly instead. "But everyone in the village made a fuss over him. I remember me and my other brother being jealous of him."

"What were their names?" she asked him, looking as if she were aching to go to him, too. Dammit that Adams was here.

"I do not remember their names."

He noted the glistening tears that lit her eyes. She felt sad for him, sad that the *Scots* had done this to him.

He looked away. His lie was too big.

Adams told of his dear baby sister, Edith, who had been wed at fifteen to a Scottish laird and taken to the Highlands.

"I remember when she left," Braya said quietly, staring into the flames. "'Twas the same year Raggie died."

"Aye," Adams murmured, then finished his apple. "'Twas difficult for all of us."

"Let us go find her when this is all over." Torin was sure he'd gone mad, for only a madman would make such plans with a man he would most likely have to kill. His gaze slipped to Braya. She was smiling. She liked the idea. Of course she would. He'd like for her to come as well.

"When what is all over?" Adams asked.

Braya was looking at him over the flames, waiting for his answer.

He gave it. "After the Scots have taken Carlisle."

Her glorious blue eyes lit with fire from within, as hot as the flames between them. "We cannot let them."

His eyes on her darkened beneath his furrowed brow. "You would prefer Bennett over a Scot after all he has done to you and your family?" Now, he waited for her answer. He hoped she didn't hate Scots so much.

"How do we know the Scots will not be worse?" she asked earnestly. "You of all people know how cruel and savage they are."

"As I told your family in the great hall, the Scots are not known for killing border reivers. If they know the Hetheringtons are a thousand strong and there are others who would fight at your family's side, the Scots will leave you alone."

"How can they be trusted?" she argued.

He couldn't tell her the truth; that it was the English who had taken everything from him. He couldn't defend the Scots without giving himself away. She would hate him. He wasn't ready for that.

"Perhaps they will not use your father as a pawn to fight their battles. They might not have his daughter kidnapped and tied to a damned bed and struck as if she were not the most delicate of beings."

She smiled, beguiling him senseless with her dimple. "I'm not so delicate."

"You are to me," he said quietly so that only she might hear.

When the Armstrongs had taken her, he thought he would go mad. He did not for a moment think she was dead or in danger of dying. He would have gone blind with fury if he had. He was not going to lose her, too.

Was this love that he felt for her? He had to speak to Adams alone. What would he do if it was? He wasn't sure he wanted to leave her. Ever.

And the tragedy of it all was that he would lose her because of who he was and what it had made him.

"We should get some sleep," he told her tenderly. He reached his hand out to touch her bruise and looked into her eyes. "I will watch over you."

She smiled and laid waste to his heart. "And I will watch over you."

"And I will watch over the horses," Adams called out softly from his place against the tree.

The three of them laughed and watched the stars for a little while longer.

Torin didn't get much sleep thinking about what he would tell Lord Rothbury when he arrived at Lismoor. The earl more than likely believed Torin was a Scot since he was fighting for Robert.

Fighting for Robert.

He opened his eyes and watched Braya while she slept across from him, across the flames. He should take her to Bothwell Castle, but it was in Scotland and too far to travel to and come back in time to fight.

Besides, she should know the truth.

Tomorrow, he thought, after he penned a letter to Rothbury, he would tell her.

LORD ROTHBURY, NICHOLAS MacPherson of Lismoor, known to some as William Stone, reread the missive he received from Commander

Gray of the Bruce's army out loud.

He sat at a table in the gathering hall in the rear tower with Cain, his brother, who was visiting with his wife, Aleysia, for the birth of Nicholas' first babe. With them also was Father Timothy and Nicholas' close friend, Sir Richard.

"I have no idea who Gray is," he told the others. "If he is in Robert's service, why does he not know my true name?"

"The two that he travels with are English, my lord," Father Timothy reminded him after hearing the letter. "He says he's a spy of sorts, so 'tis likely they dinna know he's a Scot, or that ye are one. If he's workin' fer the Bruce, best to go along with it when they get here."

"I wish he had penned why he was coming," Nicholas scowled. "I do not fancy the idea of strangers in my home when my wife gives birth. Worse, what if Carlisle's guards are pursuing them?"

"Let them bring the whole English army," his brother said in his naturally lilting, challenging voice. "I'm here."

Nicholas nodded and smiled. He could fight, thanks to his brother teaching him, and he commanded a proper guard, but he was a more diplomatic earl. Besides, no one fought like Cain. If there might be fighting, Nicholas was glad his brother was here.

Putting thoughts of the English and his Scot's comrades to rest for now, he folded the parchment and shoved it into his gray woolen doublet. "Let us return to the keep and my wife. Soon, I am to be a father."

"Mayhap not *too* soon, Brother," Cain laughed, coming around the table and tossing his arm over Nicholas' shoulder. "It has only been five hours. Remember, it took almost a score and three hours fer my son to arrive."

"I remember it as if it occurred yesterday instead of two years ago," Nicholas told him with a frown darkening his eyes to smoky silver. They had traveled to Invergarry for the birth of Cain and Aleysia's first babe. "Mattie remembers it as well. She's been afraid because of it. Now she is going through it. Why can I not be there with her?"

"Aleysia and Mattie's maids are with her," Richard reminded him as they left the gathering hall. "They know what to do. You do not."

Cain leaned in closer to his ear. "I went to Aleysia's side when she was havin' Tristan. She nearly tore oot my eyes. The things she said, I think I will never ferget."

Nicholas moved away and stared at him in the dimly lit hall, looking less sure than he had a moment ago. Until Cain laughed again and pounded him in the chest.

Nicholas thought he preferred it when Cain had always been solemn and serious. "I think I shall go to my wife anyway."

Father Timothy held up his hand to protest. "I dinna think ye should—"

"Do it," whispered Cain, coming close again.

"You will distract the women," Sir Richard said, thinking to stop him as they reached the massive doors, and then the narrow door of the tower.

Before they left, Cain pulled him in by the shoulder and looked him in the eye. "Are ye brave enough, little brother?"

Nicholas nodded. Aye, he was. He smiled when Cain smiled at him.

"Then go." His brother gave him a shove toward the door. "And remember this is yer castle when my wife tells ye to get oot."

Nicholas hurried out of the tower and down the stone stairs. He'd wanted to go to her since this painful task had begun, but there had been much to do. Father Timothy, the lover of celebrations, had begun planning an hour after her pains started. Since the priest didn't live here, but in Invergarry with Cain and his family, he did not know who to go to for anything, and much of the female staff was with Mattie, so he ended up going to Nicholas.

He crossed the short walkway and moved quickly toward the keep. He wondered as he went what his life would be like as a father.

He couldn't help but smile thinking about all that had changed in the past two and a half years. He was no longer a servant but an earl, and he wasn't going to spend his life with Julianna, as he had always dreamed, but with Mattie, a woman who loved him passionately, a woman who had taken the place of every other. She crept into his heart when he thought he would never love again and sang a new song.

He entered the keep, ready to help her start their new life together, eager and ready for it.

He didn't waste a moment on Rauf, his steward, when Rauf demanded to know how the cook was supposed to prepare so much food in so little time.

He didn't let his thoughts wander too much to the three people who would soon be arriving and if an army might be arriving with them.

He saw Emma, Tristan's nurse, chasing the lad down the hall. His heart swelled with love for his family, and he hurried past Emma and called out that Cain was on his way.

When he reached the door to his bedchamber, someone—Mattie—wailed in agony. Nicholas nearly pushed the door down. He wanted to run inside but stood beneath the doorframe for a moment, paralyzed with uncertainty about what to do next.

Aleysia and the other women stared at him, startled. He expected Cain's spirited Norman wife to shout at him, but she said nothing as he entered and hurried to his wife.

"My dove, I am here." He stepped up onto the bed and leaned over her.

Her pale blonde hair was damp with sweat. There were dark circles under her eyes and her skin was pale. She barely had time to smile at him before another wave of pain gripped her.

He tried to comfort her, but failed. Still, in the end, he was thankful he had gone to her. Thankful he was there to hold her while she left him and his baby son alone on the earth.

CHAPTER NINETEEN

T ORIN CROUCHED AT the edge of a small cliff and looked down at the River Coquet and Braya bathing in it. He knew he should turn away, but the sight of her caught him by surprise when he was searching for berries for breakfast and mesmerized him.

It didn't matter that she wasn't facing him. Her long, creamy back, draped in waves of light, shimmering gold, and the alluring curve of her waist, set his blood to racing and made his muscles tighten. Part of him wanted to continue gazing at her, making him wish he could paint or put to words what he thought of her and how he saw her, like a living flower, perfectly crafted by God.

The other part of him wanted to tear off his clothes and dive down to her...hold her and kiss her, take her deeper into the waves and make love to her. But first—

She turned and looked up suddenly, as if she'd sensed his gaze.

Instinctively, he backed away and then fled.

Hell! He shook his head as he scurried away like the coward he was. Why was he running away? Why did the thought of facing her now make him want to keep on running? He should go back. No. He already looked foolish. He would not avoid her though. The thought of not being with her riled him and worried him at the same time. He was going to have to get used to not being with her soon enough. He didn't want to rush the inevitable along if he didn't have to.

He made his way down the steep hill and around to the riverbank. He would find her, apologize, and then meet her back at the campsite.

She was out of the water and dressed in her chemise when he arrived. The thin linen clung to her wet body.

Torin swallowed and commanded his eyes to look away. They refused.

"I did not mean to—" Hell, he could barely think and finally turned away when she reached for her léine. "I was searching for berries and I came upon—forgive me for staring, but you are like sunshine finally breaking through the clouds."

"Torin." Her voice rolled across his ears like the current of a rippling brook.

He turned to her just as she reached him. She closed her arms around his neck and fit herself perfectly against his body. Could she feel his heart beating against her?

"Torin, there is something I must tell you," she said, looking into his eyes. "I...I am in love with you."

Nothing in his life could have ever prepared him for this. He hadn't loved or been loved in twenty years. He was afraid of it. In fact, it was the *only* thing he feared. No. He feared losing it, losing her. He wanted to believe he was in love with her. Better that than going out of his mind and ending up on the road, begging for mercy when he'd never granted any. Until recently.

"Braya." He dipped his head to her and breathed across her lips. "I—"

"No," she pleaded. "Let us say no more."

He closed his arms around her slim waist and pulled her in close. She felt right in his arms. He felt restored in hers.

She opened her mouth to his and clutched his mantle in both

hands as he pressed her to him. He swept his tongue inside her, gently brushing it over hers in a dance that freed his soul and captured him whole at the same time.

His slid his hands down her elegant back and rested them on the soft mounds of her bum. His muscles tightened. His kiss grew deeper. All he had to do was lift her up, free himself from his breeches, and have her right here. Right now.

But he was no brute. Not with women. He smiled against her teeth. Even women who would try to slay him.

"What is amusing about this?" She laughed and pulled away from him with a playful smile tilting her rosy, swollen lips. Swollen from him.

He growled from deep in his throat and closed his eyes, and then laughed when she poked him in the guts and traipsed away toward the water.

He untied his mantle, pulled off his léine, and kicked off his boots. She wagged her finger at him, telling him not to follow. Of course he would, as soon as he got out of his belt. He laughed and shook his head at himself that she could make him so pitiful he would forget how to remove his damned belt!

Finally! He flung it aside and gave chase. When he got close, she squeaked and kicked water at him. He bent and splashed her back until she screamed and ran again. He chased her through the shallow bank, over pebbles and other stones, feeling better than he ever had in his life.

He stopped suddenly and stared down at the water. Something swam across his legs. His smile faded and he lifted his arms in the air.

Braya stopped and watched him. "What are you doing?"

He swept his damp curls away from his eyes and cast her a worried look. "I felt something brush across my legs."

"'Twas just a fish," she said. He could hear the humor in her voice and almost admired how hard she worked at keeping it away. "Why do you look so alarmed?"

"I do not like what I cannot see."

"Can you see this?" she asked, scooping handfuls of water and tossing them at him.

When he leaped after her, she screamed and laughed and fell into his arms.

He kissed her with exquisite care, delighting in how she touched his bare shoulders. Her fingers tracing the angles in his arms made him ache for more than kisses.

"Remember the race, my lord," she said with a teasing smile. "Will you let me beat you to the castle, or take me as your wife?"

"I will take you as my wife," he murmured, bending to capture her and her mouth once again.

But...he couldn't take her with so much between them, and he couldn't reach the castle first while he had so many secrets.

"But Braya, hear me. I...I...live with a great...shame." He released her and ran his hand down his face. "It plagues me every day."

"What are you ashamed of, my love?" she asked, concern filling her gaze while she ran her fingers over his jaw.

He couldn't do this. He didn't want to admit it, hear it coming from his lips.

But he needed to. And she was the only one he wanted to tell. "I left them." He said it. He used to dream about saying it, confessing it out loud. He always wondered if it would change anything. It did. "I ran away while my enemies burned down my house and killed my entire family. I ran away."

Tears filled her eyes instantly. He loved that she would shed them for him. He'd never had the understanding ear of anyone before. Even if he'd had one, he would never have spoken this out loud. Not even to Avalon.

"What could you have done, Torin?" she asked him, touching his face with both of her soft hands now. "You were but a babe. You were not the man you are now. You cannot blame that child for choices he made after living for only five years. 'Tis not fair, Torin. You are feeding the shame instead of slaying it."

"I *am* slaying it by killing my enemy."

"No." She shook her head. "It will never be enough."

"What will, then?" he asked, hoping she had an answer.

She tossed her arms around him again and walked with him back to the shore. "I do not know what will. You were a helpless babe, Torin. Your father could not stop them Why do you think you could have?"

He thought about it and then shook his head. "I do not know." He laughed at it, and she laughed with him.

Would telling her he was a soldier of Robert the Bruce go this well?

He looked for his belt with his sword and knives. They were all gone. He stepped in front of a dripping wet, beautiful Braya Hetherington.

She shoved him away and retrieved a knife from a pocket in her breeches. Something dropped out of the trees.

Not something. Someone.

He heard Braya expel a strangled sound at the big brutish, long-haired Scot landing on his two feet to their right, a long claymore in his right hand. He was dressed in a long-sleeved léine and belted Highland plaid. Hell, he was daunting enough to make Torin wish they hadn't come here.

"Commander Gray," the Highlander sang, coming closer, unafraid. "Lord Rothbury received yer letter. He regrets that he is not seein' anyone at this time."

"And who are you?" Torin asked him.

"Commander Cainnech MacPherson."

Adams appeared on his horse with Avalon and Archer close by. He leaped from his saddle and pushed forward, his sword drawn. "Where is Lord Rothbury? What have you done with him?"

"Gray," Commander MacPherson's voice went flat and laced with warning. But it was his glacial blue eyes that convinced Torin he spoke the truth. "Control yer man's tongue before he loses it."

"Why, I—" Adams raged and moved forward.

"Put yer sword away," the Highlander warned on a deadly whisper, "before ye lose yer arm as well."

"Adams!" Torin shouted at him to get his attention. When he had, he shook his head. "Let us be of a sound mind."

Adams finally nodded and sheathed his blade.

"Our clothes." Torin turned back to the Highlander. He missed his plaid, his pride. He was a Highlander, too. He knew how savage they were. They didn't need to be fighting this man.

MacPherson tossed them their clothes but kept their weapons. "Ye can have these back when ye leave, which ye will do now. Hurry, before I decide to take yer horse. I assume the glorious white and chestnut mare is yers?"

Torin nodded then quickly warned him that Avalon would take his fingers.

"Avalon?" the commander frowned at him. "Where have I heard that name before?" He didn't wait for an answer but swished his hand in front of his face and waved them away. "Go."

They needed to get inside. Adams was cranky from sleeping against a tree all night. Torin had seen Braya rubbing her back earlier.

"I need to speak to Rothbury, Commander," Torin insisted. He would tell him the Scots were coming. "To him and him alone. 'Tis of the—"

MacPherson's blade cut the air and came to a stop at Torin's throat. "I said Lord Rothbury is not seein' anyone today."

"Commander."

The Highlander slipped his sharp gaze to Braya, who had somehow managed to move behind him when they were not aware. He ignored the knife she held to his throat and smiled.

"Do not think I am afraid to kill you, Scot," she warned. "Move your blade away from him or die."

Hell, Torin thought, this was no time to grin.

"Gray, is she yer woman?" MacPherson demanded, looking irritated now.

Torin set his eyes on her. She was already looking at him, waiting to hear his reply with dreadful anticipation.

"Aye," he said without taking his eyes from hers. "She is my woman. Do not harm her."

Her expression softened on him, and her grip on the hilt of her knife loosened.

Torin wasn't certain how Commander MacPherson could tell, but he moved before any of them took their next breaths. His arm shot up. His broad fingers clamped around Braya's wrist, lowering it and her knife from his throat. Almost at the same time, and without letting her go, he stepped behind her, managing somehow not to break her arm, and captured her other wrist as well.

"Drop it," he commanded.

She had no choice but to obey.

Torin had seen enough. He stepped forward, but Adams rushed in swinging his sword.

"No!" Torin stretched out his arm. Braya blocked the Highlander's body. There was nothing Adams could do with his sword without hurting Braya!

MacPherson closed one arm around Braya and brought her down with him in a low crouch. He swung one leg out, catching Adams behind his ankles and sweeping him completely off his feet.

Adams landed on his back with a hard thud.

"I do not wish to hurt ye," the deadly Highlander said to his felled opponent.

"Ah, well, 'tis too late for that," Adams groaned when he tried to rise.

Torin helped him stand while the commander released Braya and dusted off his plaid.

"I can do this all day, lass," MacPherson told her. "Believe me, I have had plenty of practice."

Torin went to stand beside her, ensuring there would be no more surprises from anyone. He couldn't be angry with the commander. He'd protected himself against her, and himself and Braya against Adams.

"You practice often," Torin remarked.

"Every day. We must." He looked as if he had something more to say, like, aye, do you agree? But he said nothing more and flicked his gaze to Braya when she spoke next.

"What is a Highlander doing with Lord Rothbury? Has Rothbury turned traitor then?"

The commander sized her up with curious eyes. "There isna much of ye. Is there? Ye are more dangerous than ye look."

"Commander—"

"Now get yer arses oot of here."

"Commander," Torin moved forward. "My friend needs a bed."

MacPherson settled his eyes on him and, for an instant, Torin thought he'd seen him before—another time when he hadn't turned Torin's blood cold. He'd never seen anyone move the way MacPherson just had. He wanted to practice with him, not make an enemy of him.

"What is it ye dinna—" the commander stopped speaking when Torin's brooch caught the light and nearly blinded the Highlander. "Where..." he reached out to the brooch. Torin stepped back. The commander's eyes glinted on him. "Where did ye come by such an odd thing?"

Hell. He should have put on his mantle and kept the brooch covered. Should he tell him a story he'd made up, or the truth?

MacPherson hadn't hurt Braya. He'd protected her. Mayhap he was the kind of man who understood these things. "'Tis worthless. It has value only to me."

"Why?"

"Why do you wish to know?" Torin challenged.

"Did ye rob it?"

"No," Torin answered, not sure why he felt insulted. "'Twas my mother's."

Thankfully, that put an end to the commander's questions. In fact, he appeared quite...shaken. His eyes glistened like sapphire seas beneath the full moon. He traced them along Torin's face, soaking him in, admiring the strength of his shoulders.

"Commander?" Torin raised his brows. He was beginning to feel a bit uncomfortable, as if the Highlander were trying to gain entrance into Torin's innermost thoughts.

MacPherson blinked out of whatever he was thinking about and then smiled. "Get yer horses and come with me."

Whatever had just happened to change his mind, Torin was glad for it.

MacPherson was quiet while he led them to Lismoor Castle, but Torin caught him staring at him and his brooch while they rounded another hill, where more men became visible in the warm evening mist.

"What is it that you are looking for, Commander?" Torin asked boldly when he caught the commander staring at him yet again.

"Where are ye from?"

"Why? Why do you ask me that?"

MacPherson didn't answer as they reached the outside wall of the small fortress. They followed him inside and brought their horses to the stable. After that, they climbed a set of stone steps and came to giant wooden doors to the east and a walkway to the west, leading to a tower. He stopped and turned to Braya and Adams. "Ye both go inside with Amish and Father Timothy here."

They turned to find more men behind and around them.

Torin recognized the priest's robes and went to him.

"Not ye, Gray," MacPherson called out. "Ye stay here. There are things I must ask ye."

"No," Torin called back. "We all go in together or none of us will go at all and Rothbury will lose vital information about our country."

The commander laughed and then glanced at Adams, clutching his side. "You stay here or they sleep in the forest tonight."

Torin didn't take too much time thinking about his answer. "Go with them!" he called out to Braya and Adams.

They went, but Braya stopped and looked over her shoulder. She met his gaze and then wiped her eyes as she entered Lismoor first.

CHAPTER TWENTY

ORIN DIDN'T KNOW where the hell MacPherson was leading him or why. He looked back but could no longer see Braya. Damn it, he hadn't wanted to leave her. He'd done it for Adams. This was what caring got you.

He looked around. Lismoor was guarded well. How had Rothbury gained so many men?

William Stone. Torin had always thought him an Englishman who had turned traitor on his king. If that was true, why did even Highlanders follow him?

"How do you know the earl?" Torin asked him as they crossed the walkway.

"He is my brother."

Torin stopped. The earl was a Highlander? "When did he take Lismoor?"

"Two years ago." the Highlander told him with a slant of his mouth. "And he didna take it. He is not a warrior at heart. But he can fight when he has to, and fight well."

"Two years ago. I do not understand. I was told that William Stone was the earl."

"He is, but his true name is Nicholas. Nicholas MacPherson." The commander stared at him as if he were waiting for some sort of reaction from Torin.

Torin smiled then picked up his steps again. The earl must use Stone when the king needed him to sound more English. Hell. How would he explain this to Braya and Adams?

"That sweeping move you used was very impressive," he told the commander. "Where did you learn it?"

"My wife taught it to me."

Torin laughed. "Your wife?"

"Aye. She is the most ferocious woman I have ever met. Dinna cross her."

Torin shook his head. "I will not."

They reached the tower and climbed a row of narrow stairs to a door that led to another set of heavy wooden doors. They stopped, and MacPherson turned to him in the dim light before they entered.

"My mother had a brooch just like that one," he began. "My father forged it fer her."

Torin wasn't sure if his heart was beating. What was MacPherson saying? Why was he talking about his mother having a brooch like Torin's?

"The brooches are similar," Torin told him. Were they going inside to talk or not?

"I remember the day he made it," the commander went on. Torin wasn't sure why he felt as if the world was about to change, or why it scared the hell out of him.

"'Twas a surprise." The Highlander smiled, as if he were there, reliving that day. "She had no idea he had been craftin' it fer her. But we knew. My brother and I." He paused to take a deep breath.

Torin didn't breathe at all.

"Fergive me," the commander begged with a short laugh. "I dinna remember how ye signed yer name on yer letter to the earl. Is it

Thomas?"

"Torin."

Commander MacPherson's eyes grew moist. Torin felt as if he were in a dream. One he'd had hundreds of times before. But it couldn't be. It couldn't be. He refused to allow his mind to entertain the idea that this could be one of his brothers. It was all just a strange manner of events—as events were sometimes wont to be. 'Twas just a brooch. There had to be a hundred of them like it. But there was only one. He had always referred to his father as a blacksmith. He had made it. There was only one.

"At first," the commander continued, clearly trying to keep his voice from quavering, "my father couldna find her to give her the brooch."

Torin's eyes fill with tears as a memory flashed across his mind. He swallowed back the rush of emotions, including guilt and shame threatening to erupt from his long forgotten heart before he spoke. "We were in the garden."

"Aye, aye, ye were in the garden with her. Ye always were, Brother." The commander held Torin by the face, a rough, strong hand on either cheek, and stared into his eyes. "Och, hell, 'tis ye. 'Tis ye, Torin." He dragged Torin into his tight embrace. "We thought we would never find ye. I am Cainnech, yer brother."

Cainnech, his brother. This was real. He remembered. Nothing was more proof than that. The man squeezing the air from him was real. Cainnech, his brother. Aye. Torin recognized the strength in his brother's eyes and the defiant, determined dip of his brow.

He lifted his arms around Mac—MacPherson.

He was Torin MacPherson. He had forgotten, but now it gave him a sense of belonging. He was a MacPherson and he had his brother back.

He had two.

"Is Lord Rothbury my brother as well?" he asked, withdrawing from their embrace.

"Aye," Cainnech told him, his smile fading. "The babe."

Torin shook his head in disbelief. "How did he survive? How did *you* survive? Where have you been?"

"They are long conversations we will have. But now, Nicky needs to see ye." Cainnech stepped away and ran his hand down his face. "There was a tragedy early this morn. Nicky's beloved wife died givin' him his son. We buried her this afternoon. He is grief stricken. I canna comfort him. I believe God sent ye here to us to help him."

"Where is he?"

Cainnech pointed to the doors. "He is in the gatherin' hall, stayin' as far away as possible from his babe and from the constant condolences. Losin' Mattie has taken much from him. Mayhap gettin' *ye* back will help heal him."

Torin swiped his hands across his eyes and nodded, and then, with his heart racing, followed Cainnech through the doors.

Now Torin understood why Cainnech had been staring at him earlier because he couldn't keep his eyes off his brother now. Their coloring was different, but Torin saw traces of himself in the subtle nuances of the commander's expressions.

Cainnech MacPherson was a fearsome warrior. Torin was sure that any who came against him would die where they stood. He was impressive, even in the confidence of his gait.

"Do you fight for King Robert?" he asked quietly just before they entered the hall.

"Not as much as I used to. If I am needed, I will come. Now, tell me, what ye are doin' in Northumberland."

"Infiltrating Carlisle Castle," Torin told him. "I am the first one in and the last one out. The king is soon to arrive to take the stronghold. I need to be there."

His brother stared at him and hooked his brow and one corner of his mouth into an upward slant. "Then what are ye doin' at Lismoor?"

"Keeping Miss Hetherington safe. She is a skilled warrior and a firm enemy of the Scots. She is also a...ehm...a reiver."

"An outlaw!" his brother threw back his head and laughed. "Come! We must tell Nicholas."

They entered the large hall, furnished in heavy, dark walnut. An enormous, cooled hearth was carved into the northern wall. There was no need of a fire on this warm summer day.

Torin looked toward the front of the hall, but the two largest chairs were empty.

Cainnech began walking toward the back of the hall, to a chair in the shadows, and a man who sat alone.

"What is it?" The young man drawled when Torin and Cainnech approached. "Leave me alone, Cain."

"Nicky, Commander Gray has arrived."

Torin's baby brother looked up at him. "I am sorry, Commander. I do not want to see anyone."

Torin slipped into the bench on the other side of him. "You have my deepest sympathies, my lord."

The Earl of Rothbury sat forward, exposing his face to Torin.

Torin didn't remember him, but he looked much more like Cainnech than Torin did. His eyes were slightly more silver than blue, and bloodshot and swollen.

"Long live your son," Torin said, holding up a cup that someone set in his hands a moment ago.

Cainnech cheered along. Nicholas lifted his cup but only stared at Torin.

"I have seen you before" Nicholas insisted, "in Berwick. Two years ago. You were there before the attack."

"Aye. I was," Torin told them.

"You were at Berwick?" Cainnech asked him. "At the massacre of the villagers?"

"No," Torin said quickly. "Not that. I was there. I took down the castle and killed Governor Feathers. But then I left to take his daughter to safety. I—"

"His daughter?"

"Aye, Julianna. I took her to an abbey in—"

"I know where 'tis," Nicholas told him, looking as if he were haunted by more than the death of his wife. "I spoke to her there."

"You know the governor's daughter?"

He nodded, looking off into the distance. "I did. I lived in Berwick Castle all my life."

Torin's heart sank. Oh no! He'd just found his brothers only to learn that he'd destroyed the family of one of them. Now, he didn't want to tell Nicholas MacPherson who he was. Now, he wanted the ground to split wide and swallow him whole. "You were adopted by the Feathers?"

"No," Nicholas said hollowly. "I was purchased by them. For a stone. I was a servant until the siege."

He grew up a slave? Purchased for a stone? William Stone. It was the name the English had given him. Torin closed his eyes, hating the English even more for casting them on these paths. "Did Feathers treat you well?"

"No. He did not," Torin's youngest brother told him, making Torin glad he had killed him. "Sometimes Julianna made being alive bearable, so...thank you for saving her."

Torin wanted to drop his head into his hands and sigh with relief that he hadn't done something to make his brothers hate him.

"I do not remember seeing you there," he admitted to Nicholas.

His brother shrugged. "I was not permitted into the great hall, or into any of the governor's private rooms. I stayed mostly in the servants' quarters or in the stables."

Torin nodded, feeling ill, and slipped his gaze to Cain, who looked the same. Their brother had been a slave.

"What are you doing here?" Nicholas asked him, his voice hardening to a threat of warning. "In my castle? Are you here to try to kill me as you did to the governor?"

"Nicky," Cainnech said gently. "He is Torin, our brother. He carries the bronze moth Father fashioned fer Mother."

Torin pointed to his brooch.

"I do not remember any moth," Nicholas sighed into his cup.

"I do," Cainnech told him, sitting beside him. "And that is it. He is Torin, our brother. He remembers Mother and her garden." He turned to smile at Torin and, for the hundredth time, Torin let it sink in that he had his brothers back.

"Torin?" Nicholas stood up, as if coming awake. He looked at Cain first. "You are certain? We have only your memory to go by."

"Aye," Cain said, "I am certain."

Nicholas' eyes were pools of moonlit seas spilling over his long lashes onto his cheeks. "Torin? We have been searching for you."

Torin rose and made his way around the table and into the embrace of his brothers.

He was home. Finally. Everything he had ever dreamed of was here. Everything he ever wanted. A family...

Everything but Braya. He wanted to tell her about finding his brothers and the joy of today. It made him feel a bit guilty that he was so elated when his brother's heart was broken. Braya would tell him that perhaps Nicholas needed a fresh, light heart in his life right now.

"Brothers, I must go see to Miss Hetherington. I promised her safety and have abandoned her."

"Miss Hetherington?" Nicholas asked, then answered his own question. "Ah, one of the two of whom you penned me about. She is English?"

"She is," Torin confirmed.

"An outlaw who attacked me," Cainnech informed him with a glint of amusement in his eye. "And," he said, folding his arms over his chest and looking at Torin. "Ye are in love with her."

"I think so, Cainnech. I am inexperienced in matters of the heart."

"Cain," his older brother corrected. Then, "I wasna askin'. Ye *are* in love with her."

"I am?"

"Aye."

"How do you know?" Torin asked him.

"It doesna matter how I know, lad. It matters how ye know. Think aboot how it makes ye feel to think of her with someone else. Or if she were go—" He cast an apologetic glance at Nicky. "Either way, ye should see to her."

Torin nodded, and then looked at them both. "She does not know I am a Scot."

"Nicholas had already surmised that much from yer letter," Cain told him, putting his arm around Torin's shoulder "There is much I am curious aboot. I am sure ye and Nicholas feel the same way."

"Aye," Nicholas agreed. "Let us meet up later tonight when your guests have gone to sleep."

Torin nodded then turned toward the youngest, noting that the youngest was also the tallest. "Come with us. Introduce me to my nephew, aye?"

"Aye," Nicholas said, bringing smiles to his brothers' faces. "Cain has a son as well. Young Tristan, and another on the way."

Torin had nephews and a sister-in-marriage. He hoped he wasn't still dreaming and if he was, let him stay asleep.

They walked him to the keep and met a priest on the way.

"Ye had better come quickly," he called out before reaching them so none of them knew who he was referring to. "That wee veil of a lass ye just allowed in here has stabbed Amish in the leg!"

CHAPTER TWENTY-ONE

B RAYA DIDN'T CARE who this castle belonged to—Englishman, Highlander, or the damned king himself! She wanted answers. Where had they taken Torin? If she and Mr. Adams were not prisoners, then why wouldn't they take her to him?

She produced a knife she'd lifted from the table in the great hall and pointed it at them. "My friend needs a bed!" she shouted. "What kind of people are you that you cannot see when a man needs to rest?"

When the big, redheaded, scarred-faced Highlander called Amish came at her, she stabbed him. What the hell was she supposed to do? No one was helping. The priest was trying to help, but he wouldn't give her any answers about Torin and she'd had enough.

Four men tried to grab her. Poor Mr. Adams tried to stop them. He'd been injured earlier with the other hulking Highlander who dropped out of the trees, so unfortunately he was of little help.

She wasn't Torin, and she couldn't fight off four men.

But she could avoid them and try to strike one at a time. She'd done it plenty of times in the games. She had never been pinned to the ground in any competition. It meant death, so she learned how to escape first, and then how to fight.

She saw an opening between the men now and ran through it. She was slight of build and light as a breath on her feet. She came around and sliced at one.

"That is enough!" a woman called out with authority.

Ah, finally, the hostess of this place. Perhaps now she would get some answers. The four oafs obeyed the woman when she ordered them to put away their swords and axes and moved out of her way. Braya wanted to see the woman who commanded such savage looking men.

She was with child, about six months in. She was breathtaking with a pale, clear complexion and a long black braid draping her shoulder. Her eyes were big and green and sharp as steel on Braya.

"Amish, go have Duncan look at you," she commanded and, miraculously, Amish, the redheaded brute, went without quarrel.

The woman's gaze never left Braya. "Who are you and how did you get into the castle?"

"We arrived with Sir Torin Gray. He was once in service to the Lord of Rothbury, your husband."

"The earl is not my husband," the woman said in a less authoritative tone. She sounded sadder. Deeply so.

Braya was sorry for whatever it was, but she wanted Torin and she wanted him now. "We were accosted on the way here by a fiendish Highlander who leaped out of the trees—"

"That one is my husband," the woman told her with the slightest of smiles curling her lips.

"Oh." Braya felt foolish for calling him a fiendish Highlander. "Are you a Scot?"

"Norman," the Highlander's wife said. "I do remember some talk about Commander Gray coming here and Lord Rothbury not wanting to see anyone after his wife—"

"Our friend, the good Mr. Adams, was injured by your husband." She pointed to him now leaning weakly against the wall.

"—died giving birth to his son."

Braya stopped and stared at her, stunned to hear such horrific news. Oh, she had no idea! The poor man. "We did not know," she managed to say. "My best friend and cousin recently had a little girl. 'Twas a difficult birth. I do not know what I would have done if she had died." Her eyes filled with tears. What would poor William have done?

The hall was quiet for a moment and then the woman spoke. "Katie, bring two men with you and get this man to a bed and then send for the physician."

"Aye, my lady." A mature woman with a gray braid beneath a barbet and headband stepped forward. She moved quickly, choosing two of the men to help carry Mr. Adams away.

Braya had to hope and pray they wouldn't hurt him. But...some of them were Scots.

"Thank you." Braya thought it more prudent to be nice than to fight. She would have no chance against so many. Where the hell was Torin? First he had disappeared, now Mr. Adams was gone. She was alone. She was no fool—besides, she didn't want to fight with a pregnant woman. "I am very sorry about Lady Rothbury," she said while the beautiful woman sniffed and wiped her teary eyes. "Was she a friend of yours?"

"She was my very best friend."

Braya couldn't imagine the horror. She wiped her eyes as well.

"I am sorry you were treated so poorly here," the dark-haired woman said. "We have all suffered a great lose. You must forgive our terrible manners."

"Of course." Braya stepped forward, wanting to comfort her. "I am Miss Braya Hetherington of Carlisle."

"Braya!" Torin's voice tore through the great hall as he entered with the priest and two other men. One of them was the plaid-wearing Highlander, who ran to his wife to make certain she hadn't been harmed. The other looked almost exactly like him with shorter, curlier hair and a squarer, dimpled jaw. Their eyes were the same color, deep blue and silver, with brows that dipped lower in the center and flowed naturally upward at the outer corners—much like Torin's. He was also dressed in a plaid, but underneath he wore a blue coat and black pants with shiny boots.

The three of them were more handsome than all the men Braya had ever seen in her life. The Highlander slanted his mouth at her in a curious fashion that made her look at Torin. He smiled as well! The only one not smiling was the Highlander's neater, less amused twin, though on closer inspection, he appeared a little younger.

Braya was so happy to see Torin she didn't care who was smiling. She forgot everyone else and ran into his arms. "I did not know where they had taken you," she cried, crushed against him. "I did not know if they had killed you."

"Why would we kill him?" the brutish Highlander asked her.

"I do not know," she retorted, lifting her head from Torin's warm chest. "Why would you practically break my friend's back?"

"He attacked me," the savage defended.

"I attacked you," Braya argued softly, "and you did not try to break my back. Although I will admit, I thought you had broken my wrist when you swept around me."

"What is this?" the Highlander's wife gaped at her. "You attacked him?"

Braya didn't care if this woman was six months into pregnancy, part of her was afraid. "He attacked us first," she defended, hoping it was enough.

The Highlander's wife smiled at her and then turned to her husband and gave his arm a hard pinch. He writhed and glowered at his wife, then clamped his jaw to hold back his anger.

"How could you let someone who attacked *you* into Lismoor, unaccompanied straight through this hall, where your wife sat grieving, too unwell to even care for your own son for overlong?"

Though her voice rose from a murmured growl to a fevered snarl, her husband didn't back down. "They were not unaccompanied. Amish and Father Timothy were with them."

"Amish has been stabbed in the leg and Father Timothy ran to find you." She turned to the priest. "Thank you, by the way, Father."

The priest smiled, forgiving her instantly.

"Adams?" Torin plunged ahead, letting her go.

"I had him taken to a room to be looked after," said the raven-haired beauty, stopping him. "I will have you taken to him after one of you tells me what is going on."

"My beloved wife, Aleysia," the Highlander said, back to smiling.

Torin had already backed up, taking Braya with him. Now, he tried to shove Braya behind him.

She held her ground and turned to him. "Go on. Introduce me."

Torin laughed and suddenly reminded her of a predator that had just discovered its prey. He introduced her to the Highlander, Commander Cainnech MacPherson.

Commander MacPherson tilted his head at her and smiled. "Ye will tell me later how ye managed to stab my commander. There is only one other warrior besides me who can take down Amish, and that is my wife." He turned and smiled at her. "I am impressed with yer skill."

She swallowed and her eyes instinctively went to Torin. He winked at her. He understood what it meant to her to have her skill be acknowledged by a man—a warrior. He had understood from the first moment they were in the same hall together and the warden had ignored her presence. He knew what it meant to her to have her father praise her for helping to save her family against the Armstrongs.

She smiled at him then spread it to the commander. "Thank you, my lord."

"The Earl of Rothbury," Torin continued with the introduction.

"Nicholas MacPherson, Cainnech's brother."

"Nicholas MacPherson?" Braya asked, confused. "I thought William Stone was the earl."

"He is," said Rothbury. "I am." He smiled slightly and began to start over, but Aleysia, the Highlander's wife, stopped him.

"Why have you intruded on this family at this difficult time?" she asked Torin matter-of-factly.

Braya looked away. None of them had known of the tragedy that had befallen the earl, or Lismoor. She felt terrible for being here and for fighting Lismoor's men.

"I need the earl's help with matters regarding Scotland," Torin told Aleysia.

She stared at him, studying him, and if Torin was lying, he would have succumbed to her scrutiny, Braya was sure of it.

"These matters are so urgent that you—"

Commander MacPherson leaned in and said something low in his wife's ear. She remained still for a moment and then, just like that, sighed and threw up her hands. "Never mind any of it. I just want to see my son. Cainnech, take me to him, please. Edith," she called out to another maid, "take Miss Hetherington to one of the empty rooms above stairs so she can rest after her journey. Sir Torin." She paused for just a moment, as if something caught in her throat when she looked at him. "Father Timothy will find you a room in the keep. If…you are staying, something more can be arranged. Or you may want to come to—"

"Come, my love," he said to his now docile wife. "I think I hear Tristan cryin'."

He ushered her away and another woman stood in Aleysia's place. "I am Edith. Come with me."

"I will come for you shortly," Torin told her. "We will check on Adams after that, aye."

"Where are you going now?" She let him go and frowned at him.

"I have a few more things to see to with the earl." He moved in closer and dipped his mouth to her ear. "He lost his wife this morn."

She looked toward the earl and her heart broke again for him. He had a babe now. Did he know how to be a father? "My deepest sympathy, my lord," she offered gently. "'Tis good to spend time with a friend."

He and Torin had known each other. Rothbury probably enjoyed seeing his old friend again. She wondered what it was exactly that Torin had done in his service. She would remember to ask Torin later. For now, she hated leaving him.

When he reached for her hand, she let him take it and watched, smiling like a dreamy fool, as he kissed her knuckles.

"I will return to you," he promised, straightening. "You and Adams are safe here."

She nodded. Even after she stabbed Amish? Well, time would tell. She would be ready for any kind of attack.

She watched Torin leave with the earl and the priest, then followed Edith out of the great hall through a different entrance by which she'd entered the first time. She descended three stone steps to a web of corridors and two other stone stairways. They took one that led to some smaller rooms, which were castles compared to her small corner of the hall at home. Her bed was built for a queen, with four heavy wood posters and colorful coverings atop a feather mattress as plush as clouds. She fell into it with a sigh of sheer delight. Her straw mattress wasn't bad and it was always fresh, but this—this was heavenly.

Oh, she could sleep here for days. In fact, she could sleep here now. Edith said a few things about…she didn't remember. She wanted to refresh herself before seeing Torin, but she couldn't bring herself to rise from the bed—and she didn't ask Edith for help. She hadn't slept since she was kidnapped, and after sleeping, or trying to sleep, on the cold hard ground of the forest last night, she fell into a deep slumber, the kind a body needed to relax. She dreamed of an army of Scots thundering across the fields, breaching a castle that was neither Lismoor nor Carlisle. One turned on his horse, his curls blowing across his face, his plaid snapping behind him in the wind like a pennant. He held an axe high over his head and brought it down when he saw her. It was Torin.

TORIN LET A nurse hand him a wee babe swaddled in white wool with black stripes. He held his nephew, Elias MacPherson, gently while tears filled his eyes that such a tiny being didn't have his mother. This was his family. What he'd hoped and prayed for his whole life.

"He is so small," he remarked and smiled at his brother. "He looks like you."

"Aye. Mattie was…was…" His voice broke on a sob and Torin waited while his brother gathered himself again. "She was very blonde. Very beautiful."

Elias' nurse returned and took him from Torin's arms. Nicholas did not hold him. Torin wanted to ask him what he would do now, but it was too soon for Nicholas to know and he shouldn't be rushed.

"So, Torin," the priest finally spoke to him. He'd been staring, but hadn't said much until now. "Ye had no idea all these years that Cainnech served in the same army ye did."

Torin shook his head. He liked Father Timothy. He had kind, expressive eyes and a generous smile. "No. I did not remember their names or even our surname. I thought my brothers were dead."

"I always believed ye were wily enough to make it out there," Cain said, coming into the nursery and hearing them. He was bent over and held his son by the hand as they walked together. "He doesna like to be carried. He has his own mind like his mother."

"And his father," Father Timothy pointed out.

"What d'ye mean, old man," Cain argued. "I am calm and even-tempered."

The priest laughed and Nicholas followed. "You are about as even tempered as a wolf with mange."

Cain gave their youngest brother a hurt look then forgot them and leaned downed to his son. "Meet yer uncle, Torin."

"God is good," Father Timothy declared, smiling at them.

"God is good," Cain repeated and looked up at Nicholas, who said nothing.

"Greetings, Tristan," Torin said and could no longer remember why he'd been so angry all his life.

The brothers sat with Father Timothy and wee Tristan and talked about their lives away from each other. Cain told them about having Father Timothy with him during the very worst times of his life.

Nicholas had had Julianna Feathers.

Torin realized he'd had no one. Florie for a few years, and then no one. He'd learned to rely on himself and his own prowess and had become the Bruce's *Shadow*.

"Hell, I have heard of ye," Cain told him. "Ye are spoken of verra highly among Robert's men."

It was nice to hear, but Torin had problems, so after finding Braya's room and her sound asleep in her bed, and after visiting with Adams for a while, he returned to his brothers in the gathering hall of the keep. A few tankards of whisky aided in telling them his concerns. "I believe I have fallen in love with Miss Hetherington and I fear telling her the truth."

He told them about Ragenald and her family hating Robert's men, and that he wanted to return to Carlisle and see this through. He told them of his promise to his five-year-old self, and they cried together. They laughed together, too, and many times during the evening Nicholas told them he was glad they were there.

"Listen to me, Torin," Cain said, and then shook his head in disbelief. "I still canna believe I am speakin' to ye, little brother."

"Nor can I," Torin laughed with him and clanged another cup to his in a toast. They'd hoped to get Nicholas drunk but, by the end of the evening, they were all deep in their cups.

They walked back to the keep together, and Torin bid his brothers goodnight then tiptoed to Braya's room.

He lit a candle and checked on her. She was still asleep, but when he moved to leave, she was there, in the dark at his back, clutching his arm, stopping him from going.

"Stay."

He didn't blow out the candle when he bolted the door instead of leaving through it, but lit four more candles around the bed, so he could see her better when he undressed her.

CHAPTER TWENTY-TWO

S HE MISSED HIM. She'd spent the day worrying about him and imagining different ways of them coming to tell her he was dead.

She would have gone mad if they told her that. She loved being with him. She loved making him smile, and laugh, and making his gaze go all warm and heated. She trusted in her own capabilities most of the time, but she felt safe with him. She'd watched him fight. He was magnificent while he took down the Armstrongs—both times! And then, just when she struggled for her last breath, he saved her.

She loved him. She loved his melancholy, lonely heart and wanted nothing more than to make him happy. She couldn't wait to be with him, and when he finally came to her room, she wasn't about to let him go.

"Stay."

He bolted the door and lit more candles around the bed until the room was bathed in soft golden light. He didn't wait until she stepped into the light to undress her, but moved in front of her. He leaned down to kiss her and then began unlacing her kirtle. She had awakened earlier, refreshed herself, and changed clothes, hoping he would come find her.

He smelled of peat and whisky. She drank him in and grew heady on his kisses. She didn't remember him pulling off her kirtle. She may have done the pulling—or that may have been her chemise. Either way, all her clothes ended up strewn across the floor. She stood naked before him save for her knee-high hose. She didn't care. She couldn't think as he fit his arm behind her back and bent to draw her nipple into his mouth.

His lips were wet and warm, and his teeth gently scratched her sensitive bud. She arched a little to offer him more. He took it, dragging her upward so that he could suckle and tease more thoroughly.

She cried out softly as a dull ache that began below her belly traveled downward, between her legs, and became the focus of all her thoughts until his mouth on her made her want to beg for more— something to answer this hunger.

Answering her passion, he scooped up the rest of her and carried her to her bed. "I warn you," she told him, clenching fistfuls of his hair. "'Tis more comfortable than a cloud. You may fall asleep."

He laughed softly and set her down on the bed. "How could I fall asleep with you in my arms?"

She moaned as she sank and then remembered him and tried to hide herself with her hands.

He stood over her at the edge of the bed and looked as if he might jump in after her. "Dinn—" He stopped and shook his head at himself then began again. "Do not cover what I am emblazoning on my mind. One day, I will pay an artist to paint you using my memory." He was quiet for a moment longer then yanked his léine over his head and kicked off his boots.

Braya watched, mesmerized by the shape of him, the sound of his breath, heavy and quick. He moved into the light and her own breath stalled. How could she have touched such a heart as Torin's? She knew he had ghosts from his past. She didn't care. He was merciful and kind, and so very, very beautiful.

She smiled at him to ease the sudden uncertainty in his eyes. She didn't want to stop. To prove it, she tugged at the laces of his breeches.

Encouraged by her boldness, he nearly tore them off and flung them aside.

The downy-feathered mattress and dozens of pillows strewn all about it surrounded her. He pushed some out of his way and climbed over her, between her legs. He lowered his head to her mouth. His hot, demanding kisses robbed her of breath and logic. He traced a trail of kisses down her chin to her breasts, stopping at each one to give it the attention it demanded. He raked his teeth over her soft, flat belly and rose up on his knees.

She was quite shocked to see the very noticeable change in him. It was as if a very significant part of his body had come alive. For her. She knew it wasn't finished growing. Millie had told her a man's cock could get harder than steel. Braya had doubted it.

Torin lifted one of her legs and set her foot on his chest. He found her languid gaze and smiled at her as he began to untie the string holding up her hose. He did the same to both legs, rolling the hose over her knee and down her calf, to her feet, which he kissed.

He was getting harder. Bigger. She was growing a little concerned that he may be too big. Then what?

He didn't give her time to worry about it but slipped his fingers down her inner thigh and touched her where she ached. She startled, unsure if his touch should feel like a hot brand.

She groaned and licked her dry lips.

As if he couldn't control the need to kiss her mouth, he sank down on her and pressed her to the hard, yielding muscles of his body. She bucked when she felt his fingers still at her crux, his arm between them. He was readying her, wetting her to receive him.

She squeezed her eyes shut, waiting for him to get it over with.

"Braya," he whispered close to her ears.

She opened her eyes to see him smiling at her. "Do not be afraid, lass. I will be patient."

"You are bigger than I imagined."

"Made even bigger yet from the sound of your soft, sensual voice against my ears."

He flicked his fingertips over the engorged bud between her thighs. She spread her legs wider and threw back her head. He caught her cries in his mouth and dipped his finger into her.

"You are so tight," he said through clenched teeth. He guided the tip of his lance to her opening and pushed gently. He bit his lip to keep himself from thrusting into her.

Braya wasn't afraid. She knew Torin wouldn't do anything to deliberately hurt her. She wanted this, to give herself to him. She didn't know much about having a lover. She'd been too busy learning to take men on the field, not in her bed. What she knew, she learned second-hand from Millie and Lucy, and her other male cousins. She knew what men liked, though she blushed at the thought of taking him into her mouth.

She relaxed beneath him. Why shouldn't she relax? He was heavy, but not so much that he crushed her. He was warm and hard every-where.

She ran her palms over his sculpted shoulders, the thick sinew that corded his arms.

She wanted more of him, all of him, and closed her legs around his.

He looked at her with something untamed and finally free in the silvery-green glint of his eyes. He smiled, and in that smile she saw his heart, exposed for her alone.

She opened to him, and he took her with slow, deliberate ease, staying close to her, telling her how beautiful she was to him.

"Be my wife, Braya," he ground out, finally breaking through her barrier.

"Aye," then a gasp as a lance of pain shot through her. He was too big. Too hot. Then the pain was gone and pleasure made her head spin; it made her conjure thoughts of keeping him forever locked in the steel embrace of her sheathe and thighs.

"I could hold you to me forever," she threatened with laughter curling her lips.

He closed his eyes and withdrew almost completely. She laughed and tried to hold him, tightening her grip, undulating her hips beneath his. He was too powerful.

Then he opened his eyes and fastened them on her. "'Tis not the cage that will hold me to you, Braya, but something...deeper." He surged into her, deep and long, letting her draw him in, hold on tight. She did, while he plunged in and then out, again and again until she clawed at him and trembled in his embrace.

He took her hips in his hands and turned over, lying on his back and letting her straddle him. She laughed softly with surprise and thought about how deeply she was impaled on him.

He licked his sultry mouth and began moving her hips in his hands. "You are going to like this, my love," he promised confidently and pulled his thick arms over his head.

Ah, she had him to the hilt. Here was her power. She leaned down and cupped his nape in her hand then pulled him up. She ran her other hand over his tightly knotted belly and up through the curls on the back of his head. She held on as she rose up on her haunches and wielded her power like a queen, until nothing of them remained.

TORIN HELD BRAYA in her overstuffed bed and listened to the rhythm of her breath as evening turned into midnight. Was she asleep? He hadn't told her the truth, and now...hell, he'd been drunk, too weak to resist her. He didn't want to resist her. He wanted to do exactly what he'd done. He wanted to be with her, always in her bed, inside her body. If Bennett touched her, he'd rip him limb from limb. Torin loved her. Somehow, she'd penetrated his walls and took him down like a trained general. What was he to do now?

He thought she was asleep. She wasn't. She moved like a breeze over him, covering him with her pale yellow tresses. She kissed his chest, his shoulders, and neck. She climbed atop his hips and looked around, as if she'd reached the top of a mountain and was taking in the sights. Torin laughed and cupped her buttocks in his hands. She was soft on the outside, hard and tight on the inside.

It didn't take him long to get hard enough to impale her. He didn't. He let her rub herself up and down his shaft. He watched her and vowed to himself to always remember how she looked, naked and beautiful, delighting in him.

She slipped upward on him. She was wet and ready to be taken. He shifted his hips, and when she rode downward again, he pushed inside her.

She squeezed her eyes shut and did not cry out. He didn't let her go as he flipped them over and covered her body with his. He made love to her, looking into her eyes, telling her what she meant to him. He plunged deep, taking his time, every touch a curious caress.

He'd received half of his family back today and lost his heart completely to an English outlaw.

Her knees bent and laid flat on both sides of her. He fit perfectly, entwining their arms over her head and kissing her as searing fire enveloped him. He moved slowly, spilling himself while flames licked him, and the line between pain and pleasure ceased to exist.

Later, he lay atop her, both of them sprawled out on the bed and on each other.

"Did you know the earl was a Scot?"

Torin blinked, too tired to answer. "No," he said honestly.

"Did he know you hate the Scots?" she asked. "Is that why he did not tell you?"

Damn it, he wanted to tell her before they...how the hell was he supposed to tell her now? "Braya?"

"Did you tell him what they did to your family, Torin? He would probably never want to admit to being a Scot again."

He shifted uneasily on the bed. She would hate him. She would hate him even more now. She'd slept with a Scot. Mayhap, he should wait until after the war for Carlisle. If he died, he wouldn't have to tell her anything.

"Aye, he knows what happened to my family."

"There, you see?" she said with her cheek pressed to his chest and her eyes closed. "He was ashamed."

"Aye."

"I do pity him though," she said softly. "The poor man."

Aye, Nicky had been through much. Sold at two and raised as a Scottish servant in an English governor's household. Oh, had Torin known two years ago when he'd taken Berwick that his youngest brother was living in the servants' quarters, being beaten for stealing a kiss from the governor's daughter, Torin would have rescued him. But Cain had saved him. Hell, his heart swelled with pride that they were his brothers.

"I do not like Cainnech MacPherson, though. He is a brute."

Torin shrugged and smiled, thinking about his oldest brother. "He is not so bad."

"Perhaps not." Her voice fell softly over his chest. "I am told High-landers are the most savage among them all."

Torin stared at the ceiling. It broke his healing heart that she hated Scots so. Would she even give him a chance? He was a Highlander, here to bring war. Even his manner of speech was a lie.

And knowing all of that, he'd still made love to her. He closed his eyes. He didn't blame her if she tried to kill him, or vowed never to speak to him again. He should not have come here drunk.

"Braya," he whispered into the air. "I am sorry that I stayed."

She rose up off him, and her hair falling over one side of her horrified face made him want to run for the door.

"Why would you say that, Torin? Was I terrible? Was—"

"No," he told her, leaning up on his elbows. He knew he was supposed to be feeling remorse right now, but he wanted to smile at her. It was tremendously difficult not to. "You were...hell, you were...perfect, like a burning lute playing a song only I could hear, and we danced together to it."

She smiled. He relaxed. He didn't know why he would do whatever he could to make her happy.

"But you wish we had not done it?" she asked, looking just as troubled.

"I wish we had not done it while I was so deep in my cups. You deserve more than that. So much more than what you got from me."

"No, Torin." She held her fingers to his lips. "What you gave me was everything I've ever wanted. Please." She shook her head to quiet him when he would have spoken. "Let us enjoy this moment. How many more will we have? I do not want to speak of Scots or young widowers or sadness. Tell me again about Avalon. The isle of apples."

He smiled that she remembered. Aye, she was right. He didn't want to think about all the reasons he shouldn't be here. All the reasons he should leave. He was happy for the first time in his life. The little boy was quiet.

He told her again about the nine sisters who ruled Avalon, including Morgen, who, according to the poet Geoffrey of Monmouth, exceeded her sisters in beauty and the healing art. "She was first of the nine," he told her, knowing the tale in its entirety, "and could change her shape and cleave to the air on new wings. When she wished it, she slipped down from the air onto our shores."

"I am surprised you did not call the horse Morgen," Braya remarked, looking up at him. "She often reminds me of a magical being."

"I wanted her to remember where she came from," he told her in a quiet voice. "If a word is going to be spoken to her often, I want it to remind her of her home in case she is here too long and forgets."

Braya smiled dreamily. "Do you think she will take us home with her when she goes?"

"I wish she would take us tonight," he murmured, then kissed her head and closed his eyes to sleep.

He would tell her the truth in the morning. He couldn't do it now. He wanted to sleep with her in his arms and wake up next to her in the morning.

She'd done something to him, changed him. His whole life he'd dreamed of his brothers. He'd prayed that they'd lived and not died in the flames that night. He would never have found them if he hadn't been trying to keep Braya away from Bennett. She'd brought good things into his life, including laughter. Most importantly, he didn't feel weighed down with shame and guilt for the first time since he was a child. He felt free to love, and he loved her.

"Torin?"

"Aye?"

"I won the race. We made a bargain."

"Aye, love. I will put you out of my thoughts tomorrow."

She laughed softly and poked him in the side, then she kissed him and told him about her brother Raggie until he fell asleep.

CHAPTER TWENTY-THREE

Braya opened her eyes to sunlight streaming into her unshuttered windows. For a moment, she forgot where she was. She remembered, sighing with delight at the comfort of her bed. She became aware of a heavy arm strewn across her belly, a long, even heavier leg tossed over hers. She smiled from the innermost depths of her heart and turned to look at Torin sleeping beside her.

Oh, but she loved his face. His beguiling curls falling over his sleeping eyes. His shapely lips were relaxed and waiting to be kissed. Did she want to disturb him? He looked quite peaceful.

In fact, since he returned with the earl and the earl's Highland brother yesterday, he seemed less melancholy—until he looked at her. Was she making him unhappy for some reason? Even last night after they had lain together, he'd regretted coming to her room. Why? Why would he ask her to be his wife if she made him sad?

And why wasn't he angry with the earl for deceiving him all these years. Nicholas MacPherson was a Scot, a Highlander, though he did not dress or speak like one. How could Torin forgive him after what the Scots had done to his family?

She wanted to wake him up and ask him, but she wasn't sure she wanted an answer.

She was being silly. He wasn't unhappy around her. She made him laugh, and if she had her way, she would make him laugh until they grew old together.

And, of course, he forgave the earl. They had been friends. The earl hadn't killed his family. He had lost his beloved wife though, and Torin was just trying to help him through the day. She hoped he had, but perhaps now was the time to go. She wasn't comfortable around Scots.

But they had been nothing but nice to her. The commander had even complimented her on her skill. And her bed was so damned comfortable.

"You are beautiful in the morn." Torin's deep, groggy voice swept through her and warmed her insides.

"I have not even combed my hair."

"Then do not comb it," he told her, closing his eyes again. "'Tis perfect."

He was perfect, Braya thought, gazing at him.

"Ah!" he said, opening his eyes. "You were correct about this bed. I want to sleep for another sennight."

She brushed her fingers through his curls and smiled at him. "Shall we stay in bed all day?"

"I would love to." He laughed and pulled her closer. He was so much bigger than she and quickly covered her.

A rap came at the door. Again, harder this time when neither of them moved to answer it.

"Gray! Open the door!" It was Adams. "I know you are in there."

"What the hell is he doing out of bed?" Torin asked Braya while he left the bed and stumbled into his breeches.

"He must be feeling better," she guessed and climbed out of bed wrapped in the colorful bed coverings. She stood behind the door when Torin went barefoot and bare-chested to it and swung it open.

"Adams, what are you doing out—"

"Where is she?" Braya's family friend demanded. "Does she know, Gray? Does she know that you are a Scot? That you came to Carlisle to prepare it for defeat against the Bruce's soldiers?"

Surely she was dreaming. This was not happening. Torin was a Scot? A spy for the Bruce? No! No! He was here to bring…war? She shook her head. She didn't believe it.

"Braya!" Mr. Adams shouted.

She didn't care what Mr. Adams thought of how she was dressed; she stepped out from around the door. "I am here, Mr. Adams. Who told you such a vile thing?"

"I discovered the truth quite by accident," he told her and then stared at Torin. "The earl's babe has a nurse, and she came to have a word with Edith, who was bringing me food. She told Edith all about how you are the earl's long lost brother and how even Commander MacPherson believed it since he introduced you to his son as Uncle Torin!"

His brothers? She couldn't comprehend what he was telling her. He was the Highlanders' brother? No. She'd brought him to her family! Helped them trust him! She'd trusted him. She let him—no!

"Braya," Torin tried. "Let us speak alone."

She turned to him with a hardening gaze and her heart shattering at her feet. "Then 'tis all true."

"Aye, but I beg you, give me a chance to—"

She slapped him hard in the face. "Get out!"

She turned away before she struck him again. Tears spilled down her face as she moved to get his boots and his léine. She threw them at him and screamed for him to get out again when he didn't move fast enough.

"Braya. I will not go," he said. "I would speak with you."

Well, if he wouldn't leave, she would!

With a quick adjustment to her wrappings, she pushed past him and Mr. Adams and stormed out of the room.

She had no idea where she was going. She realized too late that she should have dressed herself properly first, but she had wanted to get away from Torin. And now he hurried after her, while Mr. Adams moved at a slower rate. She would not be stopped. She would leave Lismoor in her blanket, get on Archer, and ride home!

Another door opened and Aleysia, wife of the Highlander, stepped out of a room toting her sleepy son by the hand.

When she saw Braya garbed in bed coverings, Torin hurrying down the hall after her in just breeches, and Mr. Adams out of his sickbed, she drew back her son toddling before her.

"What in the blazes is going on here? Miss Hetherington, where are you off to?"

"I am going home," Braya stopped to tell her.

"Dressed in a blanket?" Aleysia asked with a raised raven brow.

"My lady." Torin stopped beside Braya. She moved a step farther away from him. "Forgive our indecency," he said, pulling his léine over his head and shoving his arms into the sleeves. "We had words—"

Braya turned to him, gaping. "We had words? You are a Scot, a *soldier* for the Bruce, and you kept it from me all this time!"

Aleysia looked at her in her blanket and Torin, trying to dress. She shook her head at him. "Go find Father Timothy. He is very good with things like this."

"Like what?" Braya asked. "A man who vows you can trust him and turns out to be a lying—"

"Braya," he tried, putting a hand to her shoulder.

She slapped his hand away and returned her attention to Aleysia, mostly so that Torin wouldn't see the tears she shed for him. "Lady MacPherson, your husband should not believe this man's claims that he is his brother. He cannot be trusted!" She had to turn away lest he see her fall apart.

The Highlander's wife put her arms around Braya and ushered her toward the door to her chambers. "Come inside," she offered gently. "Not either of you!" she scolded Torin and Mr. Adams while Braya wept into her hands. "You have upset her enough!"

She wasn't about to stand around and listen to their defense, so she picked up her son and, turning on her heel, pulled Braya into the room and slammed the door shut in their faces.

When Braya entered the room, she stopped and almost walked out of it again when she saw the commander sitting in a chair and pulling on his boots.

He held up his hand. "Dinna bother, I am goin'." He stood up and came toward them. "I heard." He motioned toward the door. "He didna claim to be anyone, lass. He has proven who he is to me and Nicholas."

"But the Scots killed his family."

"No, the English killed our parents."

Lies. All lies. All to bring war.

"Thank you for your kindness, Commander, my lady, but I will be leaving as soon as I can dress."

The Highlander sighed and shook his head. "He has lost much. Now, he will lose ye as well."

She turned away. He should have thought of that sooner. She fought her brother over him. She made a fool of her father by having Torin come to the town hall to apologize for—oh, dear God, her cousins. "He killed my cousins."

"Pardon?"

She didn't answer but yanked open the door and hurried into the hall. He was still there, waiting for her.

"My cousins! What happened that night, Torin? I will have the truth!"

His face paled. He looked ill.

Braya stopped in her tracks. "What?" Oh, she didn't want to think it, to hear it! "You murdered them in cold blood?"

"No!" Mr. Adams exclaimed, lest guilt fall on him, too. "That is not what happened! They attacked me and the others!"

But Torin said nothing, and it was more damning than any false defense he could have come up with. She was glad he didn't try. She would have lifted one of those knives the commander had shoved under his belt a few moments earlier and stabbed Torin with it.

"I am leaving, Torin," she said coolly and with false calm. Beneath the surface, a labyrinth of writhing emotion threatened to erupt. "Allow me to dress and prepare for the journey with Mr. Adams. Do not follow me or 'twill become a battle between us and one of us will die. I will return home, even if it means I must marry the warden. For he would be better than you."

She squared her shoulders and waited for him to move out of her way. When he did, she returned to her room alone and locked the door.

She dressed while her belly twisted with an ache she'd never known before. He was not real. He was not real. Of course, he wanted her family to stay away from the Scots. He knew Carlisle would win with the reivers on its side. She had to tell her family.

Oh, her family. What would she tell them? How would they forgive her after she told them what she had once suspected but had been too horrible to believe, so she hadn't? He'd killed her cousins to make himself appear the hero to the guards. Aye! To gain entrance into Carlisle for his deadly purpose!

Her father would never forgive her. He would tell her that she thought with her heart and that was why 'twas better to be a man. He was correct, at least about one thing. She had made her decisions with her heart and not her head. She had trusted him. She had seen him enjoy the sweet fragrance of a flower. He'd shown patience with his horse and mercy to a man who didn't deserve it, and she thought he was a different kind of man.

But he wasn't. He thirsted for blood. He hungered for battle.

And since he wanted one so bad, she would give it to him.

She had much to think on during her trip home with Mr. Adams. At first they didn't speak much, taking solace in each other's silence. But Torin's betrayal cut them both.

"Perhaps he had agreed to *fight* us *with* your cousins and then turned on them," Mr. Adams ventured. "But they did not seem to know him. Though 'twas dark and my eyes are not as good as they once were."

Braya shook her head. "I do not know what he did or how he was involved, but he was. He lied about it. I could tell when I asked him. Nothing he said was the truth."

"I do not know about that."

She drew in a deep breath. If Mr. Adams tried to convince her that Torin's feelings for her were real, she would tell him she didn't care. It didn't change anything.

"He told us the truth about his brothers."

Her heart faltered a little and she cursed it. He'd found his brothers. Truly, it was a miracle. A joyous one. She wanted to be happy for him, but her heart was too broken and all she could see were the lies.

"The commander told me 'twas the English who killed their parents."

Mr. Adams nodded. "I guessed as much once I knew the truth. He must have much hatred in him for the English."

"He watched them kill his father," Braya told him hollowly. "He has haunting memories."

"Aye. He must be very torn about recent events."

Aye, Braya silently agreed then slipped her glare to Adams. "Why are you giving him your pity? He is undeserving of it."

"Pity or no," Mr. Adams stated, "he found his brothers and lost you in the same day."

"And if he follows me," she told him, "he will lose his life today as well.

Mr. Adams remained silent but stared at her. "You love him."

"I was a fool," she cried and wiped her eyes. "I trusted him and fell in love with a shadow."

"I trusted him, too, Braya. I refuse to believe that we were both so wrong about a man. There is good in him."

Instead of answering—for she wasn't sure she had anything to say that wasn't a scathing oath—she flicked Archer's reins and pushed onward, away from the deceit, away from Torin Gray…MacPherson.

CHAPTER TWENTY-FOUR

B RAYA DIDN'T THINK the pain could get any worse, but she was wrong. The more the initial shock wore off, the worse she felt. Telling her father didn't help any—even with Mr. Adams there with her. She couldn't tell Galien or the others yet. She could not take the ridicule she was sure would come to her after insisting that he was innocent and having him apologize to all.

But none of that was the worst part. No. The worst part was that she'd given herself to him. She'd agreed to wed him. She'd lain in bed with him and...she couldn't think of it. She didn't want to remember how wanton she had been for him. The thought of it shocked and shamed her. Was Torin so cruel that he would not only deceive her but would use her to satisfy his own lustful desires?

But he had been sorry he came to her.

I wish we had not done it while I was so deep in my cups. You deserve more than that. So much more than what you got from me.

Was he sorry he had deceived her? Or was his regret just another lie?

You were...hell, you were...perfect, like a burning lute playing a song only I could hear, and we danced together to it.

She remembered his voice, so meaningful, so sensual—his touch, so tender and patient. She wanted it back, and she was angry with him for taking it from her.

She closed her eyes and wept for the thousandth time today.

"Braya?"

She opened her eyes and wiped them at the sound of Galien's voice.

"May I come in?" he asked, surprisingly gently.

When she nodded, he sat near her on the floor beside her straw mattress behind the curtained partition that separated her room from the rest of the house. "I spoke to Father."

She groaned inwardly and prepared herself for whatever her brother was going to say. She wouldn't mind if he ridiculed her for trusting a Scot if her heart didn't feel as if it were being ripped out.

"So, Gray has an agenda."

"Aye," she said weakly. That was a nice way to say it. "Aye. You were correct about him all along. I should have listened to you."

He swayed a little. If he had been standing, Braya thought he would have fallen over. "I…I wish I had been wrong."

She smiled and swiped a tear from her cheek.

"You care for him." It wasn't a question he put to her.

First she shook her head, and then she wept harder and nodded.

He didn't say anything for a time but simply sat with her and pulled her in closer while she wept—which only made her weep harder. He hadn't trusted Torin, and she hadn't listened to him.

"He…he lied to me, Galien," she told him through sobs and tears. "The Scots have taken over every stronghold. They want Carlisle as well. We cannot let them have it."

"Aye," he said, his dark gray eyes somber, "but if we fight, we will be fighting against him. *You* will be fighting against him. I do not think 'tis wise."

She eyed him, unsure if her brother had been replaced while she was away with someone who looked like him. "Since when do you care what is wise?"

He smiled. "Since my sister is involved. Braya, you are a skilled fighter. Better than most—"

She lifted her head and gaped at him. Was she hearing him right? Though her heart was aching, she couldn't help but smile.

"—but your heart is involved," he continued. "Being hurt or angry with him is very different than killing him on the battlefield. If we do fight against the Scots, I do not think you should come with us."

She sat up. "But I—"

He shook his head. "No. Father agrees. 'Tis too dangerous."

Braya bolted from her mattress and stood over him. "What are you saying, Galien?" she asked angrily. "That I will not kill him given the chance?"

"I'm saying that you *cannot* kill him," he replied. "As much as I hate to say this, I think you are in love with him. You fell asleep in his arms, Braya. 'Tis the first time I have seen you trust someone so far."

When she opened her mouth to protest loving the Highland warrior, he held up his hand. "I was not finished. Now that we know the truth, we must ask ourselves if he will bring the Scots to us. I do not think he will."

He held up his hand again and pushed open her curtain then waited for her to leave. "You will have your turn before Father, but at least hear me, Sister."

She nodded and remained quiet.

"When he wanted to go into the Armstrongs' village alone, he asked me to trust him, and I saw something in his eyes that convinced me that you meant much to him. He rescued you from John Armstrong and saved you from them on the castle battlements, and both times his gaze on you spoke volumes about his heart. The Scot loves you."

"So what are you saying?" she asked him, reaching the kitchen. "We let the Scots fight Carlisle on their own?"

"Even with our help, Carlisle may not win," her father answered from his seat at the table. "If the rest of the Bruce's men fight like him, no one will have a chance."

"If you want peace, Sister, staying out of the fight will help get it. Gray will not bring his army against you."

"And our cousins?" she turned to ask him as he leaned his hip on the table. "Do you still believe his innocence?"

"I never did," Galien answered.

"It does not matter," their father huffed. "We pardoned him. Killing him in cold blood now would make you a murderer in the Marches."

"But Father," she went to him and sat in the seat beside him, "the Bruce's soldiers killed Ragenald. You would have a Scottish warden?"

He looked at her and then at his wife and son. "Aye. I would rather a Scot over Bennett, whose intentions toward you are evil."

She shook her head, unable to believe her ears! She turned to her brother. Galien? Galien spoke of peace? She…for war? War against Torin. The Hetheringtons had relatives who were Scots. She didn't care who the warden was, as long as he wasn't Bennett. She agreed with them, so why was her blood boiling in anger toward them?

Her family didn't seem to care that Torin had fooled them all— even the border guards. He came here for war and pretended to be peaceful…merciful. She wanted to do whatever would hurt him. She didn't need her family to do it. In fact, she didn't want her family to fight and die, especially against Torin. She had a logical thought every so often when Torin's handsome face and lying tongue weren't haunting her and remembered the safety of her family.

But logic was no match for a wounded heart, and she thought about hurting him, killing him if she had the chance.

"He may not even return," she said, closing her arms around herself. She didn't know which was worse. Killing him and never seeing him again, or him choosing to stay away. "I told you. He found his brothers. He will likely stay in Rothbury, and when the Scots come to our village, he will not be there to stop them."

Her father looked a bit worried about that and turned to Galien. "Bring Rob Adams here. We need to include him in this decision."

Galien went, but not before Braya pulled him by the sleeve of his jack. "What has come over you? You are agreeable and sensible. Why the sudden change?"

"I think we will be safe if the Scots win. If Carlisle wins, I want to bring the battle and the rest of the Hetheringtons there and make sure Bennett dies for what he tried to do to you. I am not always a reckless fool, Sister. Contrary to what you think." He smiled and winked at her and headed out.

"Braya."

She turned to her father.

"You must remain hidden. No one knows you are here. I want to keep it that way."

"I wanted to check on Millie."

He shook his head. "No, my dear. If Bennett gets a whiff of you, he may try something else."

"Let him! I—"

"Braya!" Her father held up his hand. "Go back to your bed and rest. You have been through much. You are not thinking clearly."

She balled her hands into fists, but she said nothing.

She was thinking just perfectly. Better than she had in a sennight.

Without another word, she left the kitchen and returned to her room and her small, prickly bed. She remembered her bed at Lismoor and fought the stinging burn of tears forming in her eyes. She loved him. She loved him still. She'd let him touch her, know her, breathe and taste her. And he had been lying to her to entire time. How could he have kissed her with such meaning knowing they were enemies? How could he have lain with her, asking her to wed him, knowing he was a lie?

She stayed in bed the rest of the day, and when night fell and her parents were asleep, she donned a fresh pair of black breeches and a léine beneath her jack and left the house.

She thought she might just go and visit Millie and the babe. Millie and Will would never tell the warden she'd returned. She was sure it would be safe and, besides, she needed a friend's ear.

It was the lights in the distance, closer than stars, moving in formation, coming from the north that made her change her direction and head to the stable for Archer.

Her blood ran cold. The Scots had come to Carlisle.

He would be there with his king, perhaps with his brothers. What would she do if she saw him? She hadn't taken a weapon. She could go back and possibly wake her father. No, she kept going.

She wanted to see him one last time.

Before she found a knife and plunged it into him.

TORIN MOVED FAST when word came of the Scot's army moving toward Carlisle. He was glad his brothers came with him, but he especially did not want them fighting the Hetheringtons.

He was surprised the king hadn't granted his request for more time. This was bad. Nothing was in place. He was to poison the guards' supper, their water, killing his enemies like a plague. He knew who kept the keys to the weapons room and he was supposed to be in possession of the key by now. Nothing had been done. Would it matter? The Scot's army was so much more skilled than the border guards. The Bruce's men would be victorious.

Would Adams fight? Would the Hetheringtons? It felt as if his blood drained from his face and refused to return until he saw Braya alive. He prayed her family wasn't fighting. Damn it, she wasn't supposed to leave the safety of Lismoor now!

They caught up to the army, and after learning the king wasn't with them, they broke away from the march and rode hard until evening came.

But Torin could not sleep and rose up again while his brothers slept beneath the stars. He traveled on to Hetherington territory alone with Avalon—though he didn't push his dearest friend but let her take him at her own pace.

While they traveled, he thought of Braya. He should have told her the truth the moment he felt something for her. It was too late for that now. He was going to make certain she was safe.

But he was too late. He learned promptly from Braya's mother that her daughter had disappeared sometime in the night and the men had gone to the castle to find her.

His heart thudded in his ears. Why did they look for her at the castle?

"Because," her mother told him, "she was most likely looking for you."

He closed his eyes and pulled at his hair. This wasn't going to end well. How was he going to protect her? Her father and brother? Hell.

He promised her mother that he would do his best to bring them all home and left to go get them.

As dawn approached, he searched outside the city, along the Eden, but found nothing. He hoped her father had found her and she wasn't alone.

He was going to have to go inside the castle. What if Bennett had found her? What if Adams had told the other men about him? He couldn't take the whole damned guard on alone.

He was going to have to find a way in without being noticed. It was what he was good at.

The east gate.

Leaving Avalon beside the river to refresh herself and rest, he entered the castle on foot, his sword raised and ready, through the east gate. No one saw him.

But someone did.

"Torin."

He saw her standing beyond the gate cloaked in her hooded mantle. Her silken voice echoed on the empty walkway.

Lowering his blade, he walked toward her as the sun rose over the horizon. Light blended with mist, casting her in an ethereal glow as she lowered her hood. She was his laughter, his joy, and he would do anything not to lose her. More, not to harm her.

"I was doing my duty," he told her. "You and your family were not part of the plan."

"The plan?" she mocked.

"Aye, Braya. An army does not attack without a plan." He stood close. He could smell her, look into her clear blue eyes. He wanted to drag her into his arms. His muscles cramped with the need. He remembered how she felt atop him, beneath him, held close to his heart. "You were not part of it. I was not supposed to fall in love with you, lass. I never thought I would—with anyone."

"If you loved me, Torin, you would have told me the truth. Are you such a coward?"

"Aye," he told her. "Aye. I am. I was afraid of losing you. I knew you would never—"

She stepped forward and slapped his face. The crack sounded throughout the outer ward and drew two other men from the shadows, and then another.

His brothers. Galien.

"You knew I would never stay with you. You deceived me and used me for your own selfish desire."

"No," he contended. "I fell in love with your smile and your spirit. I did not know what to do. I was a coward. Forgive me, Braya."

"What do we have here?"

They both turned at the sound of Bennett's voice. Geoffrey Mitchell stood slightly behind him as he stepped into view. He shoved another man forward and held a knife to his throat. It was Rowley Hetherington. He'd been beaten, his left eye swollen shut.

"Father!" Braya rushed toward him and ended up in Bennett's arms instead.

"Bennett," Galien shouted. "I will kill you!"

"You will stay where you are if you want your family to live." He was finished with Galien and turned his attention to Braya. "Miss Hetherington." He closed his arm tighter around her, capturing her arms so that she could not move them. "I have sent for the priest."

"Bennett," Torin's voice was like an axe falling on the back of someone's neck. "Let her go before I kill you where you stand."

The warning was menacing, making Braya's eyes widen.

"I have her and her father, Gray. Whatever you do, one of them will die."

Braya stomped on his foot, but he moved it swiftly and her heel just missed his toes.

Bennett smiled at her struggle to be free and held his knife to her throat with the hand he no longer wanted. His cheeks grew round and red. "Oh, I have imagined you in my bed for a long time, little pigeon. I have wanted you beneath me crying out my name—"

Little pigeon. Torin didn't move. He wasn't certain he was breathing. His vision was filled with red. Bennett. Bennett was one of the men in his house eighteen years ago. He was the one who…

Torin's eyes were wide and unblinking as he charged like a wild bull set loose.

Bennett turned his attention to him, horrified at the speed at which Torin moved. Her captor had no time to do anything to Braya with his blade.

Torin clamped his fingers around Bennett's wrist at her throat and pulled his arm away. His eyes were like flames. He could feel the fire rising up in him, spilling out with the rage of twenty-two years.

Still holding Bennett's wrist, he moved to block Braya with his back as he raised his sword and swiped off Bennett's arm.

Blood splattered across Torin's mantle.

Braya quickly moved away when Bennett released her, screaming and trying to grasp his wound and not her.

Geoffrey Mitchell released Rowley Hetherington and leaped forward. Torin took him by the collar and plunged his blade into Mitchell's throat.

He was vaguely aware of Hetherington rushing to his daughter and her brother joining them.

He turned back to Bennett, pointing his bloody sword at him. He felt as if he were going mad. Finally taking the plunge over the precipice. He would show no mercy this time.

"Twenty-two years ago ye burned down a small cottage in Invergarry." He pushed the tip of his blade under Bennett's chin. He could no longer control how he spoke or how he looked. "D'ye remember? Ye will answer or I will cut off yer other arm."

Bennett whimpered and closed his eyes.

"Ye raided the home of a man and his wife and their three young lads," Torin said, helping him remember. When Bennett said nothing, Torin raised his sword.

"Aye. Aye, I remember," Bennett cried, opening his eyes to look at him. He must have known he wasn't going to get out of this alive, for he grew bold to ask. "Which one are you?"

Torin's sword swayed. His arm trembled. In an instant, he grew more aware of who was there. Braya, his brothers, Braya's family.

Torin gritted his teeth then exhaled. "I am the one who ran away."

"Torin," Cainnech called out. "I remember this bastard. Kill him or I will."

"The three of us will," Torin called back, keeping his searing gaze on the warden.

"Ye called her little pigeon," Torin continued. "She was our MOTHER!" he screamed in Bennett's face.

He turned to Braya and her family. "Meet us by the river. Go! The army is comin'!"

He turned back to Bennett when no one remained but his brothers. "Who else among you that day still lives?"

"Adams," Bennett told him. "Rob Adams."

Torin's head spun and his hands closed into tight fists. Adams. His friend. He thought he might be ill and turned away as his brother stepped forward.

"I am the one you sold," Nicholas said, holding a long knife in his hand.

"I am the one ye kept with ye on the battlefield," Cainnech told him and ran him through in the guts with his claymore.

Nicholas plunged his knife into Bennett's eye.

Torin felt a long, guttural groan coming up from his depths. He let it out, releasing so much, and then cut Bennett from his groin to his neck.

Adams. He lifted his bloody face from Bennett to the doors.

CHAPTER TWENTY-FIVE

FROM HER PLACE hidden in the trees with her father and brother, Braya watched the Scot's army enter Carlisle's massive outer gate after it was opened from inside. She still didn't know if it was right for her family not to fight for Carlisle. What if a Scottish warden was worse than Bennett?

Oh, but how could anyone be worse than Bennett? Her heart wrenched within for Torin, for his brothers. To remember a man by a sickly sweet endearment he had called his mother was too hard to comprehend, so Braya gave up trying.

Torin had so many demons to give up, so many shadows. Would finding the man who was guilty for Torin's life and killing him be enough? And what of her and Torin? Could she forgive him for not telling her he was her enemy? Her father's enemy?

She turned Archer toward him now, so thankful that he lived. "Father, you have not yet told me what you think of Torin."

"He is a spy."

"Aye, he is."

"I assume Bennett and his men killed his family."

"He was five," Braya told him. "Orphans raised him until he was ten." Was any of it true? Aye. It was difficult for him to speak of it. And after seeing the fury he'd kept leashed for so long released, she believed him.

Her father and brother were quiet.

"Do you think he is dead?" Galien asked, his eyes searching the battlements.

No. She shook her head. "He is an expert fighter."

They both nodded, probably remembering how quickly he took hold of Bennett and disarmed him—in every sense of the word.

"Where is Mr. Adams?" she asked. "Do you think he will fight Torin?"

"I do not know where he is," her father replied, then spit out a little blood. "My tooth is loose."

"I have never seen so many Scots," Galien said on a dreadful breath. He spotted a rider approaching and held up his sword.

Braya watched and saw that it was Cainnech MacPherson.

"Torin wants me to escort ye all home," he called out, coming closer.

Braya shook her head. "I am not going home. Where is Torin? He lives then?"

"Aye, he lives," he said, reaching her.

"Good. I can still kill him," she muttered.

The Highlander smiled.

"What if they follow us?" Galien asked. "We will stand no chance."

"No one is goin' to follow ye," Cainnech assured and shooed them forward. "There is nothin' fer ye to do here."

"I am not going home, Commander." Braya squared her shoulders. "And I do not appreciate your brother ordering me about. I am not his wife. I do not belong to him."

"Braya—" her father implored.

"No. Father, he broke my heart because, aye, I do have one—and I do sometimes let it rule me. Perhaps 'tis ruling me now, but I want to speak to him. I have things I would say to him. I am not going."

"He will come to ye," MacPherson insisted.

She shook her head. "I wish to go to him. Where is he?"

The commander laughed. It struck her how beautiful and menacing the brothers were. "I find no humor in this, Commander. I ask you again, where is he?"

His brother sighed. "Ye would be the cause of keepin' yer father here? He willna leave withoot ye."

"Then the sooner you take me to Torin, the quicker we can go home." Her eyes sparkled and her chin lifted with challenge.

The commander looked her over in her saddle from boot to flaxen crown and smiled again, shaking his head. "My brother never stood a chance." Then he laughed.

"All right. Come with me," he gave in to her. Then Cain looked at her father and brother. "Ye two stay here. I will help her if she needs it."

Braya appreciated his words. Yet again. Perhaps the savage wasn't so bad after all.

Her father pleaded with her not to go, but he was in no condition to stop her. Surprisingly, Galien remained still and promised to take him home.

She followed on Archer and caught up to the commander quickly. "Is the warden dead?"

"Aye, and in hell," he said, slowing down.

She didn't bring Bennett up again, letting him stay dead. She realized he was responsible for not only Torin's suffering, but for Cainnech's and Nicholas' as well. She was sorry for them.

But the commander seemed a bit more light-humored than his brothers. At least more than the earl. Torin had begun to laugh of late.

"But you live," she remarked with a knowing hint in her eyes.

"Some of us do."

She knew he was speaking of his brothers. She couldn't help the poor widowed earl, but… "Your brother, Torin, will be fine after today, I think."

"How d'ye know that, lass?"

Lass. It was what she dreamed Torin had called her. "He killed his ghost."

He nodded then shrugged his broad shoulders. "And now he will have a new one."

He meant her. She didn't deny it. It wasn't her fault. "If he had told me the truth, I would not have given him a chance to feel anything for me."

"He is a soldier, whether ye like it or not. He had a duty to his king and he didna sacrifice his entire mission fer love. That is what a soldier does."

"But I did sacrifice everything," Torin said from beneath a giant oak, where he waited for them atop Avalon. He caught Braya with his gaze as she passed him and she stopped. The commander smiled and continued on.

"I let you distract me by playing with you," Torin told her, dismounting and coming toward her. "By hearing from my victims' parents what my deeds had done to them. I let you turn my eyes from my task and change my heart from revenge to mercy."

"But not to honesty?" she asked him, slipping from her saddle.

He moved to catch her. She pushed him away. "No, Torin. You…you took me," she whispered and lowered her chin, too ashamed to look at him. "You would have never had the chance if I had known who you were."

"Torin MacPherson," he said softly, dropping his hands to his sides. "If I had known who I was, I might have made better decisions."

She didn't want to pity him but how the hell could she not? He had no one who cared about him during his upbringing. No one who taught him how to love, how to…play.

"Are you saying you could have resisted me if you had known you were a MacPherson?"

He smiled at her and then closed his eyes and raked his fingers through his curls.

"Who would believe me?"

"No one from around here. That's for certain," she assured him with a chuckle. Then she sobered. "Are they all dead?"

"The guards? No. None of them are dead."

"What do you mean, none?" The army had ridden straight through those gates. Surely they had killed the guards—

"Would you like to come inside and see?"

Inside the castle overrun by Scots? No.

"No one will hurt you," he promised.

But she shook her head. Everything was going to change now. They were going to have a Scottish warden. She had no idea what that was going to be like or what it meant for her family. She refused to cry over it now, but she wished she had a weapon to swing at Torin.

"I made sure the guards were given the choice of whether to fight or to surrender. They chose to surrender, so they live—and there will be no war."

She nodded as a wave of warmth flowed over her. No war. He'd done it for her. He might be a Highlander, but he was mercif—

"Gray," Mr. Adams' voice interrupted him. "I have been searching for you while trying to avoid your brothers."

Braya dipped her brow at him. "Why were you trying to avoid his brothers?"

"You did not tell her."

"Tell me what?" Braya asked either one of them.

"I was there when his family was...when they..." Mr. Adams could not finish.

Braya was sure her ears were deceiving her. Did Torin know? He would surely kill him. She eyed him nervously.

He knew.

His gaze went dark on the older guard and he drew his sword from behind his back.

"Which one were you?" Torin asked him quietly.

"I have lived my life ashamed of that day."

"Is this the secret that nearly killed you?" Braya asked him.

He nodded.

"Which one, Adams?" Torin asked, his patience running out.

"I stood watch outside."

Braya thought to speak up, but Mr. Adams hadn't stood watch outside her cottage while his friends did unforgivable things to her family.

"I made a vow to kill everyone involved," Torin said and took hold of his hilt in both hands.

Mr. Adams closed his eyes. "Do what you must, but I am sorry for my part. I have always been sorry."

Torin looked at Braya. She smiled. It was time for the killing to stop and living to begin. "You have your brothers back," she reminded him, hoping to ease some of his pain. She forgave him for not telling her the truth, but that didn't mean she was going to let him get away with it.

"Adams." He shoved the guard with his hand and Adams opened his eyes, surprised to still be alive. "We will talk more later, aye?"

Mr. Adams' dark eyes looked a little glossy. Braya tried to hide her smile. She'd never seen him cry before. He blinked and nodded, then turned away and left.

When they were alone, Torin turned to her and found her smiling at him. "So, where will you be living?"

"I was thinking of asking the king for this place. I want to be the warden."

Her heart leaped. Oh, what could be better than that?

"Of course, I would be fair," he assured her.

"Of course," she agreed, trying to remain serious. Then, "Do you think the king would agree?"

He shrugged. "He might. He's granted me other castles."

"And who would you live here with?"

"My wife, of course."

She nodded and moved to mount Archer. "Well, I hope you and she will be very happy, Highlander."

He grasped her wrist and pulled her back into his arms. "We will be." He dipped his mouth to hers and she didn't stop him.

Later, she would—just to make him suffer. But not now. Now, she clutched fistfuls of his léine and reveled in his crushing embrace.

"Braya, you—"

"Speak naturally," she insisted with feigned disgust. "If I must get used to that wonderfully melodic tone of yours, I might as well begin now."

His full, sensual mouth slanted into a grin. "Verra well, wench. Ye are the only woman I have ever loved, or will ever love."

She looked up at him and smiled, happier than she'd ever been before. "I do not know if I believe it. You will have to prove it to me."

"I will spend the rest of my days doin' so if ye will let me," he promised. He kissed her and turned her blood to fire in a prelude of more to come. "And at night, I will take ye to Avalon."

NICHOLAS STEPPED INTO his son's room and walked over to the tiny curtained bed. The babe was asleep. Nicholas didn't want to wake him. He stared at his little face, perfect in its creation. His eyes scanned the boy's pink cheeks and bump of a nose, his tuft of black hair.

She died bringing him here.

He strove to feel something other than grief and…anger, but nothing else came.

He would leave the babe for the nurses to raise while he traveled. He needed to get away from Lismoor, away from the ghost of his beloved Mattie. She was everywhere—in the kitchen even though they had a perfectly good cook, in the great hall laughing with the villagers, smiling at him in his bed.

He closed his eyes, hiding from his son—the life he would trade to have her back again.

"Forgive me," he whispered and wiped his eye. "It seems I was not born for love." He thought of the first person he had ever loved. His forbidden Julianna. He'd lost her first, and then when he finally snatched happiness for himself with Mattie, she was taken from him, too. He shook his head. No more.

"I must go."

The babe stirred and something in him stirred with it. But his anger helped him to reject it. He turned away from his son, from Lismoor, from his life.

He needed to in order to survive. And after he'd lived in a world that wasn't designed for his protection, whether slave or free, he would return and mend whatever else was broken.

But that's another story.

The End

Printed in Great Britain
by Amazon

32812980R00149